Elizabeth

The Craigdon Family Dynasty

Book Nine

CHRIS TAYLOR

LCT Productions Pty Ltd
18364 Kamilaroi Highway, Narrabri NSW 2390

ISBN. 978-1-925119-90-9 (Paperback)

Published in the United States of America.

Books by Chris Taylor

THE MUNRO FAMILY SERIES
The Profiler
The Investigator
The Predator
The Betrayal
The Deception
The Negotiator
The Christmas Vigil
The Ransom
The Defendant
The Shooting
The Maker
(Available in Audio)

THE SYDNEY HARBOUR HOSPITAL SERIES
The Perfect Husband
The Body Thief
The Baby Snatchers
The Final Bullet
The Debt Collector
The Lab Test
The Stolen Identity
The Cliff-top Killer
The Likeable Fraudster

THE SYDNEY LEGAL SERIES
An Accidental Murderer
At the Hand of Her Father
A Woman Scorned
Lies and Deception
Ordinary Evil
The Ties That Bind
The Perfect Crime
A Toxic Inheritance
Malicious Love

THE CRAIGDON FAMILY SERIES
Callum
Joel
Isabella
Nicholas
Sophia
Flynn
Noah
Logan
Elizabeth

THE BARRINGTON FAMILY SERIES
Broken Lives
Broken Promises
Broken Bonds
Broken Spirits
Broken Vows
Broken Minds
Broken Dreams
Broken Hearts
Broken Homes

THE FAIRFAX FAMILY SERIES
A Cattleman in Disguise
A Cattleman's Quest
A Cattleman's Daughter
A Cattleman's Secret Baby
To Catch a Cattleman
The Doctor and the Cattleman
To Rescue a Cattleman
A Cattleman's Heart
For the Love of a Cattleman

BACHELORS AND BRIDES SERIES
Matilda

Austin
Farrah
Benjamin
Verity
Denver
Ebony
Tyrone
Willow

Chris Taylor writing as
BELLA CHRISTIAN

THIS IS WHERE IT ENDS SERIES
(in order)
Jessie's Story
Ryan's Story
Holly's Story
Sarah's Story
Veronica's Story

Get a FREE book when you sign up for Chris Taylor's
newsletter at: www.christaylorauthor.com.au

Love Audiobooks? Check out Chris Taylor Books on audio
on Audible.com, Amazon.com and Apple Books.

Join Chris Taylor's Facebook reader group/fan page and be
among the first to receive news of book releases, read and
review books prior to release and other amazing offers. Join
Now at: www.facebook.com/groups/1758023621144744/

Find out more about all of Chris Taylor's books, by visiting her
website at: www.christaylorauthor.com.au

Dedication

This book is dedicated to Vera Jackson. Thank you for being such a loyal and supportive reader. You make my heart smile.

And as always, to my husband, Linden. My best friend, my soul mate. I love you to the moon and back.

Acknowledgments

As usual, no book comes into being without a lot of help and support by my friends and family. A world of thanks must go to my wonderful editor, Pat Thomas. Thank you for everything that you do to make my stories even more amazing than I could ever dare to dream. To former Detective Superintendent Michael Kilfoyle, thank you for lending my story credibility. Any mistakes are wholly my own.

To Mary and all of the team at Miblart, thank you for the fantastic book cover. To my sister, Nicole Guihot and to my friends, Ally Thomson and Sue Ricardo, thank you for your excellent editorial comments, proof reading skills and suggestions. I hope you like the final result.

To Amy Atwell, Kirby and the dedicated team at Author EMS who are so much more than book formatters. Amy, once again, thank you for your magic.

To the fantastic writer organizations such as Romance Writers of Australia, Romance Writers of America and Romance Writers of New Zealand for all the help, support and encouragement they offer new and aspiring writers, including me.

To my readers, thank you for your support and love for my stories. Your encouragement and enjoyment make this journey all worthwhile.

And lastly, to my friends and family, especially my husband and children. Thank you for putting up with late dinners and even later conversations as I've emerged day after day from the sometimes scary but always enthralling world I've created on my computer.

Chapter One

Ever since her husband's untimely death a year earlier, Elizabeth Craigdon had avoided Henry's study. It was a well-appointed room, with luxurious leather couches, high backed chairs, floor-to-ceiling bookshelves and an impressive hand-carved cedar desk, but it was a place that had always been her husband's domain. She was sure, even a year after his death, the scent of his expensive cologne still hung faintly in the air, mocking her.

Theirs hadn't been a happy marriage. They'd both had affairs. Henry's were too numerous to mention. Elizabeth had only strayed once, but the love she felt for Henry's brother had continued to deepen over the years. So much so that she was still in love with Archie. Not even their children or the child they shared knew the affair that had started more than two decades ago continued. It was a bone of contention between her and Archie. He couldn't understand, now that their respective spouses were dead, why she wouldn't come clean with their now adult children.

Elizabeth couldn't explain her reluctance either. She loved Archie with all her heart. Apart from his work commitments at Craigdon Super Yachts and Elizabeth's devotion to various charities, they spent most of their time together. Even the nights. A few times they'd been caught in each other's company by one or other of the children. The hour had been late, well past the time when she could have explained their presence together in one home or the other as nothing more than a casual visit. The coward in her was grateful that so far, none of their children had pushed for answers. She wasn't sure what she'd say.

Why can't I just come out and tell them? They already know about the affair. They know Archie is Sophia's father and she's nearly twenty-two…

The thing is, everyone assumed the affair that produced Sophia had ended long ago. After all, both Elizabeth and Archie had remained in their marriages. They'd given no one reason to suspect it was still going on. But Archie was growing impatient for them to be open about their love; to live together; to do what other couples did. She understood his impatience and she hated to see him upset. Perhaps after this final meeting Henry had decreed, she'd be able to get closure and move on.

"Are you ready to start, Mrs Craigdon?"

"Yes thanks, John. I think we're all here."

She forced a tight smile for her late husband's lawyer, who'd come into the study behind her. John Edgerton Junior had been the Craigdon family lawyer for years. Slight of stature and soft of voice, he was the antithesis of Henry Craigdon. Elizabeth wasn't the only family member who'd wondered at Henry's choice for legal counsel. Still, Edgerton was more than competent and Henry had prized that above all else.

Callum came up and touched her elbow. His somber expression mirrored the tension that simmered just below the surface among the other occupants of the room. Everyone was on edge. No one was looking forward to hearing Henry's final words.

"What about Christopher?" Callum asked.

"He said he couldn't make it," she replied. "Actually, I think his exact words were that he would rather kill himself than be subjected to more self-serving bullshit from the mouth of Henry Craigdon."

Callum grimaced, but nodded in acceptance. "Fair enough." He moved away to take a seat.

"Christopher made the right move by staying away," Nicholas muttered. "I should have stayed away, too."

Elizabeth looked at her youngest son and bit her lip. She wished she could offer Nicholas some comfort that his father wouldn't be so cruel a second time, but she had no idea about the contents of his letter. As far as she knew, he might have even been more spiteful while penning his final words.

Elizabeth was relieved when Nick's fiancée, Harper Wyburn, touched him on the arm and spoke quiet words of reassurance. Nick's face marginally relaxed.

Elizabeth looked around the room and sighed. A year to the day, Edgerton had gathered the family together for the reading of Henry's will. It had been the same day as Henry's funeral. A difficult time for everyone. But twelve months down the track, time had started to heal raw wounds. Now there was every chance those wounds were about to be re-opened.

A week ago, Edgerton had called her to advise that part of Henry's final instructions included a letter he wished his lawyer to read aloud to Henry's family exactly a year after his funeral. Elizabeth had been taken aback, but wasn't surprised. Henry had always demanded the last word. She'd phoned around the family and they'd all gathered together in Henry's study.

She gazed at their faces as they slowly took seats. Their expressions were filled with a mixture of boredom, curiosity and concern. But underlying that was the fear of the unknown. They weren't quite sure what they were braced for, but they were braced just the same. They sat stiff on the leather couches, the high backed chairs and other seats that had been brought in from the dining room to accommodate the large group.

There was her eldest, Jett, and his wife, Danielle. This time, their children had been left in school. Elizabeth agreed with their decision to keep the children away. No one had a clue why Henry had insisted on this meeting, but knowing how malicious he could be, it was probably something the children best not hear.

Next to them sat Callum and his wife, Grace. They'd also elected to keep their children in school. Though Seth and Alyssa weren't Callum's biological children, he'd taken to his role as step-father with eagerness, generosity of spirit and love. Callum had recently confided that he was keen to adopt them and had already begun the process. Thankfully, Grace's ex-parents-in-law had given their blessing. It warmed Elizabeth's heart every time she heard Grace's children call him "Dad."

Elizabeth's gaze drifted further along the row of chairs. Her son, Joel, and his fiancée, Sheridan, were seated next to Grace. The loved-up couple sat with their shoulders touching and their fingers entwined. Next to them was Nicholas and Harper. They'd recently celebrated their engagement, along with Elizabeth's daughter, Isabella and Raine. It had been a splendid family affair and one that filled Elizabeth with fond memories.

Now Nicholas and Harper were expecting a baby. Everyone was delighted with the news. After the year of sadness and turmoil they'd all endured, it was nice to set all the tumult aside and concentrate on what really mattered: family and togetherness. There was no better way to do that than to celebrate new love and new life.

As Elizabeth took her seat in the front row beside Jett, she acknowledged the others in the room. Her youngest daughter Sophia, sat with her husband Jarrod. In the row behind were

Elizabeth's nephews—Flynn, Noah and Logan. They were also flanked by the women who'd stolen their hearts. Elizabeth was full of gratitude and gladness knowing the younger generation had found true love. Though she and Henry hadn't enjoyed a happy marriage, she still yearned for that kind of safety, security and contentment for the people she loved.

Archie sat slightly apart from the rest of the group. His expression was closed and dark. Elizabeth's heart ached. He'd been even more distant than usual over the past few weeks. She didn't really know why. She guessed he was still upset with her for withholding from him the fact he was Sophia's father.

He'd only found out when it was a matter of life and death and though they'd talked about it—and as far as Elizabeth was concerned, the matter had been dealt with—it appeared Archie was still battling anger and sadness over Elizabeth's deception. Either that, or there was something else entirely weighing on his mind. Something else that had kept him from her bed this past week.

Lately, between his work at Craigdon Super Yachts and her endless charity obligations, they'd barely shared half a dozen conversations and Archie always seemed to have an excuse as to why he couldn't stay the night. She wondered if this was his way of punishing her for refusing to come clean to their children; if he was trying to force her hand. A silent protest. A withdrawal of affection until he got what he wanted.

No. She refused to believe Archie would be so immature. That wasn't his way. They had a deep and abiding love for each other that spanned more than two decades. In addition, there was respect, admiration and a genuine friendship. No. Archie wouldn't stoop so low as to use those kind of tactics against her. There must be something else.

Perhaps it was simply the fact that it had been a whole year since his brother's death; that as the anniversary of Henry's passing drew nearer, Archie had been reminded of the fact that his brother was gone. But then again, Henry and Archie had never been close. More like rivals. They'd even competed for her love.

Then there was Archie's late wife, Janelle. The family had recently discovered Henry and Janelle had been having an affair at the time Janelle had been killed. It was a shocking discovery and though Elizabeth had had her suspicions, Archie had been taken completely by surprise.

"Are we ready to begin?" the lawyer asked, as he seated himself behind Henry's desk.

Elizabeth shook her head slightly to clear it of her thoughts and nodded. "Yes. Thank you, John. Let's get this over with."

The lawyer's gaze moved over the people gathered before him. He cleared his throat. The low murmur of voices fell silent.

"First, I'd like to thank you all for coming. As you're aware, Henry Craigdon was my client. I prepared and my secretary witnessed his will—the same will I read to you a year ago. What some of you might not know is that at the time of executing his will, Henry left me a letter he'd written, along with instructions that it be read to all of you a year after his death."

The lawyer paused and picked up a white envelope that lay on the desk in front of him. Once again, his gaze moved around the room. "So here we are. Like you, I have no idea about the contents of this letter. It has remained in a sealed envelope since the day Henry handed it to me." Once again, he paused and his expression turned grim. "Let's hope there aren't too many surprises," he muttered.

He slid his finger under the seal and pulled out several sheets of notepaper. Even from this distance, Elizabeth could see the lazy scrawl of Henry's handwriting. She tensed with nerves.

The lawyer seemed equally apprehensive. He drew in a deep shuddering breath that did nothing to ease the anxiety that permeated the room.

"Okay, here we go."

"To my family: So, it's been a year since I died. I hope at least some of you are still grieving, but I can understand if you're not. A few of you didn't think too highly of me. That's your loss. I didn't get the chance to say these things to you before my death, so I'm saying them now. Like it or not. I don't care.

"Jett—my firstborn. I'm so proud of you and the man you've become. You always had your heart set on being a detective. I'm so glad you got to realize your dream. And Danielle and the kids... I hope they're enjoying your inheritance. Hey, you deserved it. You always were a good and dutiful son."

Edgerton glanced in Jett's direction. Elizabeth did the same. She saw the grim resignation on Jett's face recede. He reached for Danielle's hand and she shot him a reassuring look. Some of Elizabeth's tension eased.

So far, so good...

"Callum. My second born. The night you came into this world, I didn't think you were going to survive. You were so tiny, so fragile. Every breath was an effort. I spent the night on my knees in the hospital chapel, praying for God to save you, to give you the strength to live. I made a foolish promise that night, one I had no right to make. I'm sorry I forced you into the priesthood. Though I was prepared to barter anything in return for your life, it wasn't fair to chain you to a promise I made. I could tell it wasn't your calling; that you'd only entered the seminary because of me. I was filled with guilt at the knowledge you were there under sufferance, but I couldn't bring myself to release you from that bond.

"So I did what I thought was the next best thing. I left you ten million dollars. The money was my way of releasing you from the burden of my promise. I hope you've abandoned the idea of becoming a priest and are making a good life for yourself."

Once again, Edgerton paused. Elizabeth looked in Callum's direction. He and Grace sat close together, their hands clasped, their shoulders touching. Callum looked so much more relaxed. Elizabeth breathed a quiet sigh of relief and focused once again on what the lawyer was saying.

"Joel. Headstrong, passionate, stubborn and determined. You remind me a lot of me. That's why I let you ignore my wishes that you go into the law. You would have made a fine lawyer. That's something I even considered at one time. But life took me in another direction and I was okay with that.

"I thought about sabotaging your efforts to enter the police force. I had friends at the Academy. A word in the right ear and your policing career would have been over before it began. But I decided against that. Call it a moment of weakness. God knows, I didn't have many of those. I hope you appreciate that.

"The police force needs good people like you on their side. I should know. I've dealt with plenty who are far less scrupulous. I left you ten million dollars, the same as Callum and Jett. I hope you've bought yourself something nice. Be happy, Joel."

Elizabeth slowly released the breath she'd been holding. So far, it hadn't been as bad as she'd feared. Perhaps Henry had been feeling more generous, more compassionate while he penned what would be his final words. She kept waiting for the hammer to fall.

Edgerton cleared his throat and kept reading.

"Isabella—my little girl. The keeper of my secrets. The light of my life. You'll never know how much I loved you. So much it frightened me. I wanted to give you everything. I wanted you to have the best. You were my shadow, my conscience, my co-conspirator. God, we had so much fun… At least, I hope it was as much fun for you keeping secrets as it was for me…

"I left you twenty million dollars. I hope that was enough. I gave you more than your brothers received. I did that deliberately, of course. I hope you understand you were my favorite. Live well and be happy, my darling girl. I will miss you."

Elizabeth bit down on a surge of anger.

How dare he? How dare he come right out and say it! Okay, so it had been obvious he'd favored Isabella over the others, but to be so blatant about it… Especially now, in his final words to his family, when he was no longer living among them for those he hurt, to rail against. It was so wrong, so selfish, so hurtful… So utterly Henry…narcissistic and divisive to the end.

Elizabeth glanced over her shoulder to where Isabella sat straight and tall in her chair. She stared blindly at a spot on the carpet, but her lips quivered, her eyes glinted with anger and tears ran silently down her cheeks. Raine leaned close and whispered something in her ear. She turned, offering him a shaky smile.

Elizabeth briefly closed her eyes. She didn't dare look at her other children. She couldn't bear to see their pain. It wasn't Isabella's fault. She'd never asked for special treatment. No, this was all on Henry.

You bastard…

But as anger bit hard, so came remorse. It was uncharitable to think unkindly of the dead. Still… Henry didn't make it easy. Selfish in life, selfish in death. She was grateful when Edgerton continued.

"So, my dear wife. I turn to you. I'm sure it comes as no surprise I left you nothing but our family home. I only left you that because I knew you'd get it anyway through the courts.

That's more than you deserved. If it had been up to me, I wouldn't have left you anything.

"You thought you'd been so clever keeping your feelings for Archie from me. You were a fool. As if I couldn't tell how he mooned after you, right from the very start. It was sickening to watch, but it was also fun. Archie was in love with you even before we said our vows. He stood beside me as my best man and watched the woman he loved commit herself for life to someone else. I got a kick out of it, don't you worry. Best day of my life.

"While Archie pined from a distance, you and I had a good life. In the beginning, at least. You were everything I wanted. A trophy wife. Beautiful, poised and passable in bed. But it didn't last. It couldn't last. I wasn't built to be faithful to just one woman, least of all my wife.

"Fancy being married to the wrong man. How long did it take you to realize that? Not long, I'll bet. Not with Archie always sniffing around."

Elizabeth's face flamed. She kept her gaze fixed on her hands that were now twisted in her lap. Though her family knew of her affair with Henry's brother, none of them knew the full story. She wanted to rail against Henry's accusations; tell them it wasn't like that. She'd remained faithful to her wedding vows until it became impossible.

She felt the sudden increase of tension in those around her but couldn't raise her gaze. The truth was, she *had* been unfaithful and her family would judge her for that. She only hoped that now they'd all found love, they'd understand how complicated matters of the heart could be. She silently prayed for their forgiveness while the lawyer continued to read.

"What about you, Nick? Have you done something with your sorry life? I hope you're still not moping over the fact I gave my company to Logan. See, the thing is, a scant eight years into our marriage, I was convinced my dearly beloved wife was having an affair. Though your mother always denied it, I didn't believe her.

"My brother had always sniffed around, looking like a lovesick puppy, despite having a wife of his own. I, of all people, knew how hard it was to remain faithful—hell, I was the king of affairs—so I had no problem believing that Archie had also broken his vows.

"I didn't care that he'd cheated on Janelle, but I did care he'd done it with Elizabeth. She belonged to me. It didn't matter that I was unfaithful to our marriage vows almost from the beginning. That was me. My wife was off limits.

"Awhile ago, I decided to get a DNA test. The results came back last week. What do you know? You're mine, after all. The joke's on me. Not that it makes me feel differently. I left you one million dollars and not another cent. I won't be changing my will. Your beloved Craigdon Enterprises has gone to someone else."

Elizabeth shook with anger and could barely contain her rage. Fury burned her cheeks. This time she had no problem raising her gaze to glare at the paper in Edgerton's hands. So, before he'd drawn up this will, Henry had known? He'd known Nicholas was his son and yet he'd still carried out his despicable, hurtful act. He'd left Nicholas almost nothing. A scant million dollars. And the company Nick loved so much had been left to his cousin.

She glanced in Nick's direction and her heart clenched. His face was pale, his eyes wide with shock. Though he'd had a year to come to terms with his father's callousness, the knowledge that his father had continued to punish him despite learning that he was his son was a hurtful blow well beyond what Nick had already suffered. Elizabeth burned with a rage that frightened her. Digging her fingernails into her palms, she prayed for the strength to forgive the man who'd caused them all so much pain.

Chapter Two

dgerton stopped reading. He looked up, a pained but resigned expression on his face. Elizabeth could see that the contents of the letter brought him no joy. He seemed as reluctant as the rest of them to continue.

"Would anyone like a drink?" he asked. "A glass of water? Something stronger?" he half-joked.

Elizabeth offered him a tight smile. She looked at her beloved family braced in their seats, bravely weathering the devastating barrage of blows. Their expressions revealed a mix of anger, sadness and resignation.

"I think we should just get it over with," she said and heard the quiet sighs of relief from those around her.

Edgerton nodded, clearing his throat. "As you wish." He directed his attention back to the letter.

"And so we come to Sophia. Of course, there was no doubt at all you weren't my daughter. This time, your mother didn't deny it. I put it right on her: She was having an affair with Archie and the baby was his. You arrived six months later and you were the spitting image of him. You still are. I can't believe my stupid brother is still oblivious. Even funnier, that my darling wife didn't see fit to tell her lover he was the father. Poor Archie. Always the loser.

"So I'm sure you won't blame me, Sophia, for being less than generous with your inheritance. Like Nicholas, you were lucky I left you anything at all. Only the advice of my trusty legal counsel changed my mind: He explained the law and clarified that if you challenged the will in court you'd end up with a whole lot more than I was willing to give you. So I left you enough to pay off your student loans. I hope you're grateful. It was more than I wanted you to inherit. You weren't mine. I owed you nothing.

"But then I decided to have some fun. I added the clause about inheriting the five million if you married and stayed married for at least a year. I'm sure you accepted the challenge, though I bet you struggled with it for a while. You tried so hard to win my favor, but no matter what you did, you could never change my mind. I found your earnest attempts amusing. But I knew something you didn't. You were my brother's child. A constant reminder that my wife had strayed. And Archie had stolen something from me which couldn't go unpunished.

"Five million dollars is a lot of money. Too much to ignore. I hope it's left you in a quandary. I almost feel sorry for the sap roped into marrying you. Have you had the guts to tell him you're only doing it for money? Or are you just as deceptive as your mother? Oh, that's right. Turns out she was honest about Nicholas and she didn't deny you belonged to Archie. Maybe you get your deceitful streak from me? Ha, ha.

"I can't help but wonder if you'll make it to the end. Twelve months married can seem like forever. I bet you've come to realize just how hard it is to stay faithful. Your mother and I sucked at it. I hope you have better luck."

A soft gasp filled the sudden silence. Elizabeth glanced over her shoulder to where Sophia sat softly crying. Her husband, Jarrod, looked fit to kill, but when his gaze fell on his wife his expression softened, filled with tenderness and love. He kissed her gently on the mouth and pulled her close. She gave him a wobbly, grateful smile.

Once again, Elizabeth's anger spilled over. With hands clenched into fists, she struggled not to give voice to her fury.

How dare you treat our children like this! Sophia loved you! By tacit agreement, we raised her as our daughter. And now this! A betrayal of the worst kind. I hope to God you've gotten what you deserve…

The nasty thought pulled her up short, but at that moment, she was done with feeling charitable. There would be time later to beg forgiveness from her maker. She was sure God would understand.

Edgerton glanced down at the contents of Henry's letter. From the disgust that pulled down the lawyer's lips, it was obvious he took no pleasure delivering what he was forced to read. He shot the gathering an apologetic look before continuing.

"And so we come to the question you must have all asked yourself, time and time again since my death. Why did I leave Craigdon Enterprises to Logan? Have you worked it out yet? Yes, that's right. Logan is my son."

Elizabeth froze in shock. There were audible gasps from around the room. Her gaze immediately went to Archie. Though she'd suspected as much, when Noah had approached them with the possibility, Archie had flatly refused to believe his wife had cheated on him, let alone produced a child. And yet now, when Elizabeth expected him to show some outward expression of shock, Archie's expression remained closed, his eyes shuttered. He gave no obvious sign he'd even heard the announcement.

Strange… Is he in that much shock that he's beyond any reaction?

And then another, more insidious thought occurred to her: *Did he already know?*

No, she refused to believe that. The night Noah had come over and told them about Janelle and Henry's affair, Archie had stormed off, refusing to listen. Despite the evidence, he wouldn't accept his wife of two decades had cheated on him—and with his brother, no less. Elizabeth and Archie hadn't spoken of it since.

But now there was no denying it. Or the fact the union had produced a child. It was written in black and white in Henry's handwriting. Still taut with shock, Elizabeth forced herself to listen as Edgerton continued.

"Did that shock you? Probably. Not many people knew. Yes, I had an affair with my brother's wife. Sweet Janelle. It started out as a petty act of revenge, back before Nicholas was born. I was so sure Elizabeth had cheated on me. I wanted to get even. How dare she make a fool of me with another man! And not just any man, but my brother! So naturally I did what any self-respecting male would do— I sought revenge. Who better to do that with than my brother's wife?

"So I set out to seduce Janelle. I charmed her with my wittiness. Won her over with my good looks, my humor. Our families spent a lot of time together, which made things easier. Still, it took longer than I anticipated, but eventually she capitulated. I still remember our first time together…"

Edgerton broke off. He squirmed on the seat, looking uncomfortable. Elizabeth squared her shoulders and spoke.

"Please continue, John. Let's get this whole sordid ordeal over with."

A flush of embarrassment tinged the lawyer's cheeks, but he gave a jerky nod and continued.

"I digress. Within months of our affair, she told me she was pregnant. She wasn't sure which one of us was the father. I was a little taken aback she was still sleeping with Archie. Then again, I was still being intimate with my wife. I guess we were even.

"I wanted to believe the baby was mine. You see, by that time I'd fallen in love with Janelle. Yes, the joke was on me.

She still cared deeply for Archie and didn't want to hurt him. She refused to tell him about our affair and swore me to secrecy. What could I do? I loved her. Also, she refused to leave her marriage. I guess that was fair. I wasn't prepared to leave mine either, though my reasons were a lot less noble than hers.

"We increased the time we spent together, making love whenever we could. Thank God for Harriet Young. She made it so much easier. She covered for us more times than I can count. Thank you, Harriet. You were a true friend to Janelle. And to me.

"For years we met in secret. By this time, my darling wife had confessed she'd been unfaithful and Sophia was the result. I felt justified in my affair with Janelle, though I continued to keep our secret. The subterfuge made it all the more exciting; still, there were times when I wished we could love each other openly. She was the love of my life. And then I killed her. With my stupidity, my lack of self-control, I killed her. It was an accident, but I blamed myself for her death right up until this day. If I hadn't been drinking, we might never have crashed and she'd still be alive. God! How could I have been so stupid?"

The room was so quiet, Elizabeth could hear the chirping of a bird outside the window. Everyone appeared to be holding their breath. She didn't blame them. It was the first time any of them had ever heard Henry express anything that even resembled regret. And it was all because of Janelle. Apparently the love of his life.

Edgerton kept reading aloud.

"That's why I left Flynn and Noah some money. Guilt money. I stole their mother away from them. It wasn't fair. She could have still been alive and living a happy life, going to weddings, baptisms, birthdays. Watching her sons make a life for themselves. They were her world. She loved them with everything she had. I took all of that from her when I crashed that car. All because I was drunk.

"It was also my fault she wasn't wearing a seatbelt. I asked her to go down on me. She was happy to comply. That's the kind of person she was. Always happy to put herself out for someone else. For me."

Edgerton's face flamed with embarrassment. Elizabeth was beyond caring. She just wanted the whole thing to be over with, so that they need never speak of it again. A little impatiently, she urged him to continue.

"I'm sorry about getting you into drugs, Logan. I didn't know at that time you were my son. I had my suspicions and so did your mom, but we never knew for sure. She kept up her deception with Archie right until the end. She didn't want to hurt him by throwing our affair in his face.

"Of course, when Sophia came along, I couldn't wait to tell Janelle the truth. She was devastated to discover Archie had cheated on her with Elizabeth, but she knew she'd also been deceitful. That troubled her. Deep down, she was such a good person. But she came to accept she and Archie were even. Neither owed the other anything. She refused to say anything to him. She refused to allow me to tell him the truth. Right to the end, she protected her husband. She stayed with her spouse out of respect for him and for the sake of her kids. For me? I loved the power in having my brother's wife and in punishing my wife and brother for their affair by not letting them be together.

"Logan, you were fourteen when I finally learned the truth about your parentage. By then, it had become an obsession of mine. I had to know if you were mine. Janelle insisted it didn't matter, but to me it did. Your mother stole some hair from your hairbrush. It was a simple matter after that to submit it for DNA. I'm so proud to call you my son. I wish I'd been able to do so publicly, but your mother forbade me. I honored her wishes.

"So there you have it. Like me, love me, hate me. I'm done."

As Edgerton folded the letter and set it quietly down on the desk, the occupants of the room sat frozen, no one sure of what to say. So many questions had been answered, but in some respects, Elizabeth was certain they would rather have remained oblivious.

So like old Henry. He always had to be the star of the show. A narcissist right to the end.

Elizabeth looked at those around her. Anger, devastation, resentment and pain were reflected on their faces. Nicholas was breathing hard, his face flushed. Harper held his arm and spoke quietly to him. Isabella's tears had dried, but her expression remained full of sadness. Sophia was visibly struggling to contain her hurt and anger. As Elizabeth watched, her daughter shrugged off Jarrod's arm from around her shoulders and stood and made her way over to where Elizabeth sat.

"How could he, Mom? How could he be so cruel?" she cried, her eyes flooding with tears.

Elizabeth shook her head. "I'm so sorry, honey. I don't know."

"He knew how much I loved him, how much I yearned for his acceptance, his approval. He treated me with disdain at every turn. Even his final words to me were mean and cold. He had a chance to beg my forgiveness, or at the very least, to apologize. But all I got was more of the same. It wasn't my fault he wasn't my father. I treated him like he was. I loved him like he was. And he threw it back in my face. It was like he blamed me for being Archie's daughter. What kind of sick son of a bitch does that?"

Elizabeth reached out in an attempt to soothe away Sophia's pain, but Sophia was having none of it. She moved away.

"I'm sorry, Mom. I just can't do this right now. I know we've talked about this, sorted through our feelings, but right now things are too raw for me to deal with. I hate knowing he despised me, right to the very end."

"Oh, Sophia!" Elizabeth cried, her heart breaking at the pain on her daughter's face. "He didn't despise you. It was *me* he despised. And Archie."

"Then why did he take it out on *me*?" Sophia shouted.

Elizabeth shook her head, overwhelmed with sadness. "I don't know. But it was likely to punish me because he knew how much I love you. By hurting you he was hurting me. He was like that. Cold and unforgiving. Please, God. Don't let yourself become the same. Don't give him that power."

Sophia was mutinously silent. With a last devastated look at her mother, she stormed out of the room. Jarrod, nodding in Elizabeth's direction, hurried after his wife.

Elizabeth's head ached. A pulse beat behind her eyes. The stress of the day was getting to her.

Damn you, Henry! You always had to have the last word! You've ripped open wounds that were barely healed over. Your family is once again reeling with pain. I hope you're proud of yourself…

She looked across at Archie. He was surrounded by his sons: Flynn, Noah and Logan. No, not Logan. Logan belonged to Henry. The longer she looked at her lover's family, the more she realized there was a somber air of acceptance encircling them. It wasn't the shock she expected upon discovering Logan was Henry's son. It was almost as if the four of them had known ahead of the reading of the letter today…

And maybe they had…

Convinced she was right, Elizabeth stood and made her way over to them. Archie looked up at her approach. She tried to read his mood, but his eyes were still shuttered. It was like staring at an obelisk.

"You knew, didn't you?" she stated flatly.

He didn't bother to ask her to clarify. Instead, he offered her a brief nod, his mouth tight. "Yes."

Though she'd been expecting that answer, it still shocked her. She tensed and then shook her head in disbelief. "Why didn't you tell me?"

He held her gaze almost defiantly, but offered no reply.

She stared at him in bewilderment. "Archie! I... I don't understand."

Instead of answering her, offering her reassurance, he simply stood and regarded her steadily.

"I don't suppose you do, but I'm not in the mood for explanations." He gave her a hard look. "We both know what's standing between us and it isn't this. The ball's in your court. Until you're ready to do what needs to be done, we have nothing further to discuss." He turned to his sons. "Come on, boys. Let's get out of here."

Logan shot her an apologetic look. Flynn and Noah both mumbled goodbyes, their eyes averted. Elizabeth stared after them, beyond words.

"I'm really sorry you had to go through that."

Elizabeth blinked. Edgerton stood beside her, holding Henry's folded letter in his hands. She gathered her wits and responded.

"That was Henry, wasn't it? Selfish and spiteful to the end."

Edgerton lowered his gaze and nodded. "I'm sorry," he said again.

Elizabeth's anger suddenly deserted her. Whatever the fallout from Henry's letter, it wasn't the lawyer's fault. She compressed her lips.

"Thank you, John. I appreciate this hasn't been easy for you, either."

The lawyer accepted her words with a brief nod of acknowledgement. He held the letter out to her. "Would you like to keep this?"

Elizabeth stared down at the innocent-looking sheaf of papers and shuddered. "No. You keep it. Or burn it. I don't care what you do with it. I never want to see it again."

Edgerton nodded once again. "I understand."

Belatedly remembering her manners, Elizabeth offered him refreshments. He politely declined. Relieved, she saw him out and then returned to the study where the rest of her family remained quietly talking among themselves.

Well, you did what you set out to achieve, Henry. You had the final word. Now I'm left to pick up the pieces. Again. And I will. Make no mistake. Yours will be a hollow victory…

But as she thought about her defiant response, she felt terribly uncertain. Unlike all the previous battles, this time, she wasn't sure she had the love and support of Archie…

A sudden wave of helplessness began to overwhelm her, momentarily snatching her breath. But then she remembered who she was and where she'd come from. Elizabeth Grace Louise Doherty was made from sterner stuff. This wasn't the first time she'd faced adversity and come out the other side. No, whatever Henry had hoped to achieve with his letter, there was no way she'd let it break her. Nor would she let it destroy the family she loved above everything else.

He can go and shove his malice and spite up his ass. I refuse to let it destroy me… Or the ones I love. So long, Henry Craigdon. Your reign of tyranny is over!

Chapter Three

While Sophia's and Jarrod's places at the family table remained conspicuously empty, and Archie hadn't yet returned with his sons, the rest of Elizabeth's children and their partners gathered together for a meal. It was a little past one and Elizabeth was sure some of them were hungry. It would also give them a chance to come together, reconnect and talk through what had happened.

She'd asked Amy ahead of time to prepare lunch. As they filed into the large formal dining room, the housekeeper entered bearing platters of cold meats. They were quickly followed by fresh buns, a bowl of salad leaves, sliced tomatoes, boiled eggs and a plate of sliced cheese. Butter, mayonnaise and other condiments had been set out earlier. Everything was placed on the long wooden sideboard.

"Thank you, Amy. You've gone to a lot of trouble. This looks great," Callum said quietly.

The old housekeeper's face creased with wrinkles as she smiled. "Thank you, Callum. Nothing's too much trouble for my babies. Now, eat up."

Callum and Grace started a line at the serving area. The others joined them. Fine china plates, cutlery and linen napkins stacked in a neat pile at one end. As each one filled their plates and found a spot at the table, Elizabeth stood and joined the line, allowing herself a tiny portion of food knowing it would be difficult to get much past the knot of pain in her throat. She eased out a weary sigh.

The worst part was over. Now for the inevitable dissection, mulling over and no doubt, some more heated discussion. Not that she blamed them. Her children were entitled to vent. There was much to be upset about. While they'd already discovered much of what Henry had revealed, there was still an almost palpable sense of shock in having it confirmed in his words. Anger permeated the air.

Joel pulled out a seat beside her and set his plate down in front of him. Sheridan took the chair opposite. He reached across and patted Elizabeth's hand.

"How are you doing Mom? It's been a rough day."

Hearing the kindness and genuine concern in his tone, a rush of emotion burned behind her eyes. She managed a tight smile. "You can say that again."

"What happened to Uncle Archie?"

"He… He left with your cousins." She realized what she'd said and hurried to correct herself. "I mean, your half-brother and cousins." She stared at the table. Her face burned.

"It's all right Mom." Joel's tone remained gentle. "I understand." He paused and then added, "It must have come as a shock to all of them."

"Yes. No. I mean, I'm not sure about the boys, but your uncle already knew."

Joel's eyes widened in surprise. "He knew about Logan?"

Her lips thinned. "Yes."

Joel frowned. "How? When?"

Elizabeth shook her head. "I don't know. He didn't elaborate."

"I take it he hadn't told you about Logan?"

Once again, Elizabeth's lips thinned. "No," she said grimly. "I guess that's just one more thing I'm going to have to deal with."

Joel looked sympathetic. "Don't worry Mom. I'm sure he'll come round. He's probably still feeling a bit put out about the fact you didn't tell him about Sophia."

Elizabeth sighed. "I didn't think he could be that childish, but it seems I was wrong."

"Don't be too quick to judge him," Joel said quickly. "You don't know what went on. Give him a chance to explain before you convict him of any wrongdoing."

She managed a weary smile. "Thanks, Joel. I appreciate your support. For both of us."

Joel merely shrugged. "You're my family. That's what we do. Support each other."

She blew her breath out on a sigh. "Yes. I wish your father had felt a bit more like that while he was still alive."

Joel's expression darkened. "Dad had his problems, that's for sure. I won't pretend to understand where he was coming from with all that stuff. It defies reason."

"Yes. But we're not going to let his pettiness destroy us. We Craigdons are stronger than that."

Joel smiled. "Of course we are."

"I'm annoyed that he didn't enlighten us any further about Stella Taunton," Isabella grumbled. "I mean, he left the orphanage fifteen million dollars. A significant sum. It would be nice to know his connection to the place and his reasons."

"You're right," Nicholas agreed with a grimace. "He was oh so generous with me. I'm intrigued to find out what motivated him to leave the institution so much money. None of us have ever heard of it."

"I did a little digging," Joel admitted. "All I came up with was a private company established about two years ago. Only the bare minimum of information was publicly available. Without knowing who's behind it, I came up against a brick wall."

The sound of stilettos on the travertine tiles that traversed the foyer reached all of them. A moment later, Sophia and Jarrod appeared. Elizabeth's heart jumped for joy. When Sophia immediately went up to her and gave her an awkward hug, tears came to Elizabeth's eyes.

"I'm sorry, Mom. Jarrod and I have been talking. He made me see things from your point of view. I'm sorry," Sophia said again. "I behaved badly."

Elizabeth shook her head. "No. honey. You didn't. And there's no need to apologize. I understand. It was like finding out all over again. I'm sorry you had to go through that."

Sophia grimaced. "I'm sorry, too. I wish none of us had to be subjected to that. I don't care how Daddy tried to justify his behavior. The truth is, he was an asshole. Right up to the end."

"Sophia," Jarrod admonished quietly.

Elizabeth touched Sophia's husband on the hand. "It's all right, Jarrod. Sophia's right. He was an asshole."

It was the first time she'd said the words aloud. They felt good on her tongue. She said it again, this time louder.

"Asshole. Asshole. Asshole."

Sophia cheered. "Way to go, Mom!"

The rest of those gathered around the table turned to look at her. Embarrassment heated her cheeks, but she refused to apologize for her behavior. She held their combined gazes defiantly. One by one, they began to smile. Then Callum got to his feet. He wasn't the firstborn Craigdon, but he'd always been the unofficial spokesperson for the group.

He lifted his wine glass. "I'd like to propose a toast. To Mom."

"To Mom," came a chorus of agreement. Elizabeth smiled with pleasure and pride. These were her children and their chosen life partners. Jett, Callum and Sophia had already said their vows. Joel, Nicholas and Isabella were engaged. No doubt there would be wedding bells in the near future.

Especially for Nicholas who'd announced only a week earlier that he and Harper were expecting.

With her throat clogging up with emotion, Elizabeth gazed around at her family. She took a sip from her champagne flute and smiled.

"Thank you. Thank you, all of you. We've endured a tumultuous year, but we've managed to hold it all together. I appreciate your love and support and I hope you know you have mine. Now and for always."

They turned their attention to eating and the murmur of conversation mingled with the sound of cutlery clinking against the china plates. Elizabeth thought about Christopher, her late husband's illegitimate son. Once again, Henry had completely ignored his firstborn's existence. Once again, he'd been unbelievably malicious and cruel.

"What is it, Mom?" Callum asked softly from where he was seated next to Joel.

She blinked in surprise and looked at him. He'd always been her most sensitive child, the one most in tune with her moods.

"I was just thinking about Christopher," she said honestly.

Callum's mouth twisted in a grimace. "It was a good thing he wasn't here. Once again, Dad was completely insensitive."

Elizabeth nodded. "Yes. I'm glad Christopher made the decision to stay away. He didn't need another reminder of how little his father cared for him, to the point where he completely ignored his existence. First in the will and now in the letter. It would have caused Christopher unimaginable hurt."

Joel's lip curled up in disgust. "I don't know why you're so hell-bent on worrying about Christopher's feelings, Mom. He doesn't seem to care about anyone else's."

"I understand what you're saying, Joel. And you know that better than most. You and Sheridan bore the brunt of one of Christopher's stunts. But let me say this. I think he's trying to put that bad behavior behind him. Look at what he did to help that police officer. If he hadn't done what he did, the police commissioner would have gotten away with murder. Then there's the tip he gave to Noah about Logan's girlfriend being in imminent danger. Who knows what might have happened if Christopher hadn't spoken up."

She paused and then added in a quiet tone. "I think it's time to cut him some slack. After all, none of us is perfect. We all have rough edges. Some more than others. Christopher's trying hard to be the kind of man he can be proud of. We should encourage him and give him our support."

There were various grumbles, mostly of agreement. Elizabeth had to be content with that. She didn't expect her family to embrace Christopher overnight. After all, he'd gone out of his way to put most of them offside. But lately, she'd seen a change in him and she believed very strongly that everyone deserved a second chance.

The dirty plates had been cleared away and the leftovers packed up to be taken back to Callum and Grace's soup kitchen. At Elizabeth's suggestion, they all withdrew to her music room for coffee. Amy brought in a steaming pot, along with a tray containing coffee cups, teaspoons, milk and sugar. There was also a plate of petit fours.

"Thank you, Amy. These look delicious."

"When I knew all my babies were going to be here, I baked all their favorites. I hope you approve."

Elizabeth smiled. "Absolutely. And I'm sure they do, too."

Amy departed. Elizabeth picked up the pot and began pouring. As she handed out cups of coffee, she took another moment to appreciate what she had. Most of her thirty-three years of marriage had been difficult. She'd been married to a selfish, narcissistic man. But he'd also given her six beautiful children. Well, five not counting Sophia. Her children were her life and now she had their significant others to welcome, to nurture, to love. She looked forward to the time when they provided her with grandchildren. She might have faced some difficult challenges, but she wouldn't swap her situation for the world.

A knock at the front door caught her attention. She stirred, on the verge of getting up, but then heard Amy's footsteps crossing the tiles. A moment later, the door opened and conversation could be heard. The words were too muffled for Elizabeth to hear clearly, but it sounded like the newcomer was a woman. A moment later, Amy appeared in the doorway of the music room.

"I'm sorry to interrupt, Elizabeth. But you have a visitor. I told her you were otherwise engaged, but she insisted she see you right away."

Elizabeth frowned. "Oh, did she give her name?"

"Yes. Stella. Stella Taunton."

Elizabeth froze in surprise. "Did you say, Stella Taunton?"

"Yes. Do you know her?"

"No. That is, her name's familiar, but we've never met." She looked back toward her family who were all looking equally shocked. "It seems we're going to have the pleasure of meeting Ms Taunton after all. Let's hope she can answer our questions." She turned back to Amy. "Please send her in."

Isabella was seated beside Joel on the couch. She nudged him with her elbow. "This should be interesting."

"You bet," Joel replied.

"Make sure you mind your manners," Callum admonished quietly. "We don't know anything about this woman."

"Except that she impressed Dad enough that he left her orphanage fifteen million dollars," Isabella retorted.

"She might not even know Dad," Callum insisted. "Perhaps her having the same name is merely a coincidence."

Isabella rolled her eyes. "Then why is she here, Callum? Outside Dad's house? Sorry… Now Mom's house?"

Callum was spared from replying when Amy appeared once again in the doorway of the music room. Behind her stood a young woman who looked about Nicholas' age. Elizabeth started in surprise. Stella Taunton looked nothing like she expected. Call her naïve, but Elizabeth somehow had the impression the woman whose name fronted a home for widows and orphans would be mature, matronly, over fifty at least.

The young woman who stood before her had long, brassy blond, messy hair. She wore a sapphire blue, figure-hugging, low cut dress that only emphasized her assets. She was big-breasted, slim of hip and with enough height that she'd tower over the average woman. And that was without her four-inch stiletto heels.

Hiding her shock, Elizabeth got to her feet. A whiff of cheap perfume almost made her sneeze. She resisted the urge with an effort and held out her hand toward the woman.

"I'm Elizabeth Craigdon. Welcome to Craigdon Manor."

"Stella Taunton. Nice to meet ya," the woman replied while looking avidly around. She gave Elizabeth's hand a perfunctory shake. "You're not what I expected."

Elizabeth frowned in confusion. The woman spoke like she knew her. But how could that be? Elizabeth was certain she'd never met the woman.

"What did you expect?" she heard herself ask.

Stella shrugged nonchalantly. "Oh, you know. Old, fat and frumpy."

Elizabeth was momentarily silenced by shock. Before she could respond, Stella began to move around the room, looking this way and that. She gave a low-pitched whistle.

"This is one cool house. I had no idea Henry was so loaded. I mean, I guess I should have, given everything that happened, but at the time, I didn't have a clue." She walked over to where a collection of priceless figurines stood on a shelf beside the bookcase. She picked one up and looked at it, turning it this way and that before setting it back down in place and picking up another one.

Once again, Elizabeth hid her surprise. She wondered how her husband had known this woman. She couldn't imagine Henry giving Stella the time of day, let alone fifteen million dollars, albeit to her company, or at least, to the company that bore her name.

Belatedly remembering her manners, Elizabeth invited the woman to sit down. With another nonchalant shrug, Stella crossed the room and perched on the edge of one of the sofas. Callum and Grace shuffled over to make room.

"Would you like some coffee?" Elizabeth asked.

"Sure. Why not. White with three sugars," came the flippant reply.

Elizabeth concentrated on pouring the coffee and adding the teaspoons of sugar. She didn't dare catch the eye of any of her children. She was sure they were as bemused as she was as to what this woman was doing there and how she was connected to Henry. Handing the cup to Stella, Elizabeth returned to her seat. She folded her hands in her lap and looked at the woman expectantly.

Stella slurped loudly from her cup and then set it down on the coffee table that stood between her and the opposite couch. Isabella frowned with annoyance. Sophia hid a giggle behind her hand. The rest of Elizabeth's family regarded the woman with varying degrees of anticipation and incredulity as they awaited her next move. Suddenly impatient, Elizabeth took control.

"So, Stella. I'm sure you understand our surprise at your visit. I must admit, you have us at a disadvantage. You seem to know about us, but we know nothing about you."

The woman smiled brightly. "Of course you do. You were there for the reading of the will, weren't you?"

"Y-yes," Elizabeth replied uncertainly.

"Then you know Henry left me fifteen million dollars."

"Um, no," Joel said. "He left the Stella Taunton House for Widows and Orphans fifteen million dollars. I looked into it. It's a charitable trust."

Stella smirked. "Trust, huh? Good old Henry. He was always smart as a tux."

Elizabeth's eyebrows rose in surprise. She regarded the woman steadily, doing her best to hide her concern. "What do you know about the Stella Taunton House for Widows and Orphans?" she asked.

"Just that it doesn't exist."

"Of course it does," Joel insisted. "I did a company search."

Stella rolled her eyes and grinned. "You're obviously a lot smarter than I am, so I'm gonna take your word for it. I don't know anything about what Henry did behind the scenes to make it all legit. All I know is he told me he'd taken care of me, if anything were to happen to him. Which it did. But ya already know that, right?"

Chapter Four

*E*lizabeth took refuge in her coffee and prayed her shock wasn't visible to everyone else in the room. She had a sneaking suspicion Stella knew Henry far more intimately than she would have ever guessed. To her relief, Stella appeared oblivious to her discomfort. Pasting a smile on her face, Elizabeth tried again.

"So, Stella. I'm a little confused. According to Henry's will, he bequeathed the sum of fifteen million dollars to a charity that bears your name. Do you have experience with widows and orphans?"

Stella snorted. "Do I look like someone who has experience with widows and orphans?"

Joel made a sound of disgust. "Dad intentionally deceived us, Mom. It's obvious the charity was a front." He glared at Stella. "Who are you and how did you know my father?"

Stella took her time before answering. She reached for her coffee cup and took another slurp before setting it down again. She uncrossed her legs and then crossed them again. She stared at one long, pink fingernail as if searching for the answer there. It seemed, now that the moment was upon her, she struggled to find the words. Joel's glare remained unrelenting. Members of the family were poised on the edge of their seats. Elizabeth tried not to tense, but awaited the worst. Henry had always taken malicious delight in embarrassing her.

"I'm sorry to be the one to tell you," Stella responded, "but the truth is, I was Henry's girlfriend."

Nicholas pushed away from the couch. Joel made a sound of disgust. Isabella and Sophia both stared at the woman with varying degrees of shock. Callum appeared the least affected. He looked at Stella with compassion.

"How long were the two of you together?" he asked.

She twirled a strand of hair around her finger, her bravado slipping. An expression of uncertainty passed over her face. She suddenly looked very young.

"Just over a year. We met when I was twenty-two. I was at the casino in the city with my friends. We were playing Blackjack. I was on a winning streak. Henry joined the table. He gave me a handful of hundred-dollar chips and encouraged me to put them on whatever number I liked. I finished that night with more than five thousand dollars in my pocket. It was the most money I'd had in my life. We spent that night in his hotel room. We've been together ever since. That is, until he died."

Her voice cracked with emotion and unshed tears glinted in her eyes. Elizabeth felt an involuntary wave of sympathy. It appeared Stella had genuinely cared for Henry.

The room fell silent while everyone digested what Stella had said. Elizabeth struggled with the idea her late husband had been with the woman for so long. In Elizabeth's experience, Henry was a love 'em and leave 'em kind of guy. He wasn't into anything long term. A night or two, three at the most. Sometimes his affairs lasted a week. Of course, at the time, Elizabeth had been oblivious to his fifteen-year affair with Janelle. But that had been a long time ago. Janelle had been dead ten years.

With an effort, Elizabeth finally found her voice. "So

you're saying the Stella Taunton House for Widows and Orphans, the charitable organization Henry or his lawyers set up, is a front? That it never existed?"

Stella nodded. "Right. Henry left that money to me. I'm Stella Taunton's House for Widows and Orphans. The money was meant for me."

Elizabeth shook her head, still trying to come to terms with all she'd learned. It seemed awfully generous of Henry to give the woman such a hefty amount. More than he'd left his sons. Almost as much as he'd left his favorite child. It didn't make sense.

What am I missing? There must be something more, something Stella hasn't told us…

Elizabeth voiced the question aloud, in the hope Stella might just provide the answer. Stella remained silent a long moment, staring at the carpet. She finally lifted her head.

"It wasn't just me. I guess he wanted to make sure our baby was provided for, too."

Elizabeth's jaw dropped. Her mouth gaped. Her family looked equally dumbstruck. She blinked hard. She wasn't sure she'd heard right. "E-excuse me? You and Henry have…a child?"

"Had," Stella said sadly. "I was nine weeks pregnant. I had a miscarriage only a week before Henry's death. I guess he never got round to changing his will."

"Did you tell him you'd lost the baby?" Nicholas asked.

There was an edge to his voice that seemed to irritate Stella. She narrowed her eyes at him. "Of course I did. What, you think I was trying to trap him?"

"I didn't say that," Nicholas mumbled.

"Like I said," she continued, "I suspect Henry didn't have a chance to change his will. He wasn't exactly planning on dropping dead with a heart attack." Her voice hitched. "Oh, God. I can still see his face… He looked… He looked awful.

Red in the face, then purple. Gasping for breath… Then in a matter of seconds he was gone."

Oh, God. He was with her! He was with her when he died…

The shocking thought intruded upon Elizabeth's consciousness. She stared at the woman in disbelief. Elizabeth had been told by an officer who'd attended the scene that Henry had died in a hotel room. He'd been found naked on the floor. There was evidence he'd been there with a woman, though she'd disappeared.

Elizabeth had managed to keep that bit of information out of the public arena. Not even her family knew. She hadn't seen the point. It was just another exercise in humiliation and she'd suffered enough of those at the hands of her husband. The only person outside the investigating officers who knew the truth was Christopher. And now, it appeared, Stella also did. Because she'd been there.

It was like finding out all over again. The shock, the confusion, the disbelief.

Elizabeth had been chairing a meeting for one of her favorite charities at the time the police had come calling. They'd tried the house first. Amy had told them where they could find her.

The police apparently asked at the hotel reception about her and had been directed to the small interview room where the meeting was being held. They appeared in the open doorway, hats in hands, grim expressions. They asked for her by name. She could still remember the curious glances sent her way by the other women.

She'd only been gone a few minutes. Just long enough for the police to give her the news. Though outwardly she'd remained calm and had answered their queries, she'd returned to the meeting in a daze. She barely remembered excusing herself. Of course, no one asked any questions. They were all far too well bred for that. But she'd felt their burning curiosity all the way across the room until she cleared the doorway.

All the time, the only thing on her mind had been her children. The scant details provided by the police were tawdry. She hadn't wanted her children tainted by that. Henry had died the same way he'd lived: to the fullest and to hell with the consequences.

Keeping silent about the details of his death hadn't been about protecting his reputation, but protecting the sensibilities of her offspring. Their knowing the tawdry details wouldn't change anything. Henry was dead. Now it seemed the woman who'd been with him during his final moments sat a few feet away from her, slurping coffee on her couch.

Elizabeth swallowed a sigh. What was done, was done. If what Stella told them was true, that explained Henry's generosity toward her fake charity in his will. So, the child Henry had provided for hadn't survived. Did that really make any difference? Perhaps to Christopher, who was yet to drop his lawsuit against the estate.

But Elizabeth was confident Christopher's beef against Henry and the fact he'd been left out of the will had nothing to do with money. Whether the family contested Stella's right to her inheritance or not wouldn't change anything for Christopher. What he wanted from his lawsuit wasn't money. It was recognition, love, acceptance… And the only man he wanted that from was dead.

No, the best thing was for Stella Taunton to take the money and use it however she saw fit. As long as she didn't expect anything from them, they'd be fine. In fact, the sooner Stella departed Craigdon Manor, the better.

Suddenly impatient for the woman to be gone, Elizabeth got to her feet and pasted a smile on her face.

"Well, it was nice to meet you, Stella. Let me show you out."

Stella didn't take the hint. Instead, she took another slurp from her coffee before noisily setting it back on the coffee table.

"Thank you. It's nice to feel welcome. I… I wasn't quite sure how you'd react." Her gaze moved to include the rest of Elizabeth's family. "All of you. I didn't know how much you knew about me…and Henry."

Elizabeth briefly closed her eyes and counted to ten. She offered Stella an overly bright smile. "Yes. Well, let's just say Henry died with some secrets. You weren't the only surprise."

The woman immediately looked curious. "Oh?"

Elizabeth waved her obvious interest aside. "It doesn't matter anymore. Henry's dead. There's no point in rehashing the past. The thing is, now you've met us and we know about you… Well, I'm not sure what else you require of us."

"I didn't come here asking for money," Stella replied hurriedly. "I just wanted…to meet you. Henry spoke about you—all of you," she added, looking around the room. "The way he talked about you… I… I didn't expect you to be so nice."

Elizabeth looked away, feeling guilty about her earlier uncharitable thoughts. The girl might not have been the type of woman Henry usually went for, but that didn't mean she didn't have a kind heart.

And then Stella spoke again. "I mean, I stole your father and husband away. I'm not sure how he explained his absence to you, but he spent a hell of a lot of time with me. He bought me a house, a car, clothes and perfume. He took me to shows, weekend getaways in the country. He showered me with expensive gifts." Her smile was sad and nostalgic. "He was so generous, right to the very end. One of a kind. I miss him so much."

A light of comprehension suddenly flooded Nick's face. "That explains the large withdrawals," he muttered.

Elizabeth frowned. "What are you talking about?"

Joel sat forward, his expression grim. "Craigdon Enterprises was hemorrhaging money in the months before Dad's death. Now we know why."

"How much?" Elizabeth asked, curious about the extent of Henry's generosity toward his young girlfriend.

Nick answered her. "Hundreds of thousands."

Stella shrugged nonchalantly. "Like I said, Henry was a very generous man."

Nick's expression darkened. He narrowed his eyes at Stella. "I seem to recall there was more than half a million withdrawn from one of Dad's accounts in a single day."

Elizabeth blinked in surprise. "Wow," she murmured.

Stella merely grinned. "That was probably for my house. "We found this cute little semi in Newtown. It needed some work, but that was part of the appeal. We were going to have fun renovating." She paused and her face filled with regret. "Too bad Henry died before we got it finished." A moment later, her expression brightened. "The good news is, I was able to engage a builder and finish the work we'd planned. I even managed to add an extra wing." She winked. "Fifteen million dollars buys a hell of a lot of tradesmen."

Elizabeth saw the anger flood Nick's face. Despite Harper's restraining hand on his arm, he opened his mouth, obviously intent on giving Stella a piece of his mind. Elizabeth quickly intervened.

"Stella. Like I said. It was nice to meet you. But I'm afraid I'm going to have ask you to leave. We were just in the middle of a discussion about Nick and Harper's wedding plans," she improvised. "There are still so many details to work through."

Stella immediately perked up. "A wedding! Oh, how cute! I adore weddings."

Elizabeth gritted her teeth and once again forced herself to count to ten. Fortunately, the woman finally took the hint.

With a nod of farewell to the rest of the occupants in the room, she followed Elizabeth to the exit. Amy hovered right outside the door.

Elizabeth nodded imperceptibly to her housekeeper and then turned to her late husband's girlfriend.

She offered her a tight smile. "Goodbye, Stella. Do take care. Amy will see you out." Effectively dismissed, the woman had no choice but to murmur a hasty farewell and follow the housekeeper to the front door. Elizabeth breathed a sigh of relief at the sound of the front door opening and closing. A moment later, Amy reappeared.

"Is she gone?" Elizabeth asked.

"Yes. I gave her a little parcel of petit fours and suggested she need not attend here again."

Elizabeth's shoulders slumped. She managed a smile. "Thank you, Amy. You went above and beyond."

The old woman regarded Elizabeth with fondness. "I've been taking care of this family for more years than I can count. I'm not about to stop now."

Elizabeth stepped forward and gave the woman a hug. Amy flushed with pleasure. "And that's why we love you," Elizabeth said.

She returned to the music room and poured herself a fresh cup of coffee. Nick still looked disgruntled. Elizabeth swallowed a sigh. Having been largely overlooked by his father in the will, Nicholas had done it tougher than most of her children.

He looked across at her as she regained her seat. "Is she gone?"

"Yes."

"Good."

Elizabeth winced at Nick's harsh tone. While she understood his resentment, he needed to let it go.

"Don't let Stella and what your father did affect you, Nicholas," she said quietly.

"How can I not let it affect me?" Nicholas exploded. "He left her fifteen million dollars! She's not even family! She's no one. A bit of fluff he knew for barely twelve months. It makes me sick!"

Elizabeth spoke in a low tone, silently urging him to listen. "I understand. Really, Nick. I do. But holding onto your anger and hurt isn't good for anyone, least of all you. You and Harper are having a baby! Your wedding's in a couple of months. Flynn and Jayde are celebrating their engagement with a party next week. There is so much joy and happiness around you! It's time to focus on all the good in your life and let the pain and disappointment go."

Harper touched Nick on the arm. "She's right, you know."

He opened his mouth as if to protest, but Harper pressed a finger against his lips, silencing him.

"I know Nick," she said gently. "I know better than anyone. I love you, remember? It upsets me to see you unhappy; to know how unfairly you were treated. But dwelling on our misfortunes won't change anything. And we might just be forgetting all the blessings we have. Use them to become stronger." She reached up to cup her hand around his cheek. "Please, Nick. Do it for us. And our baby."

Elizabeth teared up at the emotion in Harper's voice. Nick swallowed, obviously also affected by his fiancée's words. His gaze remained on Harper. A moment later he gave a jerky nod and then dragged her into his arms. She held him tightly for a long moment.

Elizabeth busied herself refreshing everyone's cup. The murmur of conversation recommenced. Then Joel sighed.

"So now we know about Stella Taunton. I must say, I never guessed she was Dad's girlfriend."

There was a general murmur of assent. Then Jett spoke.

"I wonder how many other ex-girlfriends he has out there. We might even have other half-brothers or sisters."

Elizabeth tensed, frozen to the spot. Isabella noticed her mother's reaction and frowned with concern.

"Jett. Please," Isabella admonished.

"I'm just saying. I mean, we all know how promiscuous Dad was. Stella said she lost a baby. How do we know there aren't others out there who survived?"

Callum looked resigned. "I guess we don't, but Dad never made mention of anyone else in his will. Stella was the only anomaly. Everyone else has been accounted for. We should give him the benefit of the doubt."

Elizabeth shot Callum a grateful look. "Callum's right. I'm sure if there were other children out there, fathered by Henry, he would have made provision for them."

"That's not necessarily true. Look at me," Nicholas muttered.

"You're right," Elizabeth said quietly. "I guess we'll never know for sure, but we can't go on wondering. There's no sense each of us driving ourselves crazy with something we can't prove. Let's leave it be. Stella has her money. That's what your father wanted. As far as the rest of you go, you can always come to me if you need money."

"It's not about the money, Mom," Nicholas grumbled. "It was never about the money."

She nodded with understanding. "I know, Nick. And I wish there was something I could do to make it up to you. We both know that's out of my control."

"I don't blame you for the way Dad drafted his will, Mom. I never have," Nick replied.

Elizabeth's heart clenched. She wished there was some way for her to take away her son's pain, but there was nothing she could do. The only person who could have made right the monstrous wrong done to Nicholas, was dead.

"What about Christopher?" Sophia piped up.

"What about him?" Isabella asked.

"He's Dad's firstborn. Dad knew all about him and yet he didn't leave him anything in the will. Not even a mention."

Elizabeth flinched. It was true. Her late husband hadn't bothered to recognize Christopher's existence—not in life and certainly not in death. It was just another reason why Christopher carried such anger toward Henry. Elizabeth blew out her breath on a weary sigh. She was so tired of dealing with the mess Henry had made of their lives.

If only he hadn't been so self-centered, so selfish. If only he'd given a moment's thought to someone other than himself. Life would have been so much easier and far less painful…

But there was no point in going there. Henry had died the way he'd lived and nothing was going to change that. It was time to put it behind them and move forward.

Chapter Five

Elizabeth's fingers moved languidly over the keys of her limited edition shiny black, baby grand piano. She played the sad, mournful song from memory. Ever since the discovery of Henry's young mistress, she'd been feeling depressed. She often turned to her piano during times of stress. Somehow, running her hands over the familiar keys made her relax. But this time it didn't seem to be working and it was all Henry's fault.

Oh, she'd known all about his infidelities—well, most of them. She was sure they'd started before the ink on their marriage certificate had dried. But she'd never met any of them. Until now, they'd remained nameless, faceless women. Call her a coward, but she'd preferred it that way. It helped her cope with the knowledge the man she'd fallen in love with and committed her life to, didn't feel the same way. Oh, he'd said the words often enough—at least, in the beginning. But his actions had spoken even louder.

She'd discovered his treachery by accident. It was only a few months into their marriage. She'd still been surrounded by the glow of love and contentment, flush with happiness. She'd thought Henry felt the same way.

She'd found the note in the pocket of his suit pants. He'd left his suit out to be dry cleaned. She'd checked the pockets for handkerchiefs, as she always did. The note was tucked up in one of the crevices. It was folded twice and smelled of perfume. Even now, she could remember the cloying scent.

At first, she'd been confused about the note. She'd read it three times over before the words had begun to sink in.

Thanks for a fantastic night. You were magnificent. Such stamina! I look forward to seeing you again. L xxx

She'd had no way of knowing who 'L' was and she hadn't wanted to know. It had been obvious Henry had spent the night with a woman. Someone who was not his wife. Elizabeth thought back to the times when Henry called her from the office, explaining he'd been caught up, was working late into the night. A few times he'd told her he was spending the night there, on the couch. That he was too tired to drive…

She'd wanted to believe him. In the early days, she had. But when it began to happen with increasing frequency, she couldn't help but be suspicious. Then she'd found the note. She could still remember sinking down onto the edge of their bed, clutching the note in her hand, her mind awhirl with questions, her heart clenching with pain.

When she'd confronted him with the note later that night, he'd laughed off her accusations and told her she was jumping to conclusions.

"It was a silly game I played with my secretary," he explained. "We were talking about a show we'd watched on TV."

"Your secretary's name is Rhonda," she'd shot back.

Henry had remained calm. "Surely you don't think I have only one?"

"What about the way she ended the note? What about the kisses?"

Henry merely shook his head, dismissing her questions. "It was a joke, Elizabeth. If you don't believe me, that's your problem. I don't want to talk about this again."

Elizabeth had reluctantly come to accept her husband's explanation—until the next time. It wasn't a note, but a scrap of lacy black underwear that had definitely not belonged to her. Once again, she'd found it in the pocket of his suit pants. She hadn't even bothered to confront him about it. What would have been the point? It had become obvious he had no intention of being honest with her and though he'd continued to share her bed, even with her lack of experience, she'd known his focus had shifted.

From then on, whenever they'd slept together, it had been clinical at best, like he was just getting the job done. Finished in a few minutes. He'd stopped caring about whether she'd come. At the time, she'd put it down to the fact he was tired and stressed. Work had been busy. He'd been spending more and more time at the office.

But as the months and years had gone by, Henry hadn't even attempted to hide his infidelities from her. By then she'd almost convinced herself she didn't care. And of course, she'd had Archie.

Dear Archie…

He was the best friend she'd ever had. She'd met him a few months after she began dating his brother. She was twenty-five. Archie was three years older. Henry had invited her home for a game of tennis. Though Elizabeth came from a wealthy family, she'd been impressed that the Craigdons had a full-sized tennis court at the back of their house, along with an in-ground pool.

And Henry had been right: Archie had been immediately besotted. His gaze had followed her around the court. He'd laughed at her jokes. He'd blushed when she gave him any attention; became awkward, tongue tied. Elizabeth had thought him adorable, but she was already half in love with his brother. She could tell from the sadness that sometimes crossed his face that he was well aware of that.

Still, they'd had fun together. Henry was often busy at work. In those early days, he'd been employed at Elizabeth's uncle's firm as an accountant. That's where the two of them had met. Sometimes they'd made plans to spend time together, only for Henry to tell her he couldn't get the time off.

Archie had always seemed to be there to help her get over her disappointment. Often the two of them would attend the function together instead. Archie was always happy to step in for his errant brother and though Elizabeth had been aware of his feelings for her, she'd always been careful to treat him as a friend. Henry had once teased her about her "lap dog."

"He fancies himself in love with you Elizabeth," Henry often joked. "Haven't you seen the way he looks at you? He's got it bad."

She'd merely brushed away Henry's comments. Henry would let it go for the moment, but there had always been a hard edge to his smile. It had made her anxious and she'd go out of her way to reassure him he was the only man for her.

Elizabeth stopped playing. The clash of piano keys was jarring in the silence. Still feeling out of sorts, she rested her hands in her lap and stared blindly into the distance.

Why, oh why didn't I see what was staring me in the face? I thought I was in love with Henry, but all along it was Archie who'd stolen my heart. I fell in love with Henry's charm and charisma. He had a way of making me feel special, like I was the only woman in the world. But it was all a front, a malicious joke… And the joke was on me…

A knock on the open music room door interrupted her sad thoughts. She looked over her shoulder and saw Amy standing in the doorway. The housekeeper was frowning.

"What is it, Amy?"

"It's Archie. He's outside. He… He asked to see you."

Elizabeth flushed with embarrassment. She understood Amy's confusion. Archie had been coming and going from Craigdon Manor for decades. Elizabeth couldn't remember the last time he'd asked for permission before entering. It just went to show how upset he was…and how much things had changed between them.

A surge of guilt washed over her. She quickly pushed it aside. Archie was the one who'd walked out on her. He was the one who'd been keeping secrets.

And so did I…

Amy returned with Archie trailing behind her. He carried a box that was brimming over with tulle and dark purple ribbons. Amy disappeared. Archie entered the room and set the box down on the coffee table.

Elizabeth stood and came toward him. He kept his gaze averted, didn't even acknowledge her presence.

"Flynn asked me to stop by and drop off some decorations for the engagement party." He glanced at her and just as quickly looked away. "It's a bit awkward now, given how things are between us, but apparently Jayde has her heart set on having the party on the grounds of Craigdon Manor. She's been making plans for weeks. I'm not going to disappoint her by telling her our situation has…changed."

Elizabeth's heart clenched. Through all the years of pain and turmoil while they'd loved each other from afar, and even later, when they conducted a stealthy affair, they'd always managed to stay united in their love for each other. She couldn't believe that now, when they could finally be together, they were at odds.

This is stupid! We love each other! We need to work things out! One of us needs to be the bigger person…

"I'm sorry Archie," she said quietly.

He shook his head, his eyes filled with sadness and resignation that scared her more than angry words.

"I don't think 'sorry' is going to cut it this time, Elizabeth."

Panic tinged with fear rushed over her. She stared at him. "Please don't talk like that."

He kept his gaze averted. "I don't know what else you want me to say."

She moved closer, her panic ratcheting up a notch. His quiet resignation was terrifying. "I want you to stand and fight for us. Tell me what's wrong. Why are you so upset? Is it because of Sophia? Is that what this is all about? I thought we worked through that?"

"It's not about Sophia," he said wearily. "Although I can't deny that shocked the hell out of me. You couldn't have hurt me more than you did by keeping the truth about Sophia from me. All these years. She's my daughter! And I never knew."

Elizabeth was flooded with a renewed sense of guilt. Though she and Archie had talked about this and she thought he'd forgiven her deceit, she understood the hurt she'd caused ran deep. It wouldn't heal as fast as she wanted it to. Still, Archie had just said this wasn't about Sophia…

"I'm sorry, Archie. I'm confused. If this isn't about Sophia, then what is it?"

Archie looked her in the eye. "Don't you want to know about Logan? How I found out he was Henry's son?"

Elizabeth blinked. "Of course. I was shocked when I realized Henry's revelation didn't come as a surprise to you. Or your sons. You all knew before the letter was read, didn't you?"

"Yes." Archie's shoulders slumped on a weary sigh. "Logan was going through some of Janelle's things. They've been stored in the attic all these years. He's never expressed any interest in them before, but I guess now he has Mia in his life… Anyway, he asked if he could look at them. I think he wanted to show Mia a picture of Janelle. Instead he found her diary. He was left in no doubt as to who his father was."

Elizabeth's heart clenched at the pain on Archie's face. "Was he the one who told you?"

Archie gave a jerky nod. "Yes. He also told his brothers.

I don't think either of them were as surprised as I was." He glanced at Elizabeth. "I know you tried to convince me that Janelle had cheated on me, but I refused to believe it. She never once gave me any indication… I thought she loved me to the end. It was one of the reasons why I felt so guilty whenever you and I were together… There were times when I hated myself."

Elizabeth bit her lip against a rush of emotion. "I wish you'd told me."

"What good would that have done?" Archie cried in anguish. "Neither of us were prepared to leave our marriages. No, I dealt with things the best I could and learned to live with the guilt."

"Would it have made a difference to you if you'd known about Henry and Janelle back then?" Elizabeth asked quietly.

Archie was silent for a long moment and then he shook his head. "No. Probably not. Maybe I would have felt less guilty, but it wouldn't have changed what I did."

"What we *both* did," Elizabeth reminded him. "I was part of it, too. I came to you of my own free will. You didn't force me to fall in love with you and you certainly didn't force me to sleep with you."

His bark of laughter was devoid of humor. "You're right, I guess. That didn't make it any easier for me. And now, when we're finally free to live openly together, to tell the world—or at least our children—about our love, you refuse to do it."

She opened her mouth to respond, to explain, to… She didn't know what she wanted to say. As the silence between them lengthened, Archie's expression filled with sadness and resignation.

He sighed wearily. "That's what I thought. After all we've endured, you don't love me enough to go public. You're more than happy to keep me in the background. I'm supposed to be content with whatever scraps of affection you're prepared to give. Always in secret. Like you're ashamed of me. Of us."

He shook his head. "I can't do it anymore, Elizabeth. I've had enough. I've spent the past thirty-eight years loving you. I'll love you until my final breath, but this…" He spread his arms wide. "I'm done."

She gaped at him, wanting desperately to wipe away the disappointment and despair, to say the words he wanted to hear. When she continued to remain silent, he turned and left.

Collapsing into a heap on the couch, Elizabeth cried like her heart was broken.

And it was.

Flynn quietly opened the door to his apartment and tiptoed across the tiles. Jayde sat with her back to him on the couch. He could hear her muttering to herself. The engagement party was less than two days away and she was driving herself mad trying to keep on top of the many last-minute details.

As he got closer, he could see she had the guest list and seating plan spread out on the coffee table in front of her. Names had been added and crossed out so many times he didn't know how she could tell which was which. He stifled a bemused chuckle and planted a kiss on her cheek.

She yelped in fright. "Flynn! Oh, my goodness! You nearly gave me a heart attack!" He grinned unrepentantly.

"Surprise!"

"What are you doing home so early? I thought you were going to be stuck in court all day."

"I thought so too. Let's just say I used my exceptional negotiating skills to mediate an agreement between the warring parties. We avoided having the judge decide."

She raised a dark eyebrow, looking skeptical. "And they both walked away happy?"

"Of course not," Flynn replied, coming around and dropping himself down beside her. "I specialize in family law.

No one's ever going to walk away happy." He shrugged. "But I do my best. Today I got lucky." He pulled her close against him and kissed her properly on the mouth. "And that means I get to come home early and snuggle with my fiancée."

She smiled and pulled slowly away. "Speaking of engagements, what's with your aunt?"

Flynn frowned. "What do you mean?"

"I stopped by Elizabeth's house earlier to drop off some more things for the party. She was polite enough, but I got the distinct impression she wasn't looking forward to hosting it."

Flynn shrugged. "No one's said anything to me. I was only speaking with Callum yesterday. He didn't say anything about her being unwell."

"*Hm.* Maybe I was imagining it. You don't think she only agreed because your father asked her, do you?"

"No. Aunt Elizabeth doesn't do anything she doesn't want to. There's no way my father has any influence over her."

Jayde shot him a dubious look. "Are you sure about that?"

Flynn frowned again. "What are you getting at?"

"Nothing. It's just that she and your father seem awfully close."

"They've known each other for a long time. And of course, at one stage they were lovers. Have you forgotten about Sophia?"

"No, but that was a long time ago. Sophia's nearly twenty-two."

Flynn drew her closer against him and nuzzled her neck. "I'm sure Aunt Elizabeth is thrilled to host our engagement celebration. There's nothing she loves more than to throw a big party. I'm not in the least concerned she's doing it out of sufferance. She's just not that kind of person."

"Okay, if you say so," Jayde mumbled, distracted.

She let her head fall back to give Flynn greater access. He kissed his way across the curve of her shoulder, her neck, her jawline. Her eyes drifted closed. At the same time, she reached for him. His lips found hers and they sighed together. As the kiss deepened, he cupped her breast through her T-shirt. Her nipple hardened beneath his touch.

She reached out and stroked his erection through his suit pants. His cock leaped, straining against his boxers.

"And this is why I worked so darn hard to get home early," he mumbled against her lips.

She continued to stroke him through his pants. "*Mm.* I can feel how hard you worked. I'm flattered."

"You ought to be. You do that to me. Every time. I can't get enough of you."

With that, Flynn gathered her in his arms. He stood and carried her to their bedroom. The mid-afternoon sunlight drifted in through the window, bathing the bed in a golden glow. He set Jayde down on the mattress and then followed her down. Their lips met in another hot kiss. He stared down at her, his heart swelling with a tenderness that was almost overwhelming.

"I love you, Jayde. Now and forever. 'Til death do us part."

She smiled softly. Her eyes were luminous with emotion. "I love you, too."

Chapter Six

Seated before her dressing table, Elizabeth stared at her reflection in the mirror and frowned. She'd done her best to hide the dark circles, but there was nothing she could do about the sadness that lingered in her eyes. It had been that way since her talk with Archie. She hadn't seen him since.

The truth was, she was scared. Scared that if they brought their love out in public, it would be diminished somehow. She'd heard of so many people who lived together and then finally tied the knot… Only to divorce a short time later. The very thought of that terrified her. She'd thought long and hard on it and this fear was what kept her from saying the words Archie wanted to hear.

Now she was preparing for his son's engagement party. In less than an hour, the guests would begin to arrive. She wasn't ready to face him or them, but she had no choice. She was hosting the party and Archie was Flynn's father, a prominent party guest. There's no way she could avoid him for the duration of the celebration.

She couldn't believe they'd come to this. To attending the same event and doing their best to avoid each other. For so many years, they'd rejoiced whenever they happened to be invited to the same function. It had meant they could spend time together, talking, dancing, drinking…without fear of anyone becoming suspicious.

Though they'd snatched private moments whenever they could over the years, it hadn't been easy. They were both from prominent families. There was always someone wanting to latch onto a scandal. Or an overzealous journalist being paid to fill the social pages with scurrilous gossip.

But somehow their love had endured and despite the challenges they'd faced and the secret she'd kept from him, she liked to think it had flourished. Three decades later and they still loved each other. That was no mean feat. And yet now their wagons were circling and they were quietly licking their wounds. They were at a horrible impasse and she was terrified she'd lose him.

Archie felt justified in his actions, refusing to reconcile with her until she went public with their love, and Elizabeth felt just as strongly that she wouldn't be pressured into doing something she wasn't ready to do. It shouldn't matter that she couldn't quite enunciate her reasons. The fact was, Archie should respect her wishes: She wasn't ready to 'out' them as a couple to the world. There had already been enough drama and upheaval.

With a sigh of resignation, Elizabeth patted down a few errant strands of white hair. She did a last check of her makeup and then pushed away from the dressing table. She wasn't going to fix anything by hiding out in her bedroom and though she was acting cowardly as far as Archie was concerned, she knew better than most how to put on an act worthy of an Oscar. No one attending tonight would guess her heart was breaking, least of all Archie. *Especially* Archie.

On a surge of determination, she stood and crossed over to her walk-in wardrobe. The gold-sequined, floor-length dress was new. She could have chosen any number of designer dresses that already filled her wardrobe, but she'd decided the formal celebration of Flynn's engagement was worthy of a new dress.

Slipping the satin-lined number over her head, she let the soft fabric slide over her skin. Reaching around, she slid up the zipper. The dress fit like a glove. She turned from side to side and viewed her reflection in the full-length mirror that hung on the wall.

She'd turned sixty last birthday, but she worked hard to keep herself in shape. She ate well and regularly exercised and was aware many people thought she was a decade younger. That made her smile. She was comfortable in her skin, particularly when she was sheathed in a dress that only emphasized her assets—and who didn't want to look younger?

Bending down, she pulled on a pair of matching gold sandals. The heels elevated her natural height an extra few inches. Checking her watch, she noted the time. She needed to get downstairs. She wanted to check on last-minute details and make sure Jayde wasn't working herself into a panic. Not that she seemed the type.

Jayde was an officer with the DEA who'd spent time working undercover. She was tough, both mentally and physically. But she hadn't organized an engagement party before and Elizabeth had seen lesser women come undone over organizing events.

What was more, Jayde's parents weren't around to provide their support. Her mother had died over a year ago from cancer. Her father was serving time in jail. Flynn's mother, Janelle, was also not around anymore, so both of them were without the help and support of a motherly figure. She guessed that's where she could and should step up.

Back before their fallout, Archie had asked her if she'd consider hosting the engagement party at her home. He'd confided that Jayde loved the beautiful, spacious grounds of Craigdon Manor and would be thrilled if Elizabeth came on board. Elizabeth was flattered to be asked and was all in on the preparations. It was only since she and Archie had fallen out that the glow had been taken off the celebration.

But now the time was upon her and she'd put on her very best smile. After all, this was about Flynn and Jayde. It was their night. She loved them both and owed it to them to make this night extra special. More than a hundred guests were expected. Some of them she knew quite well. She also looked forward to spending time with her children. She'd deal with Archie if and when she had to.

The party was in full swing. There was plenty of food, the drinks were flowing and everyone appeared to be having a good time. Elizabeth scanned the crowd of guests who were gathered around the pool.

They were bathed in the warmth of a balmy summer evening. A light breeze gently teased the women's hair. The smell of orange blossom was heavy on the air. Jayde had done a wonderful job with organizing the decorations. Thousands of fairy lights, colorful Chinese lanterns and glittering silver bells filled the trees that grew around the garden perimeter.

The effect was magical. Coupled with the murmur of conversation, the tinkle of glassware and the occasional burst of laughter created an atmosphere that was light and cheery, the perfect ambience for a party.

Further away, a DJ had set up near a makeshift dance floor not far from the pool. The beat of house music encouraged guests out on the dance floor. Unsurprisingly, Noah and his fiancée, Ayla, were already out there, dancing up a storm. The two of them were almost professional-level Latin dancers. It didn't take them long to wow the crowd.

From the corner of her eye, Elizabeth spied Archie. He stood a few yards away, half concealed behind an enormous terracotta pot that housed a large, variegated elephant ears. Her heart lurched. She hadn't seen him for more than a week. They'd gone from spending much of their days and all of their nights together to only the briefest of meetings, and all of those had been tense.

The thing was, she missed him. She missed *them*. The familiar, comfortable security. Knowing he had her back. A confidante. A lover. A friend. He was so many things to her and all of them she loved.

We'll get through this. I know we will. Maybe not tonight, but sometime… Our love's been tested before. We've always come out the other side. We just have to find the courage and the willingness to do it… I need to find the words…

Taking a deep breath, she closed the distance between them and offered him a tiny smile. "Hi, Archie. You're looking sharp. Are you enjoying the party?"

He barely inclined his head in response. "Jayde has done an amazing job."

Elizabeth's heart filled with agony at the distance she saw in his eyes. It was like she wasn't even there. Her smile faded. "Yes. Yes, she has. You must be so proud of her. She's going to make Flynn a wonderful wife."

"Yes, she is."

"Archie. Please. We need to talk."

He turned to her with eyes that were cold as snow. "I already told you. I'm done talking. You know how I feel. The ball's in your court." His tone was curt, dismissive.

Emotion overwhelmed her. She closed her eyes briefly against the force of it. When she opened them again, Archie was already making his way inside. Even from a distance, she could see the anger that held his body taut.

Oh, God. What am I going to do?

Sophia draped her arms around her husband's neck and moved to the slow beat of the music. The DJ had swapped the up-tempo Latin music for a love song. The dulcet tones of the singer were low and sweet.

Jarrod pulled her close and pressed his cheek against hers. She closed her eyes and smiled.

"I love engagement parties," she murmured. "So much love in the air. They're like weddings without the stress."

Jarrod pulled slightly back. "Do you regret not having an engagement party?"

She shook her head. "No. I mean, in different circumstances, I would definitely have done the whole engagement party thing, but we didn't exactly have a normal courtship."

Jarrod chuckled. "You can say that again. You proposed the second time we met."

Sophia poked out her tongue. "You didn't have to say yes."

"Oh, but I did. Don't you remember? I was already completely, hopelessly in love with you. I couldn't wait for you to be my wife."

Their lips met and fused in a kiss filled with love and tenderness. When they finally broke apart, both of them were slightly breathless. Jarrod stared down at her, his expression reflecting the same heated desire that coursed through her veins. Even now, after nearly six months of marriage, they still set each other on fire.

Then Jarrod smiled. "Oh, I forgot to tell you. Melinda Mattheson stopped by the police station the other day."

"How's she doing?"

"Good. Great, in fact. That's why she dropped by. She wanted to tell me that she and Travis are moving. They've found a place on the Gold Coast, within walking distance of the beach. Melinda's sister lives nearby. She has a couple of kids who can't wait to get to know their cousin better. Travis has been enrolled in a good school and has already met his teacher. He's beyond excited about it all."

Sophia smiled in genuine delight. "That's so wonderful! I'm more than happy for them. For so long it was touch and go with Travis. I remember sitting outside the ICU praying he'd pull through. What happened to him was so devastating. I can't believe his father did that." She couldn't prevent a shudder.

Jarrod tightened his arms around her and pressed a kiss against her hair. "I can't believe how close I came to losing you. If I hadn't gotten there in time, Tony would have killed—"

She cut off his words with a soft kiss. "*Shh*. No more talk of that. I'm fine. We're both fine. And so are Travis and Melinda. They're off on a new adventure. I'm so glad things are working out for them. Hopefully they'll be happy."

"Yes. I hope they'll be as happy as we are." His hand moved down and splayed across her still-flat stomach. "I can't wait to share our news."

Sophia removed his hand. "I understand your excitement. I'm excited, too. But let's wait until after the first trimester. Make sure we're in the clear. Besides, this is Flynn and Jayde's night. Let's not spoil it for them by stealing the spotlight."

Jarrod nodded. "You're right." Once again, he pulled her close and they danced in unison, lost in each other's arms and dreams of the future.

Ashton Walker brushed an invisible piece of lint off his black jeans. The clean white polo shirt was tucked neatly into his waistband. His boots were shiny, his hair freshly washed. Clean-shaven, rosy cheeked. He looked like the boy next door.

That's exactly the look he was going for. Nothing threatening. Someone who looked trustworthy. He'd learned from experience that was the most important thing.

The driveway was filled with late model luxury cars, mostly Audis, BMWs and Jaguars. There were a couple of Ferraris—both red, of course. None of the cars had a price tag of less than two hundred thousand dollars.

This sure must be some kind of swanky do…

For a moment he hesitated on his way to the front door. Perhaps he should come back in the morning, when there were less people around? The security guard at the front gate had said something about an engagement party. It was obvious there was a party in full swing. He could hear the music from there.

And then Ashton shrugged. What the hell… He'd come this far already. What happened in the next few minutes wasn't going to change because of the number of witnesses. In fact, in some ways, having witnesses to what he was about to say would make it easier for him. Elizabeth Craigdon would hardly deny the truth about him in front of a crowd of people. From what he knew of her, she was much too honest for that.

He was as ready as he'd ever be and he'd psyched himself up to get there. He'd rehearsed his opening lines until he knew them by heart. He'd always been a good actor. Hell, he could call up tears at will. No easy feat for some people.

Besides, he had this down pat. This wasn't the first time he'd landed on someone's doorstep, pretending to be their long lost son. He'd learned to project just the right amount of uncertainty, anger, fear and hope. It had always worked in the past.

What can possibly go wrong?

He grimaced. A lot of things, actually. What if the information he'd memorized was incorrect? What if Elizabeth Craigdon didn't have a son she'd given up for adoption? What if it were true, but she denied it and turned him away?

He gave a mental shrug. If that happened, he'd merely move on to the next name on his list. The thing was, he had to think positive. He'd gotten this far on positive thinking. It had stood him in good stead so far.

Mind made up, he patted a few stray hairs back in place and headed toward Craigdon Manor with a smile carefully fixed in place and just the right amount of uncertainty in his posture. He didn't want to look too confident. You never knew who might be watching through the security cameras.

Elizabeth moved like an automaton, smiling and offering nods of acknowledgement to Flynn and Jayde's guests. A cold lump of dread filled her stomach, making it impossible to eat, to drink, to do anything but go through the motions and pray for the night to end. A member of the catering team came up to her and mentioned they were nearly out of smoked salmon.

Elizabeth told her she'd call her favorite restaurant and see if they could help her out. After a few moments of pleasant conversation with the owner of the restaurant, Elizabeth explained her dilemma.

"Of course I can send some over," Raphael immediately responded. "How much do you need?"

"Whatever you can spare," Elizabeth replied. "And thank you, Raphael. I really appreciate it."

"You're a valued and much-admired customer, Elizabeth. I'm happy to be able to help out."

"Thank you. Please put it on my tab. I'll fix it up next time I'm in."

"No problem. I'll arrange for an Uber driver to get it over to you. Give me fifteen minutes. Will that do?"

Elizabeth sighed with relief. "That will be fantastic. Thank you again, Raphael. You're a lifesaver."

Crisis averted, Elizabeth put away her phone. She was just about to head back out to the party when Amy approached her from the direction of the front door.

"Elizabeth. I'm sorry to disturb you, but there's a gentleman at the door who's asking to see you. I explained you're in the middle of hosting a private party, but he insisted."

Elizabeth frowned. "Who is it?"

"He wouldn't give me his name?"

Elizabeth's frown deepened. "*Hm.* Strange. Are you sure he asked for me?"

"Yes."

"What does he look like?"

Amy shrugged. "I don't know. Dark hair with a hint of gray, blue eyes. Maybe forty."

A surge of impatience went through Elizabeth. *This is ridiculous! I don't have time for an unfamiliar, unwelcome visitor. It's all I can do to get through my duties as hostess. I don't need any more complications tonight…*

"What should I tell him?" Amy asked, anxiety tingeing her voice.

Elizabeth blew out her breath. "Oh, for heaven's sake. Who turns up at someone's house unannounced this late at night? It's the epitome of bad manners."

Amy regarded her uncertainly. "Should I send him away?"

Elizabeth compressed her lips and shook her head. "No. I'll deal with him now. Show him to the music room."

Taking a moment check her appearance in the mirror that hung in the hallway, Elizabeth made her way there. The music room was empty save for a tall, broad-shouldered man who stood with his back to her in front of the piano. He ran his fingers over the keys.

She froze. "Who are you and what are you doing here?"

The man turned slowly around. Elizabeth catalogued his features, but nothing about him was familiar.

A slow, uncertain smile tugged at his lips. "Don't tell me you don't recognize me?"

She frowned. Impatience made her irritable. "Of course I don't recognize you. Now, if you don't mind, get to the point because—if you hadn't noticed—I'm kind of busy."

"Oh, yes. An engagement party. Nice."

She narrowed her eyes at him with suspicion. "How do you know it's an engagement party?"

"The security guard outside the front gate told me."

Elizabeth relaxed infinitesimally. "Oh, I see."

The man walked closer. A bemused expression filled his face. "Are you sure you don't recognize me?"

Once again, she frowned. "No. I'm sorry. I've never seen you in my life. Who are you?"

"My name is Ashton Walker. My friends call me Ash."

The name meant nothing to her. She told him as much.

"Figures," he replied. "I guess I didn't expect you to know my name."

Impatient, she threw up her hands. "For heaven's sake! This is ridiculous! What game are you playing? I don't know you and I'm absolutely certain we've never met. Now, either state your business this minute, or leave. I have guests to attend to."

When he remained silent, she turned on her heel, intent on carrying through her threat. His voice reached her before she made it to the door.

"It's funny. The number of times I dreamed of this scene, wondering what it would be like. I always imagined this moment would be filled with more...joy."

His words gave her pause. Slowly, she turned back to face him.

His lips twisted into a grimace. "Stupid of me, really. What did I expect? That you'd greet me with open arms, be beside yourself with excitement that we'd found each other again?"

Something about the bitterness that lined his voice reverberated deep inside her.

He sounds so sad, so…disillusioned. Poor fellow…

"I'm sorry, Ashton. Ash. You have me at a disadvantage. You seem to know who I am, but I'm still completely in the dark about you and why you're here." She spread her arms wide. "Please, you need to give me more."

He walked slowly toward her. "More? I'll give you more. Tell me, does the name David Mason mean anything to you?"

Elizabeth's stomach dropped. She gulped with shock. "D-David Mason?" She hadn't thought about him for a long time. She didn't even know if he were still alive. "H-how do you know David?"

Ashton smiled. "Ah. So you remember David. How nice."

Elizabeth's mind was in turmoil. Her thoughts spun madly around. Having a complete stranger voice his name after all these years was vastly unsettling.

"What do you know about David?" she managed.

Ashton's face filled with regret. "Unfortunately, not a lot. But I do know one important thing… He's my biological father." He paused again and added: "Hello, Mom."

Chapter Seven

With Ashton's stunning words still ringing in Elizabeth's ears, he then stepped forward, opened his arms wide and hugged her. Elizabeth stood frozen with shock. She didn't even realize they were no longer alone until Isabella cleared her throat and asked, "What's going on here?"

Elizabeth leaped back like she'd been burned. Her face filled with heat. She never imagined in her wildest dreams that this was how she'd be forced to reveal her deepest, darkest secret. In fact, she'd convinced herself she'd take the secret to her grave. Though she'd never forgotten her first-born child, she'd forced herself to push his memory to the furthest part of her mind. He was lost to her forever and that's the way it was.

But now he was here, in her music room. Shiny dark hair, big blue eyes. A dimple in his cheek. He had her coloring. She stared at him, searching for signs of David, but there were none.

"Mom? What's going on? Who is this?"

Once again, Isabella's questions intruded. Elizabeth cast around frantically for some answers. Before she could say anything, her son took the decision out of her hands.

"Hi, I'm Ashton Walker. Your brother. Well, half-brother," he corrected with a disarming grin.

Isabella gaped in shock. She immediately turned accusing eyes on her mother. "Don't tell me this is another of Daddy's by-blows we didn't know about."

Elizabeth remained motionless, still trying to come to grips with the shock of having her son arrive on her doorstep. She opened her mouth, but nothing came out. Once again, Ashton stepped in.

Anger was banked in his eyes. "A by-blow? How quaint. To answer your question, no. I'm not your father's child." He glanced at Elizabeth. "This woman is my mother."

Isabella burst out into laughter. "Yeah, right. And I'm the Prime Minister's secret love child."

Ashton's gaze remained unperturbed. "You must be Isabella. The pictures I found of you on the Internet didn't alert me to how nasty you are."

Anger narrowed Isabella's gaze. "Look, buddy. I don't know who you are or what you're doing here, but one thing I do know is that you're not my mother's son." She gave him a scathing look. "You look like you're just shy of forty. Don't you think we would have heard about you by now?" She shook her head, dismissing him. "We're in the middle of a family celebration. You need to leave."

With that, Isabella looked pointedly past Elizabeth's shoulder to where Amy hovered in the open doorway. The housekeeper looked as shocked as Elizabeth felt.

"Amy? Please show this man out. He doesn't belong here," Isabella said in a dismissive tone.

Ashton shot Elizabeth a hard look. Panic warred with hope inside her veins. She couldn't deny him again. She'd been denying him all his life. It was time to bring an end to that.

"It's all right Amy," Elizabeth said in the calmest tone she could manage. "Ashton's staying."

"*What?*" Isabella shot her a look filled with confusion. "Mom! Are you feeling all right?"

Elizabeth looked at her daughter. She felt bad about the uncertainty that now clouded Isabella's beautiful face.

"I know this has come as a shock to you, Issy… Don't worry, it's come as a shock to me, too. But… Ashton is right. It appears he's my son."

Isabella continued to look confused. "But… But… I don't understand."

Elizabeth's shoulders slumped on a weary sigh. She would have preferred not to deal with this right now, but it seemed Ashton and fate had other plans.

"I'll explain everything, I promise." She looked at her son. "But Isabella's right. We're in the middle of celebrating an engagement party. Do you mind if we put this on hold until after our guests have left?"

Ashton gave her a reassuring smile. "Of course, Mom." He smiled again. "You don't mind me calling you 'Mom', do you?" Without waiting for her to reply, he added, "Please accept my apologies. If I'd known you were entertaining, I wouldn't have arrived on your doorstep like this."

Elizabeth touched him on the arm. "It's not your fault. "But I'd appreciate it if you could keep this quiet a bit longer. At least until the party has wound down. We'll talk after that. I promise." She looked at Isabella. "That goes for you, too. Please don't say anything to your brothers and sister. I want to tell them myself."

A mutinous expression filled Isabella's face, but she offered a half-hearted shrug. "Okay."

Elizabeth swallowed a sigh of relief. She'd been granted a reprieve. It wasn't for long, but it was something. Pasting a smile on her face, she turned to Amy. "Would you kindly get Ashton a drink?"

Amy nodded and blindly left the room. With a similar expression clouding her features, Isabella followed her. Elizabeth turned back to face her son.

My son… I still can't believe it… After all these years… It pains me to realize I would not even have recognized him if we'd passed on the street…

As if sensing the agony of her thoughts, Ashton stepped toward her and pulled her in against him for another hug. She resisted momentarily and then forced herself to relax.

"I'm sorry again, Mom, for barging in on you like this. I can see how shocked you are. Would you like to sit down?"

Elizabeth pulled away and smoothed out her dress. "No. I'm fine. Shocked, yes, but I'm also…happy. The last time I saw you, you were a squalling newborn, all glistening and pink. I instantly fell in love with you."

His lips twisted on a grimace. "But you didn't love me enough to keep me."

Pain sheared through Elizabeth's heart. She gasped from the impact of it. "Oh, Ashton! I'm so sorry you feel that way! It couldn't be further from the truth! I loved you with every fiber of my being…"

"And yet you gave me up," he said bitterly.

"I didn't want to! My parents… They wouldn't let me keep you. We were both so young, David and I."

Ashton looked at her with a cynical expression. When he spoke, there was scorn in his voice.

"You were twenty, Mom. Not that young. Your parents were hardly in a position to force you to do anything. You were an adult. You could have left and taken me with you. If you'd loved me enough."

His tone remained low, but there was pain and accusation behind his words. Elizabeth was flooded with guilt.

He's right. I could have left. I could have tried to raise him on my own…

She shrugged helplessly, wanting him to understand. "It wasn't a matter of not loving you enough. Please don't think that. I loved you with all my heart. But it wasn't that easy. I was still living with my parents. I had no money of my own. No skills. I thought I'd spend my life playing the piano, traveling the world, making music in some of the grandest theaters in the world." She paused and then added sadly, "David thought the same. He was a violinist at the Conservatorium of Music in Sydney. He was so talented… That's where we met….and fell in love."

Ashton looked unconvinced. "I still think you took the easy way out. You weren't ready for a baby. I interfered with your plans. You just admitted it."

Once again, Elizabeth was weighed down by guilt. Everything Ashton said was true. She bowed her head, unable to bear witness to his pain. There was nothing she could say that would convince him she'd taken the only option available to her. While it had felt that way at the time, she'd always had a sliver of doubt about her decision. Could she have tried harder to keep him, her son?

But she'd allowed her parents to talk her into giving him up. By then, David was long gone. He'd been as unprepared for the disruptions of a baby as she was and though earlier they'd promised to love each other forever, life and a baby made that promise impossible to keep. She hadn't blamed him for deserting her. It was her fault she'd gotten pregnant. He'd wanted to wait until they could get married. She'd persuaded him otherwise.

She'd been head over heels in love, sure they'd had what it took to last the distance. She'd been young and silly, with her head full of dreams. She hadn't wanted to be cautious. She hadn't wanted to wait. And then she'd had to live with the consequences. Only, she'd never dreamed they'd be so harsh or that she'd mourn the loss of her baby for the rest of her life.

Because that's how it had felt when they'd taken him from her, never to be seen by her again. It felt like he'd died. In some ways, it would have been easier if he had. At least then she'd have closure, a grave to visit. This way she'd had nothing. She wasn't even allowed to know where he'd gone, or who had adopted him. Over the years, the laws regarding adoption had undergone change and now it was possible to track down a child or a biological parent.

Curious about that, Elizabeth looked at him. "How did you find me?"

"I contacted the department of Family and Community Services. It took more than a year from when I first started looking, but finally I found you."

She frowned. "Wow. And you…didn't think to write first, before turning up?"

His answering laugh sounded strained "Yes, well, my counselor certainly urged me to do that, but I wanted it to be a surprise."

She bit her lip and then smiled. "I see. Well, it definitely was a surprise." She shook her head, still feeling overwhelmed. "I can't believe you're here."

He gave her a rueful grin. "Neither can I." He looked down and gave an embarrassed laugh. Then he looked back at her again.

"You can't imagine how many times I nearly turned back. Not just tonight, but over the months I spent trying to track you down. I didn't know if you'd want to see me. If I ever crossed your mind. I didn't know if you'd be happy to reconnect, or send me packing. I was scared. Terrified, more like it.

"All sorts of scenarios of our first meeting continuously went through my head, like a movie that never stopped. Some of the scenes were happy, some not quite so much. It tore me up inside, not knowing. But then, somehow I found the courage and I just walked right up that drive. I nearly turned around when I saw all those cars, but I knew I probably wouldn't find the courage again if I didn't do it here and now. So I knocked. And here I am."

When he held his arms out wide, as if offering himself to her, tears burned behind her eyes.

"We've lost so much time. Forty years. Come, sit down beside me. Tell me about yourself."

"Don't you have guests to deal with?"

"Yes, but right now, I want to spend a few moments with my son. We have a lot of catching up to do."

He shot her a beatific smile that lit up the blue of his eyes. Once again she searched for some sign of David, but found none. She took a seat on the couch.

Ashton followed her and sat down at the opposite end. He stretched out his long legs and sighed. "I can't believe I'm here."

She gave him a moist smile. "That makes two of us." She paused and then added, "I'm so glad to see you after all these years. You can't imagine how many times I've thought about you." Her gaze roved over him, committing everything about him to memory. "You look well. Fit and strong and healthy. Have you…had a good life?"

His lips twisted in a grimace. "Do you really want to ask me that? You gave up your right a long time ago about having any input into how I was raised."

She flushed and looked down at her hands where they sat in her lap. "You're right," she said softly around a lump that had lodged itself in her throat. Her gaze landed on her piano that stood in the far corner of the room. "Do you play?" she asked.

He followed the direction of her gaze and nodded. "Yes. I play the piano and the violin."

She gasped softly with surprise. "Wow. That's… That's wonderful."

Ashton shrugged. "I was raised in a musical family. My adoptive mother was a music teacher. She worked at the local high school. My dad—sorry, my adoptive father—was a small-time farmer. Cattle, cereal crops. We were never rich like this, but we did all right. The most important thing was, I always felt loved."

He shot Elizabeth a look that was pregnant with meaning. Once again, she was filled with guilt. Ashton immediately looked contrite.

"I'm sorry, Mom. I don't mean to make you feel bad. It's just that..." He shrugged helplessly. "I've spent all of my life thinking about you; what you were like; where you lived; whether I had any brothers and sisters; wondering why you didn't love me enough to keep me."

The tears that she'd fought to hold at bay, now slid down her cheeks. "Oh, Ashton! There's nothing I can say or do to make up for the time we've lost. All I can do is to start fresh now—become a good mother to you in whatever way I can. And maybe someday you'll forgive me."

Ashton closed his eyes briefly. When he opened them again, the pain was still there. "I'd like to think one day I'll get there, but right now... It's too much to ask. I've spent the past forty years vacillating between hating you and wanting to throw myself in your arms and never let you go. From the time I could understand, I was told I was adopted.

"I was one of the lucky ones. My adoptive parents were mostly good and kind. But I still spent thousands of hours wondering about you, wanting to meet you, to get to know you, to be loved by *you*..."

This time, Elizabeth refused to let her guilt overwhelm her. There was nothing she could do about what had happened, unless she could turn back time. Since that was impossible, she had to learn to live with the circumstances as best she could— just as she had for the past forty years.

"Are they still alive? Your adoptive parents?"

Ashton shook his head. "No. They were in late thirties when they adopted me. Dad died of cancer two years ago. I lost my mother to dementia a year later."

"I'm so sorry," Elizabeth murmured.

Ashton shrugged off her sympathy. "In some ways it was a blessing. They were both suffering. And it gave me the courage to start my search of discovery for you. It was something I never felt right about doing while they were alive."

Elizabeth offered him a shaky smile. "I'm so glad you did."

The shock of coming face to face with her son was starting to wear off. Now all she felt was joy… And apprehension at the thought of explaining him to her family. She only hoped they were as accepting of him as she was.

Of course, it was only natural that it would take time for them to warm to him. After all, they'd had no idea Ashton existed. But she'd raised her children to be good and kind and compassionate and she prayed that once over their initial surprise, they'd welcome him into the family with open arms. He deserved nothing less and she was determined to make up for lost time. Starting now.

The party had wound down. Only Elizabeth's immediate family and Archie remained. At her request, they congregated in the music room. Coffee and tea were served, along with the port. Ashton had spent the time since his initial talk with Elizabeth, mingling with the other guests. She'd made sure he had something to eat. At one point she'd seen him talking to Archie. She wondered what they'd discussed.

She flicked another glance in Archie's direction. Fatigue had etched lines into his face. His expression remained distant. It was later in the evening than she'd wanted to have this discussion, but that couldn't be helped. The guests had lingered for what seemed like forever and she could hardly shut the party down and ask them all to leave. So she'd endured a few more long hours and sighed in relief when the family finally had the house to themselves.

"Well," Elizabeth said as she began pouring coffee, "that went off smoothly, don't you think?"

There was a general murmur of agreement. Elizabeth glanced around the room. They were all there: her children and their respective partners. Callum and Grace—their children had long since been tucked up in bed in one of the guest rooms upstairs. Jett and Danielle had opted to leave their children with a babysitter. Joel and Sheridan sat side by side on the couch with their shoulders touching. They had yet to set a wedding date, but Elizabeth was confident an announcement to that effect was sure to be made soon.

Nicholas and Harper also sat together on the couch. Harper had her head resting on Nick's shoulder. He had a hand on her belly, cupping the child that lay within. Sophia and Jarrod were all loved up. They kissed and held hands like they were teenagers. Though they'd married under unusual circumstances, Elizabeth had no doubt this was a true love match. The knowledge filled her with contentment and peace. All she wanted was for her children to find true love and happiness. It appeared her prayers had been answered.

Isabella and Raine stood off to one side. Though Raine's arm was draped casually over Isabella's shoulders, there was a tension in her body that was no doubt attributable to the secret she'd been forced to keep. Elizabeth sighed inwardly. She hated that she'd asked that of Issy, but there had been no choice. There was no way she could have dealt with such shocking news in front of a crowd of strangers and it wasn't like they could retire to a different part of the house and abandon their guests.

It was supposed to be a joyous occasion, celebrating the engagement of Archie's oldest son. Elizabeth had no doubt Flynn had chosen well in a soul mate. It was obvious just by looking at them how in love they were. Elizabeth was just as happy for her nephew as she was for her children, but thankfully, the loved-up newly engaged couple had left for the night, along with the last of their guests.

Setting the coffee pot back down on the table, Elizabeth picked up her cup and took a sip. Nerves twisted in her stomach. She'd delayed the moment as long as she could. It was time to take hold of her courage and explain why she'd summoned them all there.

She glanced toward Ashton. He'd moved to the piano stool. He sat in half-shadow, removed from the rest of the group. A few of them had sent curious glances in his direction. Others appeared not to have noticed him.

Elizabeth cleared her throat. "Thank you all for joining me here. It's late and I'm sure you're all looking forward to retiring. So am I. But there's something important I need to tell you about. Or more specifically, *someone*."

A fresh wave of nerves tightened her stomach. She tried to find the words. This was going to come as such a shock to her family. Having her son arrive out of the blue had come as a shock to *her*, and she at least had known of his existence.

"Come on, Mom. Get to the point."

Elizabeth winced at the harshness of Isabella's tone. Still, she understood her daughter's antagonism. And it would probably be easier just to rip the plaster off. Drawing in a deep breath, she squared her shoulders and gazed straight out toward her gathered children.

"I have another son… One you have not yet met. His name is Ashton."

"*What?*"

The cry of alarm came from Archie. It was mirrored by similar shocked cries from her children. Only Isabella remained silent.

Archie stood, his fists clenched. His expression was a mixture of shock and anger and hurt.

"I'm sorry," Elizabeth continued, enveloping all of them

with her gaze. "Ashton was born years before I met Henry. Forty years ago, I gave him up for adoption. Tonight… Tonight he showed up here and introduced himself. And now, I'd like to introduce you all to him."

She gestured toward Ashton. He stood and moved to where she sat perched on the edge of an armchair. She looked up at him and smiled and then turned back to her family.

"This is Ashton Walker. My son."

"Who's his father?"

"Where's he been?"

"Why turn up now?"

"What does he want?"

"How do you know he's your son?"

The questions came thick and fast from all directions, all tinged with shock and even a bit of panic. It was like none of them could believe what they were seeing and hearing. She understood their reaction. It would take time and patience for them all to work through this. She just hoped they'd also be understanding. In the meantime, she owed them an explanation.

Chapter Eight

lizabeth's gaze rested on each of her children, cataloguing their shock. It was important that she give them an explanation if they were ever to accept Ashton as their half-brother and if they were ever to forgive her for keeping him a secret.

"I always wanted to be a concert pianist," she started quietly. "My parents were supportive at the time. My mother had been a talented pianist. She was pleased when I wanted to follow in her footsteps.

"When I left school at eighteen, I was fortunate enough to be offered a place at the Conservatorium of Music in Sydney. I was thrilled and excited and scared all at once. Out of thousands of applicants, they chose only a few. It was an honor to be offered a place, but I knew it wouldn't be easy. I'd be expected to work hard, to practice endless hours each day. To work on my craft, to get better each time. To excel."

She smiled. "And boy, did I work hard. I loved every minute I spent there. It was what I'd been born to do. I was surrounded by my tribe—other musicians as passionate as I was about their music. It was a heady environment, especially for a young woman. I'd never experienced anything like it. I felt like I'd come home."

"And then you fell pregnant and that was the end of your music career," Isabella offered in a dry tone.

Elizabeth grimaced. "Yes. That's exactly what happened."

"Tell us about it," Callum encouraged in a gentle tone.

Elizabeth shot him a grateful look. At least one of her children was showing her some support and understanding.

"David Mason was a violinist. Tall, fine-boned, beautiful. White-blond hair that looked like spun sugar. Eyes as green as the summer forest. He was soft spoken, gentle. I never heard him raise his voice. And he played the violin like an angel; like the maestro he was."

Elizabeth momentarily closed her eyes, swept up in her memories. It had been a long time since she'd allowed herself to think of the man who'd first stolen her heart. Her first love. The father of her first child.

"I was nineteen when I fell pregnant. David was twenty-two. You can imagine my parents' reaction. Or maybe you can't. Things were different back then. Single mothers were shunned. Good girls from good families didn't have babies out of wedlock. It's just the way it was.

"My parents reacted like most parents did back then. There was no question of an abortion—we were strict Catholics, after all. No, I would be allowed to have my baby, but I wouldn't be able to keep him."

"That must have been tough," Nicholas muttered. He drew Harper close.

Elizabeth nodded. "Yes, it was. Though I didn't like the plan one little bit, I went along with it. After all, I had nine months to try and convince them otherwise." She drew in a deep breath and eased it out before continuing.

"Unfortunately, my relationship with David wasn't as strong as I'd believed. I had to leave the conservatorium, of course, and it was difficult to see him when I wasn't in school with him.

My parents wouldn't allow him to come around and see me and there was no other way for us to meet."

She smiled wryly. "You have to remember, there were no mobile phones in those days and only one phone in our house. David didn't have a phone either. I sent him a few letters, but I never received a response. In the end, David did write me back and told me he was breaking things off. His position at the conservatorium was demanding. He couldn't afford the distraction of fighting for me and our love. He made no mention of our baby."

Her breath caught on a soft sigh. "I didn't blame him. I understood exactly how demanding a position at the conservatorium was."

"You were very forgiving," Joel muttered. "He was as responsible for your pregnancy as you were. I'm not sure I would have been as forgiving in the circumstances."

Elizabeth looked at him. She compressed her lips and shrugged. "I understand how you might feel that way, Joel. Over the years, there have been times when I looked back and realized David could have tried harder, proposed—anything to fight for us. But he was young and completely invested in his career and, dare I say it, selfish and weak. Although I didn't see that at the time."

She took another careful sip of her coffee and then set the cup back down before continuing.

"The nine months came and went and my beautiful son was born. Pink and healthy and screaming. Perfect in every way. I was allowed an hour with him. That was it. A nun came in and took him away. I never saw him again. Until this evening."

Her voice cracked with emotion. She looked at Ashton. His eyes had filled with tears. He reached out his hand toward her. She took it gratefully. He squeezed her hand in reassurance. A lump of emotion formed in her throat.

I can't believe he's here…in my house. After all these years… My son!

"What did you do afterwards?" Sophia asked curiously.

Elizabeth sighed. "I was depressed for a long time afterwards. I wouldn't leave the house. I had no thought of returning to the conservatorium. It would only remind me of David and our son. Eventually my parents had had enough. They insisted I get a job."

She gave a half-laugh that was devoid of humor. "A job! I don't know what they expected me to do. I'd gone straight from school to the conservatorium. I knew how to play the piano well, but that was about the extent of my skills. Until then, I'd been pampered and petted and spoiled all of my short life. I didn't even know how to cook. We had a houseful of servants who saw to my every need. How was I supposed to learn how to do anything?"

She sighed. "Eventually my father managed to convince his brother to let me go work in his office. Uncle Jack was an accountant. He put me on as an office junior. I ran errands, did the banking, picked up the mail. That kind of stuff."

Her lips twisted into a grimace. "My parents were pleased to have me work there, of course. By then, the only future they could see for me was to nab an eligible husband. My chances were greatly improved by working in a professional office. My uncle ran a very successful business in the eastern suburbs. He had plenty of well-heeled clients. My parents were hopeful I might catch the eye of one of them."

She looked around at her family and offered them a sad smile. "I guess they were right. That's where I met Henry. He was working there as a junior accountant. By that time I had some typing skills. I'd worked my way up to secretary and was assigned to Henry."

She sighed. "I was twenty-three. He was twenty-eight. As you know, it took a few years of courtship, but eventually I succumbed to his charms."

"Did you tell him about the baby you'd given up?" Archie asked, his voice hoarse.

Elizabeth regarded him steadily. "No. That part of my life was closed. I never expected to see my son again."

Archie made a sound of disgust in the back of his throat. He shook his head in disbelief. "You've got to be kidding! What else did you keep secret?"

Elizabeth ignored him. There were too many people around for her to get into this with Archie. It would have to wait until they were alone. She deliberately focused her gaze on her children. "By the time I agreed to marry Henry, I was in love with him. I realized what I had felt for David was more like infatuation. I had been young, innocent when I fell in love for the first time. What did I know about that?" She laughed without humor.

"Henry swept me off my feet. He promised me the world. I told him about my dream to become a concert pianist. He was supportive of this. In fact, he even bought me a piano. The limited edition black baby grand you see over there." She smiled sadly at the memory. "We were so in love back then. At least, I thought we were. The piano cost him two months' wages."

"I never knew Dad bought you that," Jett murmured.

Elizabeth nodded. "Yes. Your father could be very persuasive. His charm and persistence finally won me over. We married when I turned twenty-seven. By then I'd thrust memories of David and our baby to the furthest recesses of my mind."

Ashton made a sound in the back of his throat. Elizabeth's gaze flew to his. "I'm sorry, Ashton. That came out wrong. I thought about you so often. All the time. You were never far from my thoughts. But my life had gone in a different direction. I had a husband. Eventually more children came along. Your half-brothers and sisters. The people you see here today."

Once again, her gaze encompassed her children. "This has come as such a shock for all of you, even for me. I understand you're feeling blindsided. But none of this is Ashton's fault. Please, don't take out your anger on him."

She looked at Archie. He stood so still it was as if he were frozen to the spot. Twin spots of color on his cheeks highlighted his anger. His eyes were as cold as ice.

Her heart fell. She closed her eyes against the hurt and accusation she saw in his gaze. Even though her love affair with David had happened years before she and Archie had met, it was obvious he was upset by it. Or perhaps he was hurt that she'd never told him… Whatever. She couldn't deal with Archie right now. She had too much going on in her head already. In fact, she was tired. Her head was aching. She needed to be alone.

With that thought in mind, she stood. Ashton was immediately by her side.

"Are you all right, Mom?"

She smiled wanly and patted the back of his hand. "I'm fine. Thank you, son. It's been a long day. Tell me, where are you staying?"

"I booked a room at a hotel. I wasn't sure what kind of reception I'd get here. Besides, I didn't want to impose."

"Nonsense. You're family. My son. You must stay here. I insist."

"Are you sure?"

"Of course. We have plenty of room." She looked at Isabella. "Would you please show Ashton to one of the guest rooms? We can send a car for your belongings in the morning."

Isabella didn't look so pleased about her request, but Elizabeth was beyond caring. She was tired and overwhelmed with all that had happened. She needed to lie down.

She looked again at her family gathered around. "We've

all had a shock. It will take some time to get our heads around it. I understand some of you might need more time than others. That's fine. In the meantime, I'm going to bed. I'll see you all in the morning."

"Have a good sleep, Mom."

"Goodnight, Mom."

"Take care, Mom. Sleep well."

The kind comments from her children followed her across the room as she made her way out the door. She took the stairs slowly, all of a sudden feeling all of her years deep in her bones. Mixed with the euphoria of meeting her son again was the pain of knowing her secret, now outed, was bound to cause anger, hurt and disruption. She only hoped her family would exhibit the kindness, generosity of spirit understanding and compassion they'd been raised with and that Ashton would feel embraced by the family that hadn't known he existed until that evening.

The thought about their eventual acceptance made her smile. Her heart lightened.

I still can't believe it! My son! My precious son! After all these years, he found his way back to me!

They had so much catching up to do.

The next morning, Elizabeth woke alone and she was immediately filled with a rush of sadness and emptiness deep inside. It had been weeks since she and Archie had shared a bed. She missed the closeness, the intimacy, the feeling there was someone who loved her and had her back. She hated being at odds with him. She missed him. Things between them had become even more complicated with the arrival of Ashton the night before.

Elizabeth blew her breath out on a weary sigh. She'd spent a restless night, tossing and turning, her dreams filled with images of her infant son in the moments before he'd been taken from her. She'd woken this morning from a fitful sleep with tears drying on her cheeks. Now she had a chance to make up for lost time. It was a gift she never thought she'd have.

Throwing off the covers, she did her best to repair the damage caused by a sleepless night. She took a steaming hot shower and carefully applied her makeup. Checking her appearance in the mirror before she went downstairs, she was satisfied she'd managed to disguise most of the effects. The dark circles under her eyes were concealed with foundation and she'd squirted some eye drops into her eyes in an effort to lessen their redness. Overall, she didn't think anyone would guess she'd been awake most of the night.

A murmur of voices reached her from the breakfast room. She rounded the corner and saw her family. Sun poured in through the windows, filling the room with light. The chatter from Seth and Alyssa, Grace's children from a previous marriage, was interspersed by the murmur of adult conversation. She scanned the familiar faces. Archie's wasn't among them.

He must have gone back to his house last night…

The knowledge saddened her, but there was nothing she could do about that right now. Her gaze landed on Ashton. His luggage must have arrived because he wore different clothes than those from the night before. Her heart lightened at the knowledge he was here, taking his rightful place among her family.

I really hit the jackpot this time.

Ashton poured himself a cup of coffee from the carafe that stood on the sideboard. Next to the coffee, a hot breakfast was laid out, just waiting for the family to begin eating. Bacon and eggs, toast, sausages, grilled tomato and a large platter of fresh fruit, just for starters. It had all been prepared by the Craigdon chef.

I can't believe there are people who actually live like this! And now I'm one of them!

It reminded him he needed to play his part in order not to arouse suspicion. He could tell his arrival had already put a few of the Craigdon children off side. Isabella in particular seemed put out that he was there. She'd barely been civilized when she'd shown him to a guest room the night before. He made a mental note to double his efforts to charm Elizabeth. She was the head of the household. If she believed he was who he said he was, all would be well.

As if conjuring her up, she appeared in the doorway to the dining room. She was dressed in a sky-blue tailored blouse and navy-blue skirt. The color brought out her eyes.

"Good-morning. What a lovely day! How did everyone sleep?" Elizabeth asked, smiling.

There was a general murmur of greetings. Then Ashton spoke.

"I'm pretty sure that was the most comfortable bed I've ever slept in," he said. He wanted her to think he was a country bumpkin who'd done it a little tough. That way she was sure to feel sorry for him. Sympathy was good. It would help foster her guilt.

Elizabeth's smile widened. "I'm so glad you stayed. I hope someone got you settled?"

"Yes, thank you." Ashton turned and winked at Isabella. "Isabella was ever so gracious to show me to a room. It was right next to where Seth and Alyssa slept. Callum did warn me they were early risers..." Ashton looked in Callum's direction. "You were certainly right about that."

Ashton looked straight at Isabella. She narrowed her eyes at him. A stain of embarrassment colored her cheeks.

Take that, you nasty cow… You put me in that room on purpose… I know you did…

Unaware of the tension between him and Isabella, there

was a rumble of laughter from the others before everyone helped themselves to the bountiful breakfast.

"Would you like a cup, Mom?" Isabella asked, holding up the coffee pot.

"Yes please," Elizabeth replied. She handed Isabella her cup.

Moving to the head of the table, Elizabeth set down her cup and then filled a plate from the sideboard. Ashton made sure to sit on her right, where he was pretty sure Archie normally sat. Everyone else had left the chair vacant. If Elizabeth minded the imposition, she made no mention of it. Instead, she turned to him and offered him another smile.

"I'm so thrilled to have you here. I never thought I'd see you again."

He pretended nonchalance and shrugged. "Here I am."

"Yes, and I couldn't be happier. It's like a wonderful dream. We have so much catching up to do."

So far so good… This was going better than he'd expected. She hadn't even questioned his claim. Not even once…

"Forty years in fact," he quipped, remembering that tidbit of information he'd gleaned from his research. He forked scrambled eggs into his mouth. "*Mm,* these are so good. It must be nice having your own personal chef."

It was a deliberate dig, but he said it with such wide-eyed, country bumpkin innocence he was sure she wouldn't take offense.

Elizabeth started in on her breakfast. "Yes. Amy's a whizz in the kitchen. She's been with us for many years. She's been there for many of the important occasions. We moved here when the kids were young teens. They used to love coming home from school to a plate of her fresh brownies, or cookies, or whatever delights she'd made that day."

Ashton forced a wistful expression. "Amy's the woman who showed me in last evening?" Elizabeth nodded and

Ashton continued: "It must have been nice growing up here."

God, he was laying it on thick! Still, from the distraught look on Elizabeth's face, his dig had hit the mark. She tactfully changed the subject.

"Tell me about your adoptive parents. Where did you grow up?"

He thought of the backstory he'd hatched. "In the country. In Tamworth. It's about four hours' drive north of here. My parents still have a house there. I inherited it on my mother's death. Have you heard of Tamworth?"

"Yes, of course. The country music capital of Australia, right?"

He deliberately grimaced and then let it morph into a reluctant smile. "Right. Not exactly the kind of music I like to play, but some people get a kick out of it."

"What's your favorite instrument?"

"The piano. But the violin is a close second."

She flushed with pride. "Are you sure you're not just saying that to impress me?"

Of course I am. What do you think I am? An idiot? Everyone likes to be flattered...

"Of course not," he replied in a sincere voice.

"What kind of music do you play?"

"Classical, of course." *Just like you. Did you think I wouldn't do my research?* He deliberately opened his eyes wide. "Is there any other kind?"

Once again, she flushed with pleasure. She touched a hand to her chest and smiled at him again.

"We have so much in common. I have no doubt you're my son."

Oh, God, this is like taking candy from a baby. It shouldn't be this easy... Still, I'm not complaining.

She took another bite of eggs. "Where are you staying while you're in Sydney?"

"Like I said last night, I booked into a hotel in the city." He deliberately stared down at his plate. His tone became uncertain. "I… I wasn't sure what kind of reception I'd get from you. I wanted to make sure I had somewhere to stay."

Elizabeth looked devastated. Guilt flooded her face. It was all Ashton could do not to smile.

"Oh, Ashton! It breaks my heart to hear you thought I might have turned you away."

He lifted his gaze to hers. Right on cue, tears glinted in his eyes. "How was I to know if you'd even acknowledge my existence, let alone invite me inside? I've spent years imagining this moment and wondering how it might go. Some pretty awful scenarios passed through my mind, believe me. I wanted to prepare myself for the worst, just in case it happened."

"Well, I hope I've put your mind at ease. You're my son, my flesh and blood. You're welcome here anytime."

Jubilation poured through him. *Yes! This is way too easy! A few more tears and I'm in!*

He forced a suitably sincere and grateful expression on his face. "That's very kind of you. Thank you."

Elizabeth waved his gratitude away. "There's no need for thanks. We're family. And I won't hear of you staying in a hotel. There's plenty of room here at Craigdon Manor." She looked around at the crowd gathered around the breakfast table and gave a wry laugh. "We're a bit overcrowded at the moment, but usually I live here on my own. Grace lived here with her children for a few months before she and Callum were married and until recently, Isabella lived here, too. But she's now moved to Brisbane to be with her fiancé, so it's just me again.

"I have this huge house going to waste." She reached over and put her hand on his arm. "Please, say you'll stay with me. At least, for as long as you're in town."

Ashton deliberately hesitated. He lowered his gaze and frowned, as if in deep thought.

No sense in appearing too eager. She might get suspicious if I don't appear to give it at least a modicum of consideration...

Elizabeth tightened her hold on his arm. "Please, Ashton. It would make me very happy to share my home with you."

Hook, line and sinker...

He finally capitulated on a wry laugh. "Well, I guess... If you're certain..."

"I am," she said firmly. "In fact, you can have your own wing. You'll have plenty of privacy and for those times when we want to sit and talk... Well, we can do that, too."

Ashton hid a satisfied smile. Elizabeth clapped her hands to get everyone's attention.

"I just want to let you all know I've invited Ashton to stay here while he's in Sydney and he's agreed. How wonderful is that?"

Her announcement was met with a mixture of uncertain smiles and frowns. Ashton noticed Callum gave his mother a smile of encouragement, but Joel, Jett, Isabella and Nicholas all looked decidedly unimpressed. Sophia also appeared concerned.

I need to watch my step around them. They're not as gullible as their mother. Nor are they as riddled with guilt and so quick to believe...

He made a mental note to try harder on his long lost son act. He had a feeling he was going to enjoy his stay at Craigdon Manor. He didn't want to do anything to jeopardize that, or bring it to an end too soon. At least, not before he was ready.

After breakfast, Elizabeth retired to the music room. She barely had time to sit on the couch and pull out her needlework when her children cornered her.

"How do you know this guy's really your son? He could be anyone!" Joel exclaimed.

"He's right Mom," Isabella added. "What proof do you have?"

Already anticipating their opposition, Elizabeth remained calm. "He went through the department of Family and Community Services."

Sophia frowned. "How does that work?"

"People can apply for access to the details regarding their birth parents," Jett explained. "Unless a veto has been put in place by one or both of the biological parents, a child can get access. Even then, the veto had to be recorded prior to 2003, when the law in that regard changed."

"Oh, okay," Sophia replied. "So you didn't veto it. Does that mean you hoped he'd find you?"

"Yes. On some level I really did. And he knew about his father, David," Elizabeth continued. "He knew how to track me down. He has my coloring and plays the piano and the violin. Isn't that wonderful! He's a musician like me. I don't need any more proof than that."

Nicholas looked unconvinced. "So what if he plays instruments. He could still be anyone. Have you even heard him play?"

"No, we haven't had a chance. He only arrived last night."

"Have you looked for him on YouTube?" Isabella asked. "If he's as good as he says, he should have an online presence somewhere."

"He could be making all that stuff up, Mom!" Sophia protested. "It's not hard to get on the Internet and research someone's past."

"Yes," Joel added, "it seems kind of strange how he's turned up now. I mean, he's forty years old. The laws that were changed allowing people who were adopted to discover their biological parents came into effect years ago. What took him so long?"

"Dad's death was all over the news, including plenty of speculation about his net worth. I hate to be cynical, but you just can't overlook the fact this guy might be an imposter after a slice of that wealth," Isabella said.

"What you're saying doesn't make sense," Elizabeth protested. "How could he know I had a baby all those years ago? It was a closely guarded secret. Not many people knew."

"You can find out anything if you know the right people and if you look hard enough," Jett muttered.

Elizabeth crossed her arms over her chest and stared at her family. She clenched her teeth and set her jaw at the angle they knew meant she wasn't budging from her position.

"The reason he's taken so long to find me is out of respect for his adoptive parents. He didn't want to hurt them by taking those steps sooner. Now that they're both dead, he's free to make his inquires. Which he did. And now he's here. And for your information, he's not forty. At least, not quite. He turns forty in a couple of weeks."

"You remember his birthday?" Isabella asked.

Elizabeth's gaze remained steady. "Of course. Just as I remember all of your birthdays."

"I still don't like it," Nicholas muttered. "This guy could be anyone."

"There's one simple way we can know for sure," Joel said. "We'll ask him to submit to a DNA test."

"You'll do no such thing!" Elizabeth protested, aghast. "As if this poor man hasn't been treated badly enough! How would you feel if you'd been given up for adoption at birth? Growing up believing your birth mother didn't love you enough to keep you? How would you feel?"

To their credit, all five of them stared at the floor with guilt coloring their cheeks. Elizabeth sighed.

"I'm sorry. I know this has come as a shock to all of you. It can't be easy to discover you have a long-lost half-brother.

It was bad enough when Stella Taunton turned up and told us about the baby she and Henry lost. Now I've gone and done the same, only my baby's alive and well and he's staying right down the hall."

She stood and moved closer to where they were gathered. "I understand how difficult this is and I don't expect you to welcome Ashton with opens arm right away. These things take time. But like I said last night: None of this is his fault. Please don't blame him for my sins. He was the truly innocent party in all of this.

"He didn't ask to be born. He didn't ask to be adopted. Now he's found us—his family. The least we can do is accept him without querying his motivation or questioning his word. Okay?"

She stared at each in turn until they nodded with varying degrees of reluctance.

"Good," she said, satisfied. With that, she turned away and left the room before any of them could respond again. She'd had enough of defending her son to her children…as well as Archie the night before. He'd been none too pleased to discover she had a secret love child. Or was it that she'd kept the secret from him?

She sighed and her shoulders slumped. It was only mid-morning, but already she felt weary. She wanted to reconcile with Archie and put the tension between them behind her once and for all, but she also owed a debt of allegiance to her son.

She'd turned her back on him once in such an awful and permanent way. She refused to do it again. She might be acting irrationally, but all she wanted was to bask in the glory of having him there. It might be forty years late, but better late than never.

Chapter Nine

Ash Walker pulled his sunglasses over his eyes and settled himself comfortably in the pool chair. With the summer sun sparkling off the water and turning it into diamonds, the pool couldn't have looked more inviting. He'd been living at Craigdon Manor for a little over a week and boy, was he becoming accustomed to the lifestyle. It sure beat his usual digs.

Each morning he'd come downstairs and find Amy in the kitchen and put in an order for breakfast. By mid-morning, he usually found himself out by the pool. He'd check emails, surf the Internet and idly flick through pages on Facebook while he worked on his tan. Sometimes he played a round on the nine-hole golf course.

Amy would materialize a couple of hours later and ask what he'd like for lunch. It was a nice life and one he could get used to. And by the way things were progressing with Elizabeth that ought to be a no-brainer.

Elizabeth had meant it when she said she wanted to make up for lost time. She was constantly in attendance, wanting to know if he needed anything. Naturally, he always declined her offers. His fake reluctance had the desired effect. She showered him with gifts. Designer clothes, shoes, sunglasses. A Rolex watch. When he'd mentioned his phone was on the blink, she'd turned up with a brand new one, the latest model iPhone on the market.

Only yesterday morning when she asked about his plans, he told her he wanted to head into the city but his car had broken down. She'd smiled mysteriously. By mid-afternoon, a shiny red Porsche was parked outside. She'd seemed embarrassed by the over-the-top gift, but he'd told her it was the nicest thing anyone had ever done for him. That seemed to bring her round.

He'd even managed to squeeze out a few tears and had then gone for broke by telling her how much he'd love a dog.

"My adoptive mother was allergic to dogs. That's why I wasn't allowed to have one. With no brothers and sisters, it sure got lonely at times."

Elizabeth had looked so sad he'd actually felt a little bad about his performance. But feeling bad for him was good. The same as feeling guilty. He actively encouraged her feelings of guilt. The guiltier she felt, the more she wanted to overcompensate for all the years he'd supposedly missed out. It was all part of the game. He was living the kind of life he could only dream about. He was going to do all he could to prolong it.

A shadow fell upon him, blocking his sun. He opened his eyes and stared up at Isabella. She was breathtakingly beautiful in a glossy-magazine-model kind of way, but there was a bright intelligence in her green eyes that he knew he shouldn't underestimate. She, along with most of her siblings, had remained cool toward him. It was obvious they didn't trust him.

Not that he could blame them. He'd appeared out of nowhere and taken up residence in their mother's life—literally and figuratively. If the tables were turned, he'd be somewhat suspicious too.

He dipped his sunglasses and plastered on a friendly smile.

"Well, well, well. If it isn't my delightful sister, Isabella. To what do I owe this pleasure?"

Her manner bordered on frosty. "Cut the crap, Walker. You might have fooled my mother with your little lost son routine, but I'm not as gullible."

He pretended to be taken aback. "Wow. Say it like it is, sis. I didn't expect you to welcome me with open arms, but do you have to be downright hostile? What did I do to you?"

She gave him a scathing look. "You're an interloper. I don't believe for an instant you're my mother's long lost son and you could hurt her badly when she finds out the truth. You might have her coloring, but so do lots of people. Black hair, olive skin, blue eyes. Big deal. You look nothing like her."

His lip curled up in a wry smile. "And you do?"

She touched the cloud of platinum blond hair reflexively. "I took after my father. So what?"

He shot her a lazy look. "How do you know I didn't take after *my* father?"

"My mother told us David had fair hair, remember? As white and fine as spun sugar, I think she said." Once again, her gaze raked over him. "Doesn't sound at all like you."

He chuckled. Sparring with Isabella was so much fun. She had a fire about her that got him going. Too bad they hadn't met under different circumstances… And then he dragged his thoughts away from such dangerous territory. If he had any hope of pulling off this subterfuge, he best watch himself.

With an exaggerated yawn, he stretched his arms out over his head, elongating his body as he did so. Tall and muscular and well-built in all the right places, he was disappointed when Isabella's gaze didn't once stray to his buffed, near-naked body.

"What are you doing here, anyway?" he asked over another yawn.

Her gaze hardened. "Sorry to bore you, but I stopped by to see my mother. Is that all right with you?"

"I thought you lived in Brisbane now," he murmured, purposefully injecting a bored note into his voice.

"Not that it's any of your business, but yes. I do. I'm just down here tying up some loose ends before my wedding."

Ash clapped his hands together. "Oh, a wedding! How delightful! I love weddings."

Isabella scowled. "It's for family only."

His grin widened. "Oh, perfect. Does that mean I'll get a seat at the main table?"

Isabella made an indecipherable sound of frustration in the back of her throat. Ash merely grinned. He loved that he was able to get under her skin. Isabella Craigdon looked like she needed someone to loosen her up. She was way too tense.

"Oh, by the way, Mom went into the city. I can take a message for her if you like."

Isabella frowned. "But I saw her Audi out the front."

"Oh, yeah. You're right. She went in my Porsche. I thought since she was so generous in buying it for me, the least I could do was let her take it for a drive."

Isabella sputtered in shock. It was obvious Elizabeth hadn't told her about the recent purchase.

"She bought you a *Porsche*?"

Ashton merely smiled. "Yes. I told her it was too much, but she insisted." He threw his hands up in surrender. "What was I to do?"

"She's lost her mind," Isabella muttered under her breath. "Just wait until I see her…"

"Don't be too hard on her, Issy," he said, deliberately using her family nickname. "She's having so much fun splashing out on things for me. She's trying hard to make up for lost time."

Isabella's expression hardened. "Oh, yes. I bet she is. And you're just lapping up all the attention, right? How nice to be you."

His answering grin was unrepentant. "Absolutely! I have no complaints."

"I'll bet." With that, Isabella spun on her heel and stalked back in the direction of the house, no doubt to check if what he'd said was true.

Sure enough, a moment later he heard her call out. "Mom? Are you home?"

Isabella was fuming. She couldn't stand another minute of that insufferable man. He was supposed to be her half-brother but there was no way she was falling for that line. There was something about him that set her on edge. She'd distrusted him from the start. It was only that her mother was so determined to believe he was her long-lost son that Isabella had kept her mouth shut.

Of course, she still intended to expose him for the fraud he undoubtedly was. She just had to find a way to prove it.

"Mom?" she called again.

Amy appeared from out of the kitchen. "Hi Issy. I'm sorry, but your mom went into the city. She left an hour ago and said she wouldn't be home until dinnertime. Is there something I can help you with?"

Issy's shoulders slumped on a sigh. It seemed these days whenever she tried to talk to her mother, Elizabeth had something else on. It was all Ashton's fault. He was the reason she was always tied up. Whenever they did get to speak, it was usually "Ashton this" and "Ashton that." It was driving Issy insane. She hadn't even had the chance to tell her mom they'd set a wedding date.

Where has my mother gone? The woman who's always been so cool and calm and assessing? She's lost her head over the imposter out there who's pretending to be my half-brother…

"It's all right, Amy. I just wanted to show Mom some fabric samples. Raine and I have set a date. The wedding will be in the spring."

Amy's face was wreathed in smiles. She clapped her hands together in delight.

"Oh, Issy! How wonderful! A spring bride!" Her eyes teared up. "I was a spring bride, you know," she suddenly confided.

Isabella blinked in surprise. In all the years Amy had worked for them, she'd never once mentioned a husband.

"No, I didn't know. You never told us you were married."

The old eyes grew moister. She got a faraway look on her face. "Gerald was the love of my life. We got married early. I was nineteen. He was twenty-one. People got married young in those days."

Isabella smiled. "Yes."

"We were so in love. We couldn't wait to start our life together."

"What happened?" Isabella asked gently. She could tell from the sadness on Amy's face that things hadn't turned out well.

The old housekeeper wiped her hands on her apron and sighed. "He was killed in a plane crash. We'd only been married a few months. He was flying back from his family farm in far north-west New South Wales. They farmed cotton, along with cereal crops and cattle. A bit of everything. We had plans to move to the farm after a couple of years of marriage. We'd decided to stay in the city and enjoy all that Sydney had to offer and then move to the country when it was time to start a family. We never got the chance."

Isabella was filled with a rush of compassion. "That's terrible, Amy. You poor thing! I can't imagine losing my husband, and so soon after the wedding!" She paused and then asked, "You never remarried?"

Amy shook her head. Sadness still lingered in the air. "No. Gerald was the love of my life. There was no one else for me." She looked up. Her eyes glinted with tears. She swiped at them with the back of her hand. "That's why it was so wonderful when I secured this position. Your mother really had her hands full. So many young children demanding attention. I was happy to step in and help out. It took my mind off things."

Isabella stepped forward and hugged her. "And we love you for it. I can't imagine what life would have been like here without you."

"Aw, Issy. You're so sweet. I know it wasn't always easy for you growing up here."

Isabella compressed her lips. She was besieged by a barrage of memories. She'd called herself "the keeper of the secrets." It had been a heavy burden to carry. Until now, she didn't think anyone had noticed, but it seemed nothing escaped Amy.

Issy sighed. "You're right. There were some tough times, especially when I was too young to properly comprehend what was going on."

"I won't speak ill of the dead, but I wish your father hadn't burdened you like that. It wasn't fair."

"No, it wasn't," Isabella agreed. "But Daddy's gone now and that's that."

"Can I take a look at your fabric samples?"

Isabella brightened. Though she was still disappointed her mother wasn't there, that didn't mean she couldn't share her excitement with Amy. She gave the old housekeeper a wide grin. "Absolutely."

"I'll put the kettle on to boil and we'll have a cup of tea. White with one, right?" Amy winked.

"Right. We can sit in the breakfast room. The light's good in there."

While Amy disappeared back into the kitchen, Isabella brought her bag containing the fabric samples into the breakfast room. Setting the bag on the table, she pulled out the various swatches of fabric she was choosing between for the bridesmaids' dresses. She'd decided to ask Sophia to be her matron of honor and Raine's four sisters to be bridesmaids. She hadn't told him yet, but she was sure he'd be thrilled. He was as close to his brothers and sisters as she was to hers. This was a nice way to include them.

The sound of the opening and closing of the sliding French doors that led out into the pool area caught her attention. She looked up in time to see Ashton saunter into the kitchen. Though he disappeared from her sight, she could clearly hear him.

"I'll have a mango and pineapple smoothie, thanks Amy. Add a dash of Cointreau. Oh, and go easy on the ice. Bring it to me in the TV room. My favorite show's about to start."

Isabella tensed. Anger arced through her veins. *How dare he order Amy about like that! Like he was king of the house! He was a usurper! She was sure that's what he was!*

Silently, she vowed to renew her efforts to prove he wasn't who he claimed to be. She needed to talk to her brothers—the ones who had access to police databases and such. This situation was untenable. It certainly couldn't continue. Determination surged through her.

While the sound of the blender blocked out her conversation, she pulled out her phone. Moving away from the noise, she dialed her brother's number.

"Issy! What can I do for you?" Joel asked.

"I need a favor."

"Ask away."

"It's about Mom's boarder."

Joel chuckled. "What's Ashton done now?"

"I don't fall for his act a single minute! There's no way he's mom's long lost son. I don't care what he says. Is there some way we can find out for sure?"

"The only way to be certain is for him to submit to a DNA test. Mom refused to allow us to ask him, remember?"

"Yes, but what if we did anyway? I mean, if he is absolutely sure he is who he says he is, then what's the problem? He should be willing to give us a sample."

"We'd need something to compare it to."

"We have Mom."

"True, but we don't have any paternal DNA. Nor are we likely to get it."

"Isn't there some way you can compare by only using the maternal DNA?"

"Yes. It's called mitochondrial DNA. It's been used by law enforcement to identify bodies in the past when only the maternal parent could be located. It's not ideal, but it's better than nothing."

"All we need to do is get results that aren't a match with Mom. Who cares who his father was?"

"I guess so."

"So you're in?"

"If you mean, do you have my support to approach him with a request for DNA, the answer is yes."

She breathed a sigh of relief. "Thanks, Joel. That means a lot. Now, how do you suggest I go about it?"

"Well, like you said, if he has nothing to hide he shouldn't mind giving you a sample to test. I can get you a swab kit, if you need one. Otherwise, just get him to pull out a few strands of hair. Make sure he pulls it out by the roots. Don't use scissors."

Issy pulled a face. "I'm not stupid, Joel. I've watched my fair share of *CSI*."

He groaned. She smiled. "Just kidding." She paused and then added, "Would you mind coming with me when I ask him?"

"Sure. Two of us against one. How can he refuse?"

Issy laughed. "I'll get back to you with the time and place. Are there any days you can't make it?"

"I'm in a training course all day tomorrow, but any day after that. Where will we meet?"

"As far as I can tell, Ashton spends most of his waking hours out by the pool. I'm at Mom's house now. I've just had a run-in with him. Hence my call. If we meet here, it shouldn't be hard to track him down."

"No worries. Get back to me with a time."

"Thanks, Joel. I appreciate your support. I'll call you."

Two days later, Isabella waited impatiently outside Craigdon Manor for Joel to arrive. She'd already phoned ahead and confirmed with Amy that Ashton was at home. Her mother's car sat parked beside his shiny red Porsche. Isabella could only assume her mother was also in.

Checking her watch, Issy tapped her foot. *Joel is late.* The thought had barely formed when he turned into the drive. She watched as his car climbed the long paved driveway and eventually came to a stop.

"Sorry I'm late," he said, pulling at his tie. "I got caught up at work."

She pecked him on the cheek. "No worries. You're here now." As a detective in a busy city station, she understood that sometimes work got in the way.

"Is he here?"

"Yes."

Joel looked around him. His gaze landed on the Porsche. "Nice wheels."

Isabella grimaced. "Didn't you hear? Mom bought it for him."

Joel whistled. "No. I must have missed that memo."

Isabella compressed her lips and shook her head. "See what I mean? This has gotten way out of control!"

"Let's not jump to conclusions, Issy. There's every chance

this guy *is* Mom's son. Let's do the test and see what we find. Then we can get on our high horses."

She rolled her eyes, but walked beside him as the two of them entered the house. They avoided the music room where their mother most often hung out and headed straight to the pool. Isabella wasn't surprised to find Ashton lounging there in the sun, once again working on his tan. She deliberately stood in front of him, blocking his sun.

He opened one eye and frowned at her. "Oh. It's you again. Don't you have somewhere else to be? Mom told me you were a doctor. Shouldn't you be saving lives, or doing something equally heroic?"

His bored tone needled her as no doubt he meant it to. With a supreme act of self-control, Isabella managed to hold onto her temper. She smiled sweetly.

"Good-morning to you too, *brother*. I hope you're having a pleasant day?"

"Pleasant enough if you move aside so I can continue to take the sun."

Isabella gritted her teeth but made an effort to take a big step to one side so that the sun once again fell on Ashton. Joel moved up to stand beside her. His stance was relaxed, but Isabella could feel the tension behind his shades.

"Ashton. It's good to see you again."

Ashton turned to look up at Joel. "Which one are you again? There are so many of you, I've forgotten."

Joel tensed. His fists clenched. With an effort of will, Isabella saw him draw in a deep breath and relax.

"I'm Joel. Third from the top. Well, fourth counting our half-brother, Christopher. I'm also a cop."

It was thrown out there like a challenge. Ashton didn't react. Instead, he pushed the sunglasses off his face and regarded Joel with a smile.

"A cop, hey? Cool."

"Yes. In fact, that's the reason we're here," Joel added.

Ashton laughed. "Surely you don't think I've broken the law. Your mother invited me to stay. I'm hardly trespassing."

"You misunderstand," Isabella replied. "We're here to ask if you'll submit to a DNA test."

Once again, Ashton barely reacted. If he was concerned about the request, he didn't show it.

A single dark eyebrow quirked upwards. "Really? A DNA test? Don't you believe I'm your half-brother?"

"No," Isabella said flatly.

Ashton merely shook his head. "Dear me. I'm not sure why you think I'd make up something like that. I mean, how would I even know about it if I'm not her true eldest son?"

Isabella ground her teeth together. She had no answer for that. "I have a swab kit we can use. It's pretty simple. You swab the inside of your mouth. We collect some saliva. Test it in a lab. Then we're done."

Ashton finally reacted. His eyes flared with anger. "No."

Joel frowned. "No? If you're so sure you're my mother's long lost son, you should have no problem doing the test. What are you afraid of?"

Ashton's jaw tightened. "I'm not afraid of anything. I just don't appreciate your insinuation that I've lied about who I am. If you're so sure I'm not who I say I am, go and do some research. My adoptive parents were Todd and Jennifer Walker. They lived in Tamworth. Todd died two years ago from cancer. Jennifer died last year of dementia. They were both well-known local identities. Their deaths made the local paper." Ashton's lip curled upwards in disgust. "I'm sure a good investigator such as yourself will track down the information in no time."

"So what if he does? That only proves you were adopted!" Isabella fired back.

Ashton swung his legs off the lounger and stood. Both Joel and Isabella were tall, but Ashton was even taller. They were both forced to tilt their heads back to look him in the eye.

"This is bullshit and you know it," Ashton hissed. "You wait until Elizabeth finds out about this. She's not going to be happy her children aren't playing nice. Mark my words."

With that, he turned on his bare heel and walked away, back in the direction of the house. Isabella sighed.

"That didn't go so well," she said.

Joel grimaced. "No."

"I lost my temper."

"So did I."

Isabella grinned reluctantly. "We make a great pair, don't we?"

"Don't sweat it. We'll find another way."

A surge of determination flooded through her. She narrowed her eyes in the direction Ashton had disappeared. "I'm not going to let this go. One way or another, we're going to find out the truth."

"Here, here, sister. His refusal has definitely raised a red flag. I'm with you all the way."

Chapter Ten

Ashton glanced over his shoulder to make sure he wasn't being followed by the two well-meaning but bungling siblings who thought they could outsmart him. Ha! Not likely! He'd been swindling people for years. This wasn't the first time he'd taken on the role of long lost son. He had the act down to a fine art. It would take more than the machinations of two Craigdons to bring him down.

He found Elizabeth in the music room, seated at her piano. Her fingers passed over the keys in a light and breezy melody. She had her eyes closed, immersed in the music. It was only after she'd finished and he clapped slowly in appreciation that she opened her eyes with a start.

"Oh, Ash. I didn't realize you were there."

He smiled. "You were playing so beautifully. I didn't want to disturb you."

She shuffled over on the piano stool and patted the seat beside her. "Come. Sit down. Play something for me."

His heart skipped a beat as panic rushed through his veins, but he kept his smile firmly in place. He hadn't come this far by not perfecting the art of deceit. This would call on all of his skills.

"I'm sorry. I jammed my finger in the door earlier and it's still a little sore." He held up his index finger. Thank God he'd bandaged it a couple of days earlier as a precaution.

Elizabeth looked immediately concerned. She jumped up off the piano stool and rushed over to him.

"Oh, Ash! I'm so sorry! Is it badly hurt? Do you need an x-ray?

"No, it's just a little bruised and swollen. I'm sure it'll be fine, but I don't think I'll be playing anything for a while." He pulled a face and did his best to look disappointed.

Elizabeth smiled. "Not to worry. We have plenty of time." She paused and then suddenly frowned. "You're not in a hurry to leave, are you?"

"No, no," he assured her with just the right amount of reluctance.

Elizabeth looked relieved and then shot him another look of concern. "I'm not keeping you away from your girlfriend, am I? Or maybe even a wife?" And then she looked stricken. "Oh my goodness! I haven't even asked if you're married, or if you have children! What sort of mother am I?"

Ashton made comforting noises and moved in and gave her a hug. "Don't upset yourself, Mom. There's been so much going on. We haven't had a lot of time to really talk. Don't worry, I have no one waiting for me and I'm not needed anywhere else. For now at least, I'm all yours. We have all the time in the world to get to know each other."

Elizabeth smiled. She reached out and pushed back a hank of his hair that had fallen over his eyes.

"Good. I'm so glad. I would have been happy to welcome your family here, but I'm glad I get to keep you to myself for a little longer. Is that too awful of me?"

"Not awful at all. I know how you feel. I feel the same way. I selfishly want to steal all of your attention. I'm not proud to admit it, but I'm jealous of your other kids."

"Don't be," she said. "I have enough love for all of you."

He pulled a face. "But they've had you all their lives. I've only had you for five minutes."

She gave him a watery smile. Tears glinted in her eyes. He smiled inwardly with satisfaction.

Everything's going to plan. The old girl has no idea she's been hoodwinked. No idea at all…

"Like you said, we have all the time in the world. I'm just so glad you're here."

She linked her arm with his and started walking toward the kitchen. It was nearly lunchtime and all of a sudden he was famished. He'd forgotten to place an order, so wondered what scrumptious cordon bleu dish Amy had cooked up for them that day.

"It's a pity your other children don't feel the way you do."

Elizabeth looked up at him and frowned. "Give them time. They had no idea about you. Your arrival here has come as a shock. But they're good and generous people. They'll warm to you in time. After all, they know you had no choice in the matter of your adoption. That can be left entirely at my feet. And I take full responsibility."

Ashton pouted. "I just wish my half-brothers and sisters weren't so suspicious of me. I get that my existence came as a complete surprise, but now that I'm here and you've explained what happened… I guess I was hoping they'd come to accept me, not question my right to be here."

Elizabeth's frown deepened. "Who's questioning your right to be here?"

Ashton pretended reluctance. "I'm not going to name anyone. I don't want to cause a rift between any of you."

"Nonsense. I want to know."

Once again, Ashton pretended to prevaricate.

"Ash, please. They know my position on this. I won't stand for them attacking you in any way. Now, please tell me which one of them is causing you grief."

He let out a heavy sigh and then finally told her. "Joel. And Isabella. I get that Joel's a cop and it's in his nature to be suspicious, but what's with Isabella? I thought she was a nice girl. Kind, caring. Hell, she saves lives for a living. I guess it's just me she doesn't like."

"That's not true!" Elizabeth protested, but there was no conviction in her tone.

He regarded her steadily. "Yes, Mom. It is. And I get it, but it still hurts."

"Oh, Ashton! I'm so sorry! What did she say?"

"It's not so much what she said. She and Joel keep insisting I submit to a DNA test. They say if I don't have anything to hide, I shouldn't have a problem with it." He shook his head, making a deliberate effort to look bewildered. "The thing is, I don't have a problem with it. It's just that, it hurts me to know they don't believe me; that they think I could lie about something like this. I mean, what kind of person would do that?"

Elizabeth's expression turned grim. She shook her head in a resolute fashion. "I can't believe they're still carrying on with that DNA nonsense. It's ridiculous! How on earth would you know I'd had a son by a man named David if you weren't that child?" She paused and then added in a determined tone. "I'll speak with them. I won't put up with this any longer. I understand their instinctive distrust, but this has got to stop." She pulled out her phone from the pocket of her jeans. "I'm going to call Isabella right now."

With that, she dialed a number and held the phone up to her ear. Ash only heard her end of the conversation, but Elizabeth made it clear to her daughter she was extremely disappointed in Isabella's and Joel's behavior and that the constant badgering of Ash to submit to a DNA test was going to stop.

"Have I made myself clear?" There was a pause while she listened to Isabella's response and then said, "Good. Make sure you pass this on to Joel. I don't want to hear that either of you, or anyone else for that matter, has mentioned the words 'DNA test' to Ashton again."

With that, she ended the call and looked up at him with a smile. "There, that should be the end of it."

He managed a genuine grin. The longer she had them off his back, the longer he could stay and enjoy her hospitality. He'd settled into Craigdon Manor rather nicely. The place had a resort-like feel he'd come to relish. His most difficult decision when he woke each day was whether to lounge out by the pool or enjoy a round of golf. It would be a shame to have to give all this up before he was ready.

Maybe I could stay here forever? How good would that be?

Hiding a smile, he responded with the right amount of gratitude. "Thank you, Mom. I really appreciate that."

"No problem. Now, let's go and enjoy lunch."

Elizabeth tested the temperature of the bath water and sighed. *Perfect.* She'd already poured a generous amount of bubble bath into the wide ceramic tub and her champagne flute was full. Scented candles burned on the shelf that ran along the window, filling the room with the smell of frangipani, mango, lime and coconut. Dropping her robe, she stepped into the hot water, sinking deep until it covered her shoulders. She sighed in relief. She could almost feel the tension in her body slipping away.

It had been an emotional couple of weeks. First the last letter from Henry, penned while he was still alive and shared with them a year after his death. It still angered her that he wasn't at all sorry for the way he treated Nicholas and showed no remorse when it came to Sophia and the archaic condition he'd placed on her inheritance. The shocking discovery that he was Logan's father also continued to affect her.

She'd learned Henry and Janelle had been having an affair

for at least fifteen years. And she and Archie were on the outs now so she had no confidante to speak with and be advised by. On top of that, she was dealing with the arrival of Ashton. It was enough to make her head ache. No wonder she felt tense.

But as her thoughts centered on Ashton, a smile tugged at her lips. How thrilled she was to be having this time with her son—it was a precious gift she never thought to have. After leaving the hospital, she'd spent months curled up on her bed, crying for her lost baby. She'd fallen into a dark state. It was the reason her parents had badgered her to get a job; to rejoin society; to make new friends. They thought that might shake her from her depression.

And they'd been right. Though it took longer than they'd hoped, she'd eventually fallen in love with Henry. But she never forgot her son. Every year since the day he'd been born she celebrated his birthday in secret. She'd think about how he was. What he looked like. Whether he'd been blessed with any musical talent. Whether he had good friends, a nice family. She tortured herself with endless thoughts of him, certain she'd never see him again.

But here he was, in her home, sharing a life with her. It was a miracle that brought her joy every day. It was unfortunate her other children weren't so happy about Ashton's arrival. She understood their reticence—after all, they knew nothing about him. All they had to go on was his word. The same as she.

Of course, there were a lot of dishonest people out there and her children were right to be reluctant. She would be reluctant too, if circumstances were reversed. But Ashton knew so much about her and David. How else would he have come by that kind of information? It made no sense, unless he was her son.

Besides, how did they explain his musical talent? The fact

he played both the piano and the violin? Okay, so the woman who'd raised him was a music teacher. That certainly accounted for the exposure he might have had, but it didn't explain his talent. Surely that was something more likely inherited from his biological parents?

Am I grasping at straws? Am I so desperate to claim him as my son, to finally know he's grown up in a good and loving home, that I'm willing to overlook everything else?

No. She didn't believe she was. She didn't need a DNA test to prove he was hers. She knew he was. She could feel it in her bones. A mother would know her son, even if she were forced to choose out of a thousand people. Somehow, she'd know. Like a cow could find her calf in a herd of hundreds. It was the same with all mothers. And nobody would convince her otherwise.

And just to prove her point, she was going to celebrate his upcoming birthday by giving him a puppy. Something to love and that would keep him company, as well as keep him safe. She wasn't sure about his living arrangements in Tamworth, but everyone needed a dog. His adoptive parents hadn't allowed him one when he was growing up because of their allergies, but Elizabeth had always loved dogs. The only reason they didn't have one had been because of Henry.

Well, Henry was gone and she was free to call the shots. Starting with buying her son a puppy. She smiled at the thought. She couldn't wait to hit the animal shelters first thing in the morning. She'd buy Ashton the perfect pet.

Joel tapped his keyboard and pulled up a search engine. Ever since Ashton had dared him to look into his background, Joel had been determined to follow through. It was the cop in him that couldn't simply accept the man's word, like Joel's mother seemed inclined to do. Not that he blamed her. She saw what she wanted to see. She wanted Ashton Walker to be her son and that was that.

Like Isabella, Joel wasn't quite so enamored of his so-called half-brother. If it turned out the man was telling the truth, then so be it. Joel would accept him wholeheartedly. But no cop worth his salt took the word of a stranger without some additional evidence to back up the claim.

The first name Joel plugged in was Todd Walker. Joel included the reference to Tamworth. Sure enough, there was a small article in Tamworth's local newspaper, the Northern Daily Leader, dated a couple of years earlier that mentioned the sad passing of well-known community-minded man, Todd Walker. He'd died of cancer after a long illness. There was a passing reference to his wife and son. There were no pictures of any of them.

Okay, so Todd Walker exists… Or at least, he did up until two years ago. And he died of cancer, like Ashton said…

Next Joel typed in the details of Ashton's adoptive mother. Jennifer Walker's obituary was longer than her husband's and this time there were a couple of pictures included. Joel scanned the obituary. Once again, it referenced a well-known, well-liked member of the Tamworth community. Jennifer Walker, nee Brown, had been born in the Tamworth area seventy-seven years earlier.

She'd met and married her high school sweetheart and they'd set up a life together on a small farm on the outskirts of Tamworth. Todd Walker had been a farmer and his wife had been a music teacher at the local high school. Both were talented musicians, with Todd playing bass in a local band up until ten years before his death, when he'd been diagnosed with cancer.

Sadly, Jennifer had been suffering from dementia for several years. Her last couple of years had been spent in a local nursing home. She was being remembered fondly by her former pupils and was survived by her adopted son, Ashton Walker.

The first grainy black and white photo showed a smiling woman with upswept hair and a kind expression on her face. A piano stood in the background. The other picture was smaller, the details harder to make out. It was a photograph of Jennifer's son. The man was seated behind a desk. Though Joel conceded there was some resemblance to the man who claimed to be his mother's child, it was hard to tell from the quality of the picture.

Joel sat back in his chair and sighed. It appeared what Ashton had told them was correct. With lips compressed, he reached for his phone and called Isabella. She answered on the third ring.

"Hey. What's up?"

"I've been digging into Ashton's background."

"What did you find out?"

Joel heard the uptake in her voice. He grimaced. "Sorry to be the bearer of bad news, but it appears what he told us about his past is correct. His adoptive parents lived in Tamworth. His father died a couple of years ago. His mother a year later. I found articles in the Tamworth paper. They were both well-known and well-respected in their community."

Isabella sighed. "Darn. That's disappointing. I was sure he was playing us all for fools. There's something about him that puts me on edge. I don't like him." She paused and then added, "Even if he was adopted by those people, that doesn't prove he's our half-brother."

"That's true, but if he didn't lie about his background, there's a good chance he also isn't lying about the other."

"I want to know for sure," Isabella said with a stubbornness in her tone that Joel knew all too well. "I still want to go ahead with the DNA test."

"I don't think he's going to voluntarily hand over his saliva," Joel replied. "We already asked him, remember?"

"Then we'll steal some DNA off him if we need to. We can do that, can't we?"

Joel compressed his lips on a groan. "Yeah, I guess. It won't hold up in a court of law, but it will tell us what we want to know."

"Then what are we waiting for? Let's do it."

Joel heard the impatience in Isabella's tone and sighed. He wanted to know the truth as much as she did. Maybe more. The cop inside him wouldn't be satisfied until they had unequivocal evidence, one way or the other. That's just the way it was.

But there was also their mother's wishes to consider. She'd been far from pleased with their suggestion Ashton undergo a DNA test. It was almost like she'd made her mind up to believe him and nothing was going to budge her from that.

"What about Mom?" he asked.

"What about her? I understand that she doesn't want us to pry. I'm guessing that's because she's pinned all her hopes on this guy being her son. If we were to find out otherwise…"

Joel grimaced. "I think you're right. Still, the cop in me can't let it go. I need more than a gut feeling, or mother's intuition, or whatever nonsense Mom's relying on."

"Me, too."

Joel sighed again. "Okay, so how are we going to do this?"

"You're the detective. I thought you might have a plan."

"No, not really." He paused and then added, "The easiest thing is to steal his toothbrush. Or even some hair from his hairbrush. Like what Dad did to Logan."

"Geez. Can you believe that? I'm still trying to get my head around the fact Dad is Logan's father. I knew better than any of you about Dad's affairs. He made no secret of them, especially around me. I think he liked to flaunt them in my face. Which is really weird. Still, I had no idea about him and Aunt Janelle."

"Yeah. No wonder it came as a shock to everyone. I wonder how they managed to keep it hidden all those years?"

"Who knows? I guess we weren't looking for it either. Our families spent a lot of time together anyway. We didn't think anything of that. Remember all those family holidays we took together? The Gold Coast, the Great Barrier Reef? The driving holiday when we went all the way out to Uluru? Remember?"

"God, yes. We camped along the side of the road for weeks. You hated it!"

"So did Mom and Sophia. You try going to the toilet behind a bush! That's if you could even find one!"

Joel laughed and shook his head fondly at the memories. "We had some good times."

"Yeah," Isabella agreed softly. "But I'm not sure they outweighed the bad. I can't believe how nasty Dad was to Nick and Sophia—right down to his final words. Mean and malicious and hurtful. There's no other way to describe his actions."

"You're right. He was a prick."

"Yeah. But he was also our dad. The only one we had. For better or worse, that's what he was."

"Do you think he knew Mom had given birth to a son before they met?"

"No," Isabella said with conviction. "There's no way Mom told him anything about that. Why would she? As far as she was concerned, that part of her life was over, never to be re-visited again. She couldn't have known one day that son would grow up and come looking for her." Isabella paused and then added, "It's kind of weird, knowing we have a half-brother out there."

"He could be closer than you think. He could be living in the east wing of Mom's house."

She sighed. "True. He could be. That's why it's so

important to do the test. We need to know for sure. And if Ashton's not our long lost half-brother, I wouldn't mind finding the real one. It would be kind of cool, don't you think?"

"*Mm*," Joel replied non-committedly. He wasn't at all sure how he felt about a half-sibling out there, one he hadn't known about and one he still didn't know. "For now, let's just concentrate on Ashton," he said. "When are you visiting Mom next?"

"I can go tomorrow, if you like. I'll call her and invite myself over for lunch."

"How will you get into Ashton's suite?"

"I'll tell her I still have a few boxes of things upstairs I'd like to go through and decide what I'm freighting to Brisbane. That ought to do it."

"Good. Just make sure you know where Ashton is before you go riffling through his things. I don't want him catching on. And don't waste time while you're in there. Go straight to the bathroom and snatch his toothbrush. No doubt he keeps it on the sink. Put it into a re-sealable plastic bag. Got that?"

"Yes, detective," Isabella replied dryly.

"On second thought, maybe the hairbrush is the best bet? If you take his toothbrush, he's bound to miss it. The hairbrush—no one will notice a few hairs missing. Yes, go for the hairbrush, Issy."

"Yes, sir. I'm onto it. Leave it with me. I'll call you when I have it."

"Good girl. You know you're also going to have to steal some of Mom's?"

"Shit. Of course I am. Don't worry, I'll think of something. Maybe I can just sneak into Mom's suite as soon as I finish in Ashton's bathroom? She's in the opposite wing, but at least they're on the same floor. Yes, that would be best. Mom might get suspicious if I keep on having to go upstairs. It's not like I live there anymore."

"Right. You're staying with Sophia and Jarrod while you're in town, right?"

"Yes. I'd stay with you and Sheridan, but…you know…the dogs."

"Right."

"Don't get me wrong, I love them. They're as cute as they can be. But they can get a bit noisy, right?"

"Right."

"I don't mean—"

"It's all right, Issy. I know what you mean. And you're right. They can get a bit excited. Sheridan and I have been talking about looking for a bigger place. Somewhere with a backyard."

"Sounds like a plan," Isabella agreed. "Speaking of plans, I'd better get off the phone so I can call Mom."

"You do that. Call me as soon as you've completed your mission."

"Yes, boss."

Chapter Eleven

From the bottom of the long paved driveway, Christopher Barrington stared at the grand façade that was Craigdon Manor. Built *circa* 1927, the house displayed all the hallmarks of its impressive Art Deco architectural period, including rounded corners and stylized geometric detailing. The three-story house was set across an expansive six hectares. The manicured grounds incorporated a full-size tennis court, nine-hole golf course, heated pool and spa. It was an extraordinary home, the grandest in the neighborhood. Henry wouldn't have had it any other way.

For so many years, Christopher had hated everything the house represented and he'd been downright resentful of the people who resided there. Whenever he thought of his father, he was filled with an anger and a bitterness so foul it hurt his chest. It had always been that way, ever since he'd been told the truth about the man who'd fathered him.

It didn't matter to Henry that Christopher was his son. At every opportunity, Henry denied his existence, right to the very end. That was the reason Christopher had declined Elizabeth's invitation to attend the reading of Henry's final words. A letter Henry had written, to be read to his family a year after his death.

Well, Christopher was having none of it. The prick hadn't

even seen fit to make mention of his firstborn in his will. There was no way Christopher was going to subject himself to even more humiliation. So he'd stayed the hell away.

But lately he'd been thinking about the ongoing feud with his family. He was nearly forty-one. No wife, no children. It was time to set aside his anger and hurt, to shelve the bitterness that had filled his heart for so long and often dictated his actions. He was better than that. And it took others noticing to make Christopher aware of his value: Noah saw the goodness in him, so did Elizabeth.

Elizabeth.

He'd always been close to her. She wasn't his mother, but she'd always treated him well and with respect. She'd never denied his position in the Craigdon family and had a way of calming him down and making him see sense.

That's what had brought him to Craigdon Manor that morning. He wanted to see her and talk to her about the lawsuit and his life. For almost a year he'd been consumed with the need for revenge on Henry, intent on pursuing recognition as Henry's son, through the courts. But lately he'd been forced to concede his anger was directed at Henry more than his children and Christopher was never going to be able to even that score.

Henry's death made the whole lawsuit pointless. An exercise in futility. So what if the courts found in Christopher's favor and awarded him a portion of Henry's vast estate? It wouldn't change anything. The old prick wouldn't know. All it would do was drive an even deeper wedge between Christopher and his Craigdon siblings and the older he got, the more he realized how important family was.

With a sigh, he threw his car into lower gear and idled up the driveway. The vast lawns were freshly mowed. The flowerbeds were filled with color. Elizabeth employed a couple of gardeners, but she'd always had a green thumb. She was often out in the garden. She'd once joked with him how she loved to get her hands dirty.

Parking beside Elizabeth's silver Audi, Christopher switched off the ignition and climbed out. A fiery red Porsche was parked a short distance away. Christopher wondered which of the Craigdons owned it. Whoever it was, it must be a recent purchase. He didn't recall seeing it there before.

Forgoing the wide front steps, Christopher walked around the side of the house. Elizabeth's rose garden was there. With the warm summer sun beating down on his shoulders, he wouldn't have been surprised to find her there. It was a perfect day for gardening.

But she wasn't in the rose garden and so he continued around to the back of the house. A dog yapped and he looked up in time to see a German shepherd puppy come bounding toward him.

"Hey there buddy! Where did you come from?"

Christopher bent low and scratched the dog behind its ears. At the same time, he frowned. He couldn't ever remember seeing a dog at Craigdon Manor. Something about Henry not wanting any pets. He wondered who the dog belonged to.

"Rusty! Come here, boy. That's a good boy. Come to Daddy."

Christopher stood and watched the puppy lope back toward a stranger who looked about his age. The man's eyes were concealed behind designer sunglasses. He wore equally expensive swimming shorts. His body was long and muscular and tanned from long hours in the sun. He lounged beside the pool as if he belonged there. Christopher wondered who he was.

"Hi. I'm Christopher Barrington."

He held out his hand toward the stranger. The man gave his hand a perfunctory shake.

"Ashton Walker."

Christopher nodded in acknowledgement. "Ashton. It's nice to meet you. I hope you don't mind me asking, but what are you doing here?"

Ashton gave an easy laugh. He slid his sunglasses up on his head and winked. "What does it look like? I'm working on my tan."

Irritation stirred in Christopher's gut.

Who the hell is this smart ass and what's he doing in my step-mother's yard?

The thought had barely formed when Elizabeth appeared through the sliding doors that led back into the house. She smiled when she saw him.

"Why, Christopher! What a lovely surprise. I didn't know you were coming."

"Yes, well. I was in the neighborhood. I thought I might drop in and see how you were doing. I probably should have called."

She waved away his suggestion. "Don't be silly. You're welcome anytime."

His gaze slid to the stranger who was now playing around with the dog. Elizabeth noticed the direction of his gaze and hurried to explain.

"Christopher, this is Ashton. My son."

Christopher gaped. "Your *what?*"

Elizabeth grimaced. A faint blush turned her cheeks pink. "My son. From many years ago."

Christopher stared at her in confusion, trying to make sense of it all. "But, how? Where's he been all this time? Did Henry know?"

Elizabeth's laughter sounded strained. "My, so many questions! Why don't we go inside and I'll tell you all about it?" She glanced at the man who was apparently her son. He appeared engrossed in the puppy. "Ash? Are you coming?"

"No thanks, Mom. I'm going to get a bit more sun. Let me know when lunch is ready." With that, he dropped back down on the lounger.

Christopher followed Elizabeth into her music room, his head still spinning from her announcement. She glanced at him.

"Tea? Coffee?"

"Thank you. Coffee, please. Black, no sugar."

Elizabeth excused herself and came back a few moments later. "Amy will bring it in directly." She took a seat in one of the armchairs. Christopher perched on the couch opposite.

She shot him another glance and nervously wiped her hands on the skirt of her dress.

"I thought this would come easier each time I said it, but that doesn't seem to be the case," she said in a shaky voice.

Christopher drew in a deep breath and made a deliberate effort to relax. The shock of the past few minutes started to wear off.

"You were going to tell me about Ashton. He appears about my age..." he said and gave her an encouraging look.

It was Elizabeth's turn to blow out her breath. She twisted her hands together in her lap and then released them, only to twist them together again.

"There's no easy way to say this," she began. "I met Ashton's father while I was studying at the Conservatorium of Music. His name was David. We fell in love. I gave birth to a son when I was twenty."

Christopher's eyes widened at her revelations. "Wow."

"Yes. Wow. My parents wouldn't let me keep him. I begged them, pleaded, cried. They refused to change their mind."

Christopher frowned. "But you were over eighteen. An adult. They had no legal right to tell you what to do."

"You're right. But you have to remember, I'd lived a very

sheltered life. I'd gone from school straight to the conservatorium. My parents paid my way. My board, my tuition. Everything. I had no money of my own. I'd never needed any. They saw to my every need. They always had.

"Then when I got pregnant, they were horrified. Disappointed, angry, confused. How could I have done this to them? Did I have no shame? No sense of decency? I was raised a Catholic. A good girl, one that should know better. They filled me with guilt and then they bombarded me with all the reasons why I couldn't raise a baby. My life would be forever changed. My dream of being a world famous concert pianist dashed. They convinced me the only thing to do was to sign the adoption papers. Though it went against every maternal instinct inside me, I did it. I never expected to see my son again."

"So what happened? He just turned up?"

Elizabeth's smile was tremulous. Tears glinted in her eyes. "Yes. It's a miracle! He literally turned up on my doorstep a couple of weeks ago. He turned up the night of Flynn and Jayde's engagement party. Can you believe it?"

Christopher shook his head in bewilderment. "To be honest, no. It all seems a bit unreal. I'm sorry I missed the celebration. I was out of town. It sounds like it was… interesting, to say the least. How do you know he's your son?"

Disappointment clouded Elizabeth's expression. "Oh, Christopher! Not you, too!"

"What do you mean?"

She compressed her lips into a thin line. "It seems my children are having a hard time accepting Ashton. They're suspicious he's not who he says he is."

Christopher nodded but chose to keep his opinion to himself. He understood how his half-siblings might question the sudden appearance of their mother's "son." It did seem awfully strange.

Even though Christopher had been adopted at the age of twelve by Frank Barrington, he didn't know much about the adoption process. The paperwork had been done by his mother and he had no need to seek out information on his birth parents. He already knew who they were.

Still, he would have thought the applicant would have had to make written contact with their birth parents, or maybe a telephone call, to ascertain whether they wanted to meet, rather than just turn up on their doorstep. It seems that wasn't the case.

"And this came as a total surprise?" he asked. "You had no prior knowledge Ashton was trying to find you?"

"No, none at all. That's why it was such a shock."

"*Hm,*" Christopher responded.

Amy arrived bearing a silver tray laden with a coffee pot, mugs and a plateful of fresh pastries. She set the tray down on the coffee table before Elizabeth.

"Thank you, Amy. This looks lovely."

Once Amy had departed, Elizabeth reached for the pot and poured them both a cup. She added milk and sugar to hers.

"Thank you," Christopher said as she handed him a mug of the steaming black brew.

"Danish?" she asked, offering him the plate.

He politely declined. Elizabeth selected a mini apple Danish. She took a tiny bite of the delicate pastry, taking care not to drop any crumbs.

"So, Christopher," she said after she'd swallowed. "What brings you here?"

He shrugged. Now that the moment was upon him, he wasn't sure where to start. "Like I said, I was in the neighborhood."

She gave him a knowing smile. "You live an hour away in the opposite direction."

He conceded her point with an inclination of his head. "Yes. You're right. I came out here to see you. I… I wanted to talk to you about…about the lawsuit."

She nodded slowly. "Ah. I thought you might. If I recall correctly, your last offer was to settle the matter for eighty-five million. Is that right?"

He ducked his head. "Yes."

She took a sip from her coffee and then set the mug back down. "Why does the money mean so much to you, Christopher? Henry wasn't an honorable man and God forbid, definitely not one to be admired."

Familiar anger and hurt coursed through him. He sat forward. "He was my father! You don't know how much I wanted him to treat me like his son!" He shook his head as old memories bombarded him. "I tried to meet with him so many times over the past twenty years. He wouldn't even see me! The one time I hijacked him outside his offices, he looked at me with such disgust, such sneering arrogance… He told me to get lost, although he wasn't quite that polite about it. Then he smeared my mother's reputation; said she'd tried to trap him with the oldest trick in the book. But he was too smart to fall for that one. No way would Henry Craigdon be tricked like that. He told me in no uncertain terms that he refused to be held accountable for something he hadn't done.

"Later, after the DNA test proved beyond a doubt he was my father, he still made it clear he didn't give a toss about me. He threw me out of Craigdon Enterprises and told me not to come back. Then he added further insult by shouting at the top of his lungs in front of everyone that there was no way I'd ever see a penny of Craigdon money."

Christopher could still recall the shock and humiliation he'd felt over the encounter. Resentment had festered ever since.

Elizabeth looked appalled. "Oh, Christopher. I'm so sorry. You should never have been subjected to that."

"The thing is, I wasn't interested in his money," he said bitterly. "What I wanted was his recognition, to know he cared about me."

His voice cracked with emotion and he cursed under his breath. He didn't want to become emotional. Henry had taken enough from him as it was.

"You were treated abominably," Elizabeth agreed quietly. "I tried to make Henry see. By that time I had no influence over him. He didn't care what I thought." She made a sound in the back of her throat. "That is, if he'd ever cared at all. I'm probably deluding myself in thinking there was a time in the early days of our marriage when he valued my opinion. If it had been there, it didn't last long."

"I used to dream up ways to kill him. That's how angry I was."

"Oh, Christopher! You poor boy! Thank God you didn't go through with it."

Christopher grimaced. "The truth is, I never got the chance. He was always surrounded by security. At home. At the office. I knew it was because he was a drug dealer, but it still made it impossible for me to carry out my plan."

Elizabeth looked at him in surprise. "You knew he was a drug dealer?"

Christopher shrugged. "Yes. Of course. Didn't you?"

"No, not really. Not in a definitive way. I suspected, of course… But I had no evidence to prove it either way."

"I guess it doesn't matter now. Henry's dead. I wish that made me feel better, but it doesn't. I've been angry at him all my life. I don't want to keep feeling like this, Elizabeth. Help me. Please."

To his horror tears welled up in his eyes. He dashed at them with the back of his hand. Elizabeth murmured softly and stood and sat beside him. She put her arms around him and held him.

Hot shame at his confession burned through him, but there was also a feeling of relief. It was good to talk to someone about it, to finally get it off his chest.

"There, there, Christopher. It's all right. Let it out. You deserve that, at least."

Struggling to get control of his emotions, he at last gave up and was defeated by a sob. He cried quietly. Elizabeth continued to hold him. When he was done, she gently set him aside.

"Ash told me how devastating it was, growing up without his birth parents," she said quietly. "Not knowing who they were. Assuming they didn't love him enough to want to keep him. I understand better than most how you're feeling, Christopher. I wish there was something I could do to make it up to you. Perhaps if I get the children and nephews to agree to your lawsuit, that might go some way toward making it up to you. What do you think?"

Christopher wiped his eyes with the back of his hands and compressed his lips. "It feels so petty now. I don't know why I thought money would make up for the neglect of my father's love."

"It's not petty, Christopher," Elizabeth said gently. "It's totally understandable. But it's not like you need the money, is it?"

"No. It was never about the money. Frank has provided for me well enough. It was always about getting back at Henry for ignoring me all these years. I'm not proud to admit what I tried to do was out of spite."

"I understand. Truly, I do. Listen, how about I talk to the others and see what we can come up with? I'm sure they'll be willing to make you a decent offer. Hopefully everyone can come to an agreement and we can put this all behind us. I, for one have had enough of Henry Craigdon and his interference in all of our lives."

Christopher drew in a shaky breath and eased it out. "Sounds like a plan."

Elizabeth smiled. Moving back to her seat, she took up her coffee mug once again and sipped from it. Christopher did the same. This time, he reached for a pastry and devoured the small treat in a single bite.

"Tell me more about Ash. What does he do with himself?" he asked, genuinely curious about the stranger that had moved in with his step-mother.

Elizabeth smiled. As she started speaking, her face lit up. "He's a musician! Can you believe it! He plays the piano and the violin. Amazing! I'm not surprised, of course. His father and I were musicians."

"That's cool. Have you heard him play?"

Elizabeth's smile faltered slightly. "No, not yet. He hurt his finger. But there's plenty of time. He's not going anywhere." She paused and then added with a luminous smile, "I'm so thrilled and grateful he reached out to me. I've missed so many years of his life. He turned forty this week. I've missed the first forty years of his life! I don't want to miss anymore."

"Good for you," Christopher replied. *Perhaps I'm wrong? Perhaps this guy is the real deal…*

As if on cue, Ashton walked in. He went straight to Elizabeth and kissed her on the cheek. "Hi, Mom. What's happening?"

Elizabeth beamed, clearly pleased for the attention. Christopher watched the two of them interact. While Elizabeth was all gushing and grateful, there was something about Ash that set off Christopher's bullshit detector. Something wasn't quite right. Though the man smiled and simpered and said all the right things, there was a brittleness to his expression that made Christopher feel Ash wasn't being genuine.

"Your mother tells me you're a musician, Ashton. I'd love to hear you play."

Ashton frowned. "I wish I could, but my instruments are all packed away in storage. I didn't bring any of them with me."

"No problem," Christopher agreed with an easy smile. "Maybe you could play Elizabeth's piano? I'm sure she'd love to hear you. Right, Elizabeth?"

Elizabeth smiled brilliantly and clapped her hands. "That would be wonderful, Ash. That is, if you're finger's not too sore. I could turn the pages for you."

Ashton frowned and shook his head. "I'm sorry, Mom. Not today. I have a headache. Too much sun. I just don't feel in the mood."

Elizabeth's face fell. Her hands dropped to her lap. "Oh, okay. That's fine. We'll do it another time. Can I get you some pain killers?"

Ashton grimaced. "No, I'm okay."

Christopher watched the man closely. He was supposed to be an accomplished musician and yet nobody had heard him play. Not even his mother. Christopher felt a renewed stirring of suspicion. Still, what could he do about it? The best thing he could do would be to mind his own business. Let her children sort it out. He had enough problems to deal with.

Guilt immediately surged through him. Elizabeth deserved better than that. Swallowing a sigh, Christopher vowed silently to speak with one of his half-siblings; run the possibility that something was amiss by them; see what they thought. For now, he'd keep his suspicions to himself.

It was obvious Elizabeth was infatuated with the thought this man was her son. Christopher cared for her too much to burst her bubble unless he had irrefutable proof. Where he'd get that, he didn't know, but it was time to talk to some of the other Craigdons and come up with a way to find out if his bullshit meter was right on or needed adjusting.

Finishing his coffee, Christopher rose to leave. He'd barely stood to bid Elizabeth goodbye when Isabella appeared.

Elizabeth blinked in surprise. "Issy! What are you doing here? I wasn't expecting you."

Isabella pecked her mother on the cheek and murmured a greeting to Christopher. She glanced in Ashton's direction and then ignored him.

Interesting… So, there's no love lost between her and the man who purports to be her half-brother… Maybe I should talk to her, get her take on the situation. She might be an ally…

Friend or foe, Christopher didn't know, but either way, he vowed to get to the bottom of it for Elizabeth. The thought of protecting her made him feel good inside. That didn't happen often.

Chapter Twelve

It was all Isabella could do, not to glare at the man who claimed to be her half-brother. *Ashton Walker.* Just seeing him there, lounging all over her mother's furniture like he owned the place was enough to get her temper boiling. She shot a glance at Christopher. She was just as surprised to see him there. For so long, he'd gone out of his way to annoy the whole family. He seemed to get a kick out of playing malicious jokes on them or making them stumble. Her mother always offered some kind of excuse, but as far as Isabella was concerned, Christopher was an asshole.

Still, at least he had a legitimate claim on her family. The same couldn't be said for the new interloper. But Issy was determined to change that. She'd find proof, one way or the other. She just hoped she could live with the results. She hoped like hell the arrogant stranger who'd taken possession of her mother's time and household didn't turn out to be blood related, but if he did, at least she'd know the truth.

"Would you like some coffee?" her mother asked, reaching for the coffee pot.

Isabella schooled her expression into one of casual disinterest. "No, thanks. I just wanted to call in and go through a few of those boxes I left behind." Sticking to her script, she continued. "I want to make sure there aren't any more bits and pieces I want to take back with me to Brisbane. Raine and I are about to close the deal on a cute townhouse not far from his office. I thought I might see if there are any things that might go with our new décor. You don't mind, do you?"

"No, of course not," her mother replied. "They're your things. Take whatever you like."

Isabella smiled. "Thanks, Mom." Her gaze moved to encompass the men. "I guess I'll see you later."

Making her escape, she eased out her breath. *So far, so good…*

She hurried up the stairs. Instead of heading in the direction of the west wing that housed the suite of rooms she'd previously claimed as hers she turned left and quickly strode down the hall in the opposite direction. It didn't seem that long ago when Callum's wife Grace, had spent time there at Elizabeth's invitation. The stay had given Grace a safe and secure place to live, but it had also provided Issy's mother with company. Right now it was Ashton who was keeping her mother entertained, no doubt filling her head with all sorts of nonsense.

Issy scowled. She stopped outside the door that led to his suite of rooms. With a quick glance over her shoulder, she made sure the way was clear and then eased open the door. The room was a pigsty. Dirty clothes and wet towels lay scattered across the carpet, as if he couldn't give a toss where they fell. Plates with congealed food on them sat stacked three high on the bedside tables, along with several empty cans of beer. A half-eaten pizza sat in its box on the bedspread.

Isabella shook her head in disgust. It looked like he didn't give a damn how filthy he was or the mess he left in someone else's house. It showed a complete lack of respect. It also looked like he knew someone else would be along to collect the plates and glasses and tidy up the rest of the mess.

The pig… It's not up to Amy to clean up after him… How gross…

A fresh wave of annoyance went through her. She strode

into the adjoining bathroom where the mess continued. Toothpaste had been squirted on the sink and left to dry. Beard shavings formed a dark ring around the basin. He hadn't even bothered to rinse them off. Another two wet towels were piled in a heap on the floor.

Wanting to get the deed done and get out of there, Isabella pulled the re-sealable plastic bag that Joel had given her out of her handbag and went in search of Ashton's hairbrush. It wasn't on the sink, nor the ledge above it. She opened drawers and eventually found it. To her relief, several dark hairs clung to the bristles.

Christopher waited for Isabella to leave the room and then quickly excused himself to go to the bathroom. There was something in Isabella's expression that sparked his curiosity. *Something's going on…*

He wondered if it had anything to do with Ashton. The look she'd given the man had been decidedly unfriendly. There was only one way to find out. Christopher made his way over to the sweeping staircase and started the ascent. The thick carpet muffled his footsteps. He reached the top just as Isabella disappeared through an open doorway. Picking up his pace, he followed her inside.

The room was a mess, with clothes and food and crap all over the place. Christopher turned up his nose in disgust.

What kind of filthy pig lives like this…?

As far as Christopher knew, Isabella had moved out some time ago to move in with her fiancé, Raine, in Brisbane. Christopher hadn't heard Elizabeth had any other family members staying with her. He could only guess the room was being used by Ashton.

A noise came from the bathroom. Picking his way silently across the room, Christopher spied Isabella standing before the vanity with a hairbrush in her hand. Holding his breath, he watched while she pulled strands of hair out of the brush and poked them into a plastic bag that looked a lot like an evidence bag, the type used by the police.

What's she doing collecting hair samples? And then a lightbulb went off in his head. *She's submitting it for DNA testing… That's what she's doing… Clever girl.*

Remembering Joel's instructions, Isabella carefully pulled several strands of hair out of the brush and tucked them inside the bag. Satisfied she had enough, she returned the brush to the drawer where she'd found it.

He'll never know I've been here…

She turned to leave the room and came face to face with Christopher.

"Christopher!" she gasped, her heart beating fast. "You nearly gave me a heart attack! What are you doing here?"

Christopher stared meaningfully at the plastic bag that was still in her hands. She followed the direction of his gaze and quickly hid the bag behind her back. But she wasn't quick enough.

"I could ask you the same thing. What's in the bag?"

She gave him a blank look. "What bag?"

"Cut the crap, Issy. I saw you."

Her shoulders slumped on a sigh of defeat. "Okay. You got me. I'll tell you. I promise. But not here. We need to get out of here before we get caught."

Christopher smiled wickedly. "Is it that naughty?"

"Yes!" Issy hissed. She gave him a shove. "Now, get out of here!"

He walked back out to the bedroom and headed toward the door. He glanced over his shoulder at Isabella. She'd come to a halt beside the bed.

"I thought you were in a hurry?" he said.

"I am, but we can't go downstairs together. What if someone sees us? They'll think it's strange. You go first," she suggested. "I'll follow a few minutes later."

He shrugged. "Whatever. I'll meet you out front."

As soon as he'd cleared the doorway, Isabella slowly counted to ten. She wanted Christopher well clear of the stairwell before she followed behind him. She also needed to collect a hair sample of her mother's.

With her heart beating fast, Isabella made her way across the bedroom. She had her hand on the doorknob when she heard Christopher speaking loudly to someone on the stairs.

"Ashton, it was nice to meet you. I take it you'll be staying here for a bit?"

"Yeah," came Ashton's reply. "I thought you were going to the bathroom?"

"I was. I did. I like the one at the top of the stairs. It's always been my favorite."

Isabella's pulse took off at a gallop as she realized Ashton was close. No doubt he was headed for his room. Thinking fast, Issy ran to the walk-in wardrobe and hid herself among his clothes, praying he wouldn't come back that way. Frantic now, she tried to think up some excuse as to why she was hiding there.

As the door to his bedroom opened, she held her breath. She couldn't see him from her hiding place, but she heard him go into the bathroom, use the toilet and then flush. She listened for the sound of running water that would tell her he was washing his hands, but it seemed he hadn't bothered. The next thing she heard was the bedroom door opening and closing again. She might get away with this. She slumped against his jackets with a sigh of relief.

Her heart was pounding. She tried to slow her breathing. *That was way too close...*

Hurrying, she opened the door and peered into the hallway. The way was clear. As soon as she'd passed the stairs, she slowed her steps and eased out her breath. Her old rooms were in this part of the house, not far from her mother's. It didn't matter if someone found her here. Still, Christopher was waiting downstairs. She picked up her pace.

After ascertaining her mother's suite was empty, she hurried into the master bath. The vanity was lined with perfumes, face creams, hand creams and a couple of packets containing face masks. Once again, Issy dived into the drawers looking for her mom's hairbrush.

Her fingers closed around the wooden handle. "Bingo," she murmured and pulled it out.

Just like she had with Ashton's, Issy pulled out a handful of hair from the bristles and tucked them into a second evidence bag. She sealed the end and then slid both bags into her pocket.

Once again, after checking the way was clear, she hurried down the hallway and back down the stairs. She heard the murmur of voices coming from the direction of the music room—her mother's and a male voice that no doubt was Ashton's. Slipping off her stilettos, she padded silently across the travertine tiles that led to the foyer. Pulling open the front door, she closed it behind her.

Christopher stood beside his car, kicking idly at stones with his boot. He looked up and saw her.

Filling her lungs, she eased out the air until the panic inside her diminished some. Squaring her shoulders, she slipped her sandals back on and made her way with confidence down the wide stone steps.

Christopher smiled at her. "So, now are you going to tell me what the hell that was all about?"

For a moment, Isabella considered brushing him off. After all, it was none of his business and he hadn't exactly endeared himself to her in the past. She hadn't forgotten how he'd tried to cause all kinds of trouble for her and Raine.

But, Christopher's timely intervention with Ashton on the stairs just now had saved her ass and she owed him a modicum of gratitude.

"I guess I should thank you," she said, sounding a long way from grateful.

Christopher nodded. "Yes. You should."

"Okay. Thank you for alerting me to Ashton. I'm not sure how I would have explained my presence in his bedroom."

Christopher's lips quirked upwards in a smile. "It could have gotten tricky."

"Yes. It could have. Well… Thank you."

Isabella turned to leave, but Christopher's hand shot out and grabbed her around the arm. "Not so fast. You haven't told me what you were doing in there. Hang on. Let me guess." He pretended to think. Issy gritted her teeth.

"Oh, that's right. Collecting hair samples. You're submitting them for DNA, right?"

Issy glared at him with annoyance, but her irritation didn't last. If it weren't for Christopher, she might have been caught red-handed and they'd be back to square one. Apart from that, no doubt Ashton would have run back to her mother, only too pleased to tell tales.

Christopher's gaze remained steady on hers. Eventually Issy admitted defeat.

"Okay. Yes. We're testing Ashton's DNA. It's just a bit of insurance. So what?"

"So nothing. I agree. Apparently your mother only has this man's word to go on. I wouldn't be accepting just that. You need irrefutable proof. What better way to get it than through a DNA test."

Isabella was filled with relief. She looked at Christopher in surprise. "I hadn't expected you to be so understanding."

He shrugged. "I'm not always a prick."

Issy blushed guiltily. Christopher merely chuckled.

"Who else knows?" he asked.

"Joel and I planned it together, but most of us are suspicious of the guy. Like you said, it's hard to accept—to just take Ashton's word for it."

"Well, let me know if I can help. I have a few contacts in high places. If there's anything you need to expedite…like the results, I'm willing to do what I can."

Once again, Isabella was taken by surprise. "That's very generous of you, Christopher. I didn't think you had it in you to think of anyone but yourself."

He scowled. "I guess I deserve that, but the thing is, I really care about your mother. I don't want to see her get hurt. And I was suspicious the moment I met this guy. If he's who he says he is, then so be it. I'll be happy for her. But if he's not… He'll have to answer to me."

Christopher's expression had darkened into a frown. Sparks of anger glinted in his eyes. Isabella was a bit taken aback to realize just how much Christopher did care for her mother.

"Thank you, Christopher. I'll let you know. It's good to have you on our side. For once."

Issy couldn't resist the jibe. Christopher took it in the spirit it was intended.

"Touché," he said with grin and gave her a mock salute.

Isabella looked at him. The tension she normally felt around him had disappeared. Their conversation had been…civilized. Perhaps there was hope for them yet.

"I'll be in touch if I need anything," she said and headed toward her car.

"You do that," Christopher called after her. "Meanwhile I'll keep my eyes on him when I can."

Issy gave him a nod and a wave.

Chapter Thirteen

*E*lizabeth pulled up outside Archie's house and put the car into park. She hadn't seen him since the engagement party. More than two long weeks had passed without them speaking. They'd never gone so long. Even when they were both married to other people and trying to be discreet.

Their eroding relationship was the only blight on her horizon. She'd been so happy over the reunion with her son. Every morning she woke and thanked God for her blessings. But she also looked to the empty space beside her, the pillow that had supported Archie's beloved head, and she was overwhelmed with sadness. The irony wasn't lost on her. Now, when they were finally free to proclaim their love and happiness to the world, they were living separate lives.

She hadn't phoned ahead. She wasn't sure what kind of reception she'd get. Now she climbed out of her car, gathered her courage and strode up to the front door. Though she usually gave no more than a perfunctory knock, if she bothered to knock at all, this time she knocked briskly, loudly and waited for Archie to answer.

It seemed to take forever, but at last the wooden panel swung inward and Archie stood there glaring at her. He looked so cold and distant her heart sank.

"What do you want?" he demanded.

Elizabeth held onto her courage. She loved this man with all her heart. And he loved her! Surely they could work things out?

"Hello, Archie. May I come in?"

His expression remained cold and unrelenting. "No."

"B-but I love you! Please, Archie. Let me in so we can talk."

"No. Every time I turn around, I'm hit over the head with more secrets. My brother, my wife, now you. A son! Why didn't you ever tell me about Ashton?"

She shrugged helplessly. "Like I said before, Ashton was part of a life I'd left behind. I truly never expected to see him again. His existence was something I'd put to the furthest recesses of my mind. It was the only way I coped."

Archie looked unconvinced. "We've known each other nearly forty years! We were friends before we were lovers. You could have told me."

"I'm sorry," she choked and stared at the ground. There was no point rehashing what might have been. "Please, Archie. Can't we work this out?"

"I've told you my terms. I won't settle for anything less."

Elizabeth stared at him. "You want me to tell our children about us."

"Yes, and the rest of the world. I want to live freely with you. I want you to be my wife."

Elizabeth gasped in surprise. "You... You want to get married?"

Archie narrowed his eyes at her. "Yes. Is that so hard to believe? That's what I've always wanted. Even before you married Henry. Don't you realize I've been in love with you since the day we met?"

Elizabeth felt faint. Her heart was beating much too fast. She pressed a hand against her chest. This was beyond what she could process. What was going on was overwhelming. First with Ashton and now with Archie and the rest…

Her chest tightened on a sob as she realized she wasn't ready to give him what he wanted, what he needed. She backed away slowly, shaking her head from side to side. Tears ran down her cheeks.

Archie looked just as devastated. He stared at her, his eyes hard. And then he turned his back on her and shut the door behind him. The click of the door as it shut had such a sound of finality…it broke her heart.

With tears now blinding her vision, Elizabeth stumbled to her car. Sobs tightened her chest, clogged her throat and eventually spilled from her mouth. She managed to put the car into gear and headed down the drive, but she'd barely made it a mile down the road before she pulled over. Resting her head on the steering wheel, she cried until she was empty.

We'll get through this… We'll get through this… We've been through tough times before… We've always come out the other side, stronger in our love for each other. This time's no different…

She repeated the mantra over and over in her head and prayed she was right.

Archie parted the blinds in his study and peered out into the early evening as Elizabeth's taillights disappeared into the distance. God, how he'd wanted to take her in his arms, kiss her, tell her he loved her. Tell her everything would be all right. That somehow they'd work this out. But he was tired, so tired of pretending.

He'd loved Elizabeth for most of his adult life. He'd been twenty-five when they'd met. Henry had brought her home for a game of tennis. Archie had taken one look at the beautiful woman with the hint of sadness and vulnerability in her blue eyes and had fallen hopelessly in love. His feelings for

Elizabeth had stayed that way all these years. She'd gone ahead and married his brother, but that hadn't changed anything. He'd loved her from afar.

But Henry had been dead more than a year. There was no reason they couldn't be together now. He wasn't sure why she kept resisting the idea of going public with their love. The more time went on, the more he was convinced they were doomed to always meet in secret. He was forced to face the reality she didn't feel as strongly about him as he did about her.

There was no other explanation. Why else would she continue to resist his pleas? He wasn't being unreasonable. Both of their spouses were dead. They were free to love whom they chose.

And yet, she kept finding excuses… Well, he'd had enough. If he didn't stand his ground, he'd be lost. He'd already put his heart on the line and she'd trodden all over it. Their love was under threat of being destroyed by her callousness, or at the very least, her uncaring attitude.

Can't she see how this is killing me? Killing us? One thing's for sure. I can't keep doing this…

Ashton had found an old tennis ball when he'd been snooping around the pool shed. He now tossed it across the manicured lawn that lined the backyard of Craigdon Manor. Rusty gave an excited yap.

"Go on, boy! Go and get it!" he encouraged.

The dog danced around, grinning, but didn't go after the ball. Ash sighed. He fetched the ball and tried again.

"There you go, Rusty! Go and get it! Go on, boy! Bring back the ball!"

Still the pup looked at him, but he didn't move toward the ball. Ash swallowed a surge of frustration.

"Dumb dog."

Elizabeth had presented the pup to him as a birthday present. There had been a moment of panic when he'd realized he'd forgotten the actual date. He'd brushed it off by assuring her he'd never been big on birthday celebrations. His adoptive parents had never made a big deal of them either. Elizabeth had looked at him in horror.

"What about a cake? Surely they baked you a cake?"

"Sometimes," he replied, keeping his response purposefully vague. "But most of the time it was just another day."

Elizabeth had looked distressed enough that he'd reassured her again it was okay.

"No. No it's not," she'd said. "Everyone deserves their own special day."

And then she'd handed him the box tied with a big red ribbon. He'd opened it and found Rusty staring up at him. Despite the fact this whole thing was an act, he'd actually been moved by her present. No one had ever given him such a personal, thoughtful gift.

"Thank you, Mom. I don't know what to say."

Elizabeth smiled. "You always wanted a dog. Now you have one. The woman at the animal shelter assured me he was intelligent and loved to play. Treat him right and he'll be a good any loyal companion to you for the rest of his life," Elizabeth added.

Somehow the puppy meant more to him than any of the other gifts she'd showered him with. Of course, he was supremely happy about the car. It had cost in the vicinity of half a million dollars. A nice little paycheck when it came time to cash in.

He'd been sure to have her register it in his name. She'd insisted on paying the insurance on it and he'd agreed after a bit of hanging back. He planned to take the car with him when he left. And when he did leave he'd make sure he had more than enough money to pay that bill for years to come.

A surge of yearning went through him. Some days he was tired of this life of deception. Putting effort into relationships that ultimately ended in betrayal when the truth was revealed, as it inevitably was.

What if this time was different? What if he managed to convince Elizabeth's family he really was her son? Then this wouldn't have to end. He could stay like this forever and pretend for the rest of his life he was her son.

Would it really be that terrible to deceive the old woman for so long? Why not? She was ecstatic about the thought she'd found him. Why should he burst her bubble? He sure could get used to living this kind of lifestyle. Never having to worry about paying the rent, or where his next meal might come from. The only problem was, he knew nothing about playing the piano or the violin. He couldn't even read music. He'd have to come up with a decent excuse if he wanted Elizabeth to continue buying his act.

But everything depended upon no one finding out and with her family already suspicious, there was no guarantee of that. He realized now he'd been approaching this all wrong. He needed to charm the Craigdon children, make them want him to be their brother, even when there was a slight possibility in their minds he wasn't. No one went looking too hard for something they didn't want to find.

Yes, that's what he had to do. Win Elizabeth's children over. Have them think so highly of him, they'd never want him to leave. It was a nice dream to wish and hope for. Who knew? Maybe things would work out.

He hadn't always been a con artist. In fact, he rarely described himself as such these days. He might have started out that way, but now he preferred to think of what he did as a community service—providing lonely old people with a bit of joy, a bit of hope, when otherwise all hope had been lost.

He used to work in a dead-end job in the department of

Family and Community Services. His job was to provide information to people who requested details about their birth parents. So many sad and desperate people yearning to know about their past. Their biological parents: the mother who'd given birth to them; the father who was listed on the birth certificate but whom they'd never met.

At first he found it all very sad and emotional. Applicants would fill in a request form, providing as much information as they could. A lot of the time, they didn't even have the name of their birth parents.

That didn't matter. Ash had access to all that stuff. It was a simple matter of a few keystrokes and *voila*, there it was. He passed what was allowed to be shared on to the applicant and they did with it what they would. Some contacted their birth parents. Some didn't. Whatever. It made no difference to him.

He'd been working at the job for more than five years before an idea began to take hold. The only thing the birth parents knew about the child they'd given up for adoption was that it had happened. Most of the time, they knew if they'd given birth to a boy or a girl, but not always. Some of the church-run institutions had been quite cruel that way— refusing to confirm the gender of the baby before it was whisked away.

Of course, one thing the birth mother always knew was the date of her baby's birth. No doubt that date had been seared into her brain. As Ash spent week after week, year after year processing applications, a plan began to form.

Why should he bother with his mediocre life when he saw opportunities do so much better? What better way to bag a few riches, than to pretend to be someone's long lost son? He had access to all the information. It would be a simple matter to align himself with the details contained in so many of the records and make contact with the birth parents.

And so it had begun. Sometimes he'd gotten lucky. Other

times, not so much. Some were glad to see him and welcomed him with open arms. Others refused to acknowledge him. None of them were as wealthy as Elizabeth Craigdon, but the ones that encompassed him with love and tears showered him with gifts. They were so overjoyed to connect with him, to touch him, to kiss him, to talk to him—their long lost, beloved son.

He reveled in the attention as he accepted all the gifts. He received far more than he could have dreamed. Of course, he had no idea about the emotional trauma they'd been through and would go through again when he left. It wasn't like he cared.

He'd been born to poor white trash in the western suburbs of Sydney, and they loved him as best they could. Eve and Peter Walker still lived in the same old dump he'd grown up in. His father was a laborer. His mother worked in a shop. Dead-end people going nowhere. He couldn't wait to get away from the place.

He'd left home when he was fifteen and spent time living on the streets. He started telling everyone his parents were dead. That got him plenty of sympathy. One old lady had even invited him home for a hot meal. She'd found him scavenging out of the bins on the street outside a McDonalds. He didn't have enough money to buy food. It was humiliating to think about that now.

But that accidental meeting proved to be a godsend. Betty McCormack was a well-connected lady. She managed to get him a job in the department of Family and Community Services where her niece was the boss. It was a boring job, dealing with endless applications, but he at least got paid. Working there had also triggered the idea of pretending to be someone's long lost son.

Over the time he worked there he did a lot of billable overtime doing his research: He collected files and information on some adoptions that had potential to support his financial advancement. He did research on the players: who was where in their lives and their financial circumstances. Also on the information, if any, provided to the people searching for their connections. Or not. And he planned. Researched. Even stalked some of them to find the most advantageous marks before he'd swoop in.

Of course, the gig only lasted so long, until suspicious relatives started digging. He was always sure to leave without a trace, and long before he got found out. He gave his victims fake names, fake addresses, fake everything. Nothing he told them was true. He formulated his life story based on what he knew about the birth parents. Elizabeth Craigdon was a prime example.

In her file, someone had noted she was a talented musician. He hadn't known David was one too. The only mention of the father was his name. In Ash's experience, the biological fathers were less inclined to believe his carefully prepared speech. Neither did they bear the guilt the mothers did. That's why he now made it a practice to target only the mothers. It made his job that much easier.

Providing Elizabeth with the name of her son's father had been enough to convince her he was her son, the baby boy she'd given away. He'd perfected the art of playing on their emotions, and most of all, their guilt. He hadn't found one mother who'd given up her baby for adoption who didn't feel guilty about it. Even forty years down the track.

It made the job so much easier. They only saw what they wanted to see. They never dreamed it was all a con. Why would they? What kind of sick bastard would do that?

He grinned to himself and tossed the ball back out into the yard, calling to Rusty to fetch it. The manicured lawns stretched over several hectares, dotted with mature trees, lush garden beds and hedges. Elizabeth Craigdon was loaded.

He'd never dreamed there were people who actually lived like this.

It was obvious money was no object. Click your fingers and someone came running, eager to please. The housekeeper, gardeners, pool boys. The place even had its own nine-hole golf course.

But he needed to tread carefully. The Craigdon children were getting suspicious. Especially Isabella and the cop. Then there was Christopher. Ash could see it in their faces, hear the animosity in their voices. They didn't trust him, didn't believe him. They were protective of their mother and no doubt, their inheritance. He needed to be careful. Keep alert. He had to make sure he read the signs so he could make a run for it before he got caught. If it came to that…

He rather hoped his charm and charisma might be enough to get them on side. He needed to come up with a plan, something that would blow them away and hold them forever in his debt. Then turning him out on his ear would be the last thing on their mind…

The sound of the side gate opening snagged his attention. He looked up and spied Isabella coming around the side of the house. His initial reaction was irritation. *Great. She was back.* But then he thought of his newly-hatched idea to win her over and with a concerted effort, he plastered a friendly smile on his face.

Isabella let the gate drift closed behind her and strode across the concrete pavers that formed the path down the side of the house. She rounded the corner and came to a sudden halt. Her eyes narrowed at the sight before her.

Ashton was tossing a ball and then calling for a dog to chase after it. A puppy so cute she had to fight against melting into a smile. A German shepherd, by the look of it.

What the hell is he doing playing with a dog in our yard?

"What are you doing?" she demanded.

He winked. "What does it look like?"

"Who owns that animal?"

"His name's Rusty and he's mine."

"You can't have him here."

He continued to give her a bland look. "Why not?"

"Because… The Craigdons don't do dogs."

His answering chuckle was filled with amusement. "The Craigdons don't do dogs? What kind of crap is that?"

Her anger stirred. She glared at him, but he seemed impervious to her temper. She spun on her heel in a huff.

"Isabella! Hey! I'm sorry! Rusty was a birthday gift from your mother."

Steadfastly ignoring him, she charged into the house.

"Mom! Where are you? Mom?"

"In here," her mother replied.

Isabella headed in the direction of the voice. It sounded like it came from the music room.

"Mom?" she asked again.

"Isabella! Please stop shouting. I'm in the music room."

Issy stormed through the kitchen, past the breakfast room and down the hall until she came to the music room. She was almost panting with anger when she walked through the open doorway and found her mother seated at the piano.

"Goodness gracious! What's the matter?" Elizabeth exclaimed.

"I just saw Ashton. With that dog. What the hell's going on?"

Elizabeth sighed quietly. "He's always wanted a dog. It seems he never had one when he was young. It was his birthday last week. I bought him one."

Issy's eyes widened in shock. "So it's true. You bought it for him."

Elizabeth shrugged. "Yes, Isabella. I did."

Issy's anger found its head. "That's not fair! Why would you do that? You never let us have a dog!"

Once again, Elizabeth sighed. "Oh, Isabella. Why does that matter? It's not like you're still pining for one. And for your information, the no-dog rule was your father's, not mine. He never wanted a pet."

Her calm and reasonable tone only irritated Isabella further. "And why was that?" she shot back. "I begged him and begged him to let me get a puppy. I was about five or six. He flatly refused. He wouldn't even discuss it. What was the big deal?'

This time, Elizabeth blew her breath out. Her shoulders slumped. She suddenly looked weary. She stood and slowly made her way over to the couch. She patted the seat beside her, but Isabella was too worked up to sit.

"Tell me why Daddy didn't like animals," she said.

"It wasn't that he didn't like animals," Elizabeth replied. "In fact, when he was a young boy, he owned a dog."

Issy blinked in surprise. "Wow. I'd have never guessed."

"Your father owned a border collie he'd had since she was a pup. I think his mother had bought him the dog for his fifth birthday. Her name was Jasper. Then one day Henry noticed she was growing fatter. He took Jasper to his mother. She was as surprised as your father when she told him the dog was going to have puppies."

"Why was she surprised?"

Elizabeth shrugged. "Apparently they'd been told the dog had been spayed."

"Wow. Okay. I can understand how grandma must have been surprised then."

"Yes. Anyway, your father was thrilled, excited like any kid would be. He counted down the days until those puppies were born. He was there when Jasper gave birth. I remember him telling me he even helped deliver the last pup. Jasper was all worn out. Six puppies altogether. She was having trouble pushing the last one out. That's when your father stepped in. He saved the pup and probably Jasper's life."

Isabella stared at her mother in confusion. "I don't understand. How did he go from that caring, sensitive boy to a man who couldn't stand the thought of me having a dog?"

Elizabeth's expression turned grim. "As it turned out, Henry's father didn't want a litter of pups. He wasn't even prepared to let Henry ask around and see if anyone else wanted them. Instead he forced Henry to drown them in the ocean. He made him hold them down in a bag until they were dead. Then he had to bury them."

Isabella gasped. She stared at her mother in horror. "Oh no! Poor Daddy! Who does that to their young son?"

Elizabeth compressed her lips. "Yes. It was unspeakably cruel. For your father and for the pups. Not to mention poor Jasper who must have wondered what had happened to her babies." Elizabeth paused and then added, "Your father never forgot it. He was sure poor Jasper blamed him. She looked at him with such sadness and suspicion, he was convinced she knew he was the one responsible for killing her pups. He couldn't bear to look at her. A few weeks later, he was walking her along a busy road. He deliberately let her off her leash."

Issy pushed her hand against her mouth in an effort to contain her gasp. "Oh, no!"

Her mother nodded, sadness and resignation filling her face. "Yes. It only took a few minutes. Jasper was scared, confused. She ran straight out in front of a truck. Your father told me he was relieved when she got run over. He vowed never to own a pet again."

Guilt flooded through her. "Poor Daddy! Why didn't he tell me?"

Elizabeth looked at her askance. "Isabella, you were five. Do you really think he should have told you?"

She nodded her agreement. "I guess not."

Her mother folded her hands in her lap. "So, now you know. When Ashton told me he'd also been denied a puppy when he was a child, what was I to do? He missed out on so much because of my actions. The least I could do was buy him a dog."

Isabella hung her head. She now felt guilty about giving Ashton such a hard time over the pup. Her shoulders slumped on a sigh.

"Thanks for telling me, Mom. I really appreciate it. I mean that."

Elizabeth merely nodded.

Chapter Fourteen

After sharing a pot of tea with Isabella and listening while she brought her up to date on the wedding plans, Elizabeth saw her daughter out and then returned to the music room. The latest gift she'd found for Ashton sat on a low bench beside the piano. It was wrapped in gold paper and decorated with a shiny gold bow. She was pleased Issy hadn't spotted it. It seemed whatever Elizabeth did for her son, Isabella disapproved. But now that her daughter had left, Elizabeth couldn't wait to give him the present.

She heard the sliding door that led out to the pool area open and close. Her heart skipped a beat as excitement and anticipation zinged along her veins. She smiled wryly and silently admonished herself.

Get a grip. I'm like a kid on Christmas morning… It's only a gift…

Yes, but a very special gift and one she'd spent hours searching for. It had also cost her a pretty penny. Three hundred thousand dollars, to be exact. Not that she cared about the money. She'd lost forty years of her son's life. Nothing could make up for that. But in some small way, she hoped her latest gift might go a little way toward bridging the rift.

"Ash? Is that you?" she called.

A moment later, he appeared in the open doorway. "Yes, Mom?"

She frowned. He stood there in the same clothes he'd worn the day before and his hair was greasy and disheveled. It looked like it was in need of a wash. And Amy had reluctantly confided that his room was a pigsty. Elizabeth had waved away her concerns. It wasn't fair to judge him. She could only imagine what kind of household he'd been raised in, or what expectations there had been.

Children learned from example. Elizabeth had been a firm believer in that. But his adoptive parents were both dead and she wouldn't think ill of them. Over time, she hoped he learned to live a little tidier. Maybe she could give him a few suggestions… But that wasn't her priority now. No, all she wanted right now was to make him happy.

"Would you come in here for a minute?" she asked.

He smiled. "Of course."

She walked over to the piano and picked up the box. She presented it to him with an excited flourish. "This is for you."

He took the box and frowned down at it. "What is it?"

"Why don't you open it and see?"

"Just tell me."

"It's a surprise."

"I don't like surprises."

She touched him gently on the arm. "Please, Ashton. Just open it."

With a quiet sigh, he set the box down and tugged at the ribbon. He tossed it to the floor and then started in on the paper, tearing it to shreds. Looking almost bored, he opened the cardboard box and stared down at the violin case.

A frown marred his forehead. He looked up at her with confusion. "You bought me a violin?"

She smiled. "Not just any violin. Take a look."

He opened the case slowly and peeled back the lid.

A beautiful, shiny violin sat in its padded case. Ashton stared down at it. "Wow," he muttered. "Thanks, Mom."

Elizabeth tried to hide her disappointment. "Take it out. Have a proper look."

Ashton did as she asked. He turned the hand-crafted instrument this way and that before returning it to the case.

Elizabeth felt let down over his less-than-enthusiastic response. She forced a smile. "It's a Mathias Albani. It comes with a certificate of authenticity. It's believed to have been made around 1670."

At his continued scowl, she gave a hesitant laugh. "Of course it's not a Stradivarius, but it's still a beautiful violin. I'm sure it has a beautiful sound. Please, would you play something for me? It would give me so much pleasure."

Ashton's scowl deepened. His eyes flashed with temper. "I'm not a performing animal to execute tricks for you whenever you're bored."

Elizabeth drew back from the anger in his face. She felt unaccountably hurt and stricken that he'd taken her gift as an offense.

"I-I'm sorry if you feel that way, Ash. It wasn't my intention. I thought… I thought you'd like it. You told Christopher your instruments were all in storage. I thought you might like to have one or two here…" Her voice drifted off.

To her consternation, the irritation on his face didn't fade. "Forget about it," he muttered.

"Please, Ash. I'm so sorry. I didn't mean to upset you."

He remained stony-faced. And then his shoulders slumped. "It's not your fault. It's just that my adoptive parents forced me to play anywhere and everywhere, anytime they pleased. My mother was the worst. Being a music teacher, she liked to parade me in front of her friends. It was her way of showing off. Look at me, look at my talented son. It used to make me sick. I vowed when I left home I'd never be treated like that again."

Elizabeth was distraught. The last thing she'd wanted was to dredge up bad memories for him. "I'm sorry. I had no idea."

He compressed his lips and merely shrugged. "Yeah. Well, now you know. I'm going to go upstairs to lie down for a bit. I feel a headache coming on. Let me know when lunch is served."

With the expensive violin casually tucked under his arm, Ash made his way upstairs. Apparently it was a Mathias Albani…whoever that was. As soon as he had the chance, he'd hock the stupid thing online. No doubt she'd paid a fortune. Hand-crafted in 1670, she'd said… It should fetch a pretty penny.

Not that he'd sell it just yet. If he played his cards right and managed to allay everyone's suspicions, he might just be able to stay. And if all went to hell and his plans went awry, he'd be ready to scamper away in the night and disappear, never to be seen or heard from again. Like he'd done so many times before.

Of course he'd take the generous gifts Elizabeth had given him. They were his, after all. So what if she'd given them to him under false pretenses. It wasn't his fault the old bat wanted to buy him expensive things.

He only had another week of leave before he had to return to his dead-end job in the department. That was probably for the best. Returning to work would give him the chance to research another gullible victim; another guilt-ridden mother who'd given up her child and who'd be only too overjoyed to meet him. He only hoped he was as lucky as he had been with Elizabeth Craigdon. This had been one hell of a ride.

Elizabeth's fingers moved desultorily over the piano keys. Like she'd done so many times in the past, she turned to music in an effort to lighten her depressing mood. She thought Ashton would be overjoyed at the prospect of owning a Mathias Albani violin. They were among the finest instruments ever made. And especially one as old as the gift she'd purchased for him. It had taken several phone calls to and from her art dealer before they'd managed to secure it. Instruments like that didn't come on the market often. As a fellow musician, Elizabeth had been sure her son would appreciate the gesture. But it seemed she'd misread the situation. He hadn't reacted with gratitude at all.

She sighed. It hadn't been her intention to annoy him. In fact, just the opposite. How was she to know his adoptive parents had put pressure on him to perform to the point where he'd grown to hate it? That was so sad. It tore at her heartstrings to know he felt like that. A lot of the enjoyment she derived from music was having an audience to play for. That's what had drawn her to the conservatorium in the first place. Apart from the opportunity to learn and refine her craft with some of the best in the world, she was also expected to perform in public.

She used to relish those occasions when the conservatorium would host a public concert. The air of excitement and anticipation right before the event... The hush of the crowd as the lights fell low and the curtain opened...Even now, all these decades later, the memory still left a tingle of excitement running down her spine.

She sighed quietly. It saddened her that Ashton had been turned off that kind of thing. To think about a live performance with resentment and dread instead of the excitement and magic she'd always felt... She wondered if there was some way she could change his mind, give him an experience that would overcome the negative feelings he had.

Was there something to reignite his love of music…and of performing?

Ever since his arrival, she'd been going over and above to make him feel welcome. She'd bought him a car, a phone, shoes, clothes, a puppy. She'd given him the run of the house. She'd invited him to stay as long as he wanted. He'd made good use of the pool and the golf course. It pleased her to see him making himself at home. She admitted she was trying very hard to make up for lost time. Was she trying too hard?

He was her son after all and they'd missed out on many years together—through no fault of his own. She'd done her best. He deserved all she had to offer and that was that.

But after their last confrontation, she wanted to do more. It wasn't right that his adoptive parents had turned him against performing. Elizabeth was sure he was a brilliant musician. After all, with the blood of two talented musicians running through his veins, how could he not be?

I know! I'll take him to the opera! What better way to reignite his passion for music and performance?

She sat back on the piano stool and rested her hands on her lap, pleased with herself. Elizabeth adored the opera. There was a chance Ashton might never have been to one. How wonderful if she were to share in his first time! The possibility sent a thrill of wonder surging through her.

Unable to contain her excitement, she jumped up and hurried across the room to where she'd left her iPad. With growing anticipation, she opened a search engine and typed in "Opera Australia" and was immediately rewarded with their home page. She scrolled down the page until she found a list of current performances.

There's one showing on Friday night! Oh, it's Carmen*! How wonderful!*

She loved *Carmen*. So full of angst and tragedy. Unrequited love, fidelity, deceit… There was so much she could relate to.

But on top of that, it was a wonderful story filled with superb music that challenged all sections of the orchestra. She was sure a musician as capable and talented as Ashton would appreciate the score.

Her thoughts turned to Archie and her heart skipped a beat. The last time she'd gone to a performance at the Opera House, Archie had been her date. It was more than six months ago. They'd had a lovely time. One or two of their society friends had given them curious looks, but most understood they were two relatives enjoying a night out. After all, neither of their spouses were still living and Elizabeth had often gone to the opera with Archie, even when Henry was alive.

Anyone who knew the family was aware that Henry couldn't abide the opera. He'd once been overheard complaining loudly in the Opera House foyer that he'd rather have a root canal. Elizabeth had been completely humiliated and had tried to laugh off his comment, but she'd never asked him to accompany her there again.

Fortunately, Archie had been only too willing to go with her. It was stolen time they were able to spend together. Besides, Archie adored the opera as much as she did.

She blew out her breath on a soft sigh.

Archie...

How she missed him! How she hated being estranged from him like this! She wished now she'd told him years ago about Ashton. But when? There had never seemed the right time. Now he'd made it clear she was the one who would have to take the first step toward mending fences and that would mean going public with their love.

Then there were Sophia and Logan. Elizabeth had kept the truth from Archie about being Sophia's father, but she'd done it for Sophia's sake. And though he was hurt, that hadn't been her motivation, no matter what he thought. Archie had known he wasn't Logan's father and yet he hadn't told her.

Had he known all along? For twenty-five years?

No. She wouldn't believe that. For a year, since the question was raised after the reading of Henry's will, Archie had been adamant his wife would never have cheated on him. Even when Noah came forward with the evidence of his mother's affair with Henry. An affair they now knew had been going on for fifteen years before she died.

Archie had emphatically defended his wife's memory, refusing to even consider Noah's evidence might be right. Elizabeth didn't know what had happened to change Archie's mind, but something had. That didn't change the fact he'd kept the information to himself and she had no idea for how long. That knowledge still had the power to hurt.

Why didn't he tell me? Who was he trying to protect? It obviously wasn't Janelle…or Henry. Logan, perhaps?

She thought back to the moment when Edgerton had read out those lines in Henry's letter. She'd looked across at Archie and his sons. None of them had shown signs of shock. No, whoever and whenever it was that they'd discovered the truth, all four of them had known. And they'd deliberately kept it from her.

She didn't blame Archie's sons. They had nothing to do with this. They were oblivious to her ongoing romantic relationship with their father. It wouldn't have occurred to them to tell her about their mother's affair that had resulted in Logan.

But what hurt the most was that Archie knew and he'd said nothing to her. And now she had another secret exposed… Ashton… No wonder Archie had removed himself. He had to wonder what else she'd kept secret, what other shocks might yet be revealed. He had no way of knowing that was the end of them. All of her secrets were out.

Her emotions were in upheaval. Her thoughts kept going round and round. No matter which way she looked at it, her life was crazy and out of control.

What can I do to fix this? Does he even want it fixed? The last time I spoke to him, he was so cold, so dismissive. Have I already left it too late?

Elizabeth buried her face in her hands and held back a sob of despair. She loved Archie with all her heart, but the yawning canyon between them seemed insurmountable right now.

No! Everything inside her rebelled against that. She refused to think after all these years of love and devotion to each other they wouldn't make it to the end. They'd get through this. Of course they would. People who loved each other as long and as fiercely as they did didn't give up when the going got tough. Somehow she'd find the courage to come forward with their love, declare to their children and all the world what they meant to each other…

In the meantime, she'd take her son to the opera and introduce him to her friends. Some of them might judge her for having a baby out of wedlock, but she no longer cared about that. She wished she'd had the same kind of courage forty years earlier.

But that time had come and gone a long time ago and there was nothing she could do about that. What she could do was enjoy her son's company while she had it. She intended to make the most of it.

Archie sipped from a crystal highball glass generously filled with single malt whiskey. It was only mid-afternoon. Probably too early to hit the hard stuff, but he was beyond caring. It had been weeks since he'd spent time with Elizabeth. Weeks since they'd shared a bed. For all his determination to hold out until she came to her senses, he was punishing himself as much as her.

God, I miss her! I love her so much! This is crazy! What am I doing?

He'd been rocked by the discovery his wife of more than two decades had been having an affair most of their married life. And with his brother, no less. But now that he'd had some time to get over the shock, he'd been filled with nothing but sadness and regret. It was obvious they'd both been more unhappy in their marriage than either of them had been prepared to admit. He'd been in love with Elizabeth and Janelle had obviously fallen hard for Henry.

Though Archie and Elizabeth didn't act on their attraction until well into her marriage, the fact Henry had already convinced himself she'd been unfaithful before that had given his brother the impetus to seduce Archie's wife. It was a sad, tangled love affair that didn't have a happy ending. Janelle had died way too young, indirectly at the hands of her lover and Archie and Elizabeth weren't speaking to each other.

Archie's shoulders slumped on a sigh. He sipped at his whiskey. The aged liquor was rich and mellow and slid all too easily down his throat. It would be a simple matter to get roaring drunk and do his best to forget about his troubles for a while.

He lifted the glass to his lips again and gave the idea serious consideration. And then he shook his head. Though the thought wasn't without appeal, he couldn't stand the idea of waking with a thumping headache and the inevitable irritation and temper that would plague him for the next day or so. Sometimes the hangover just wasn't worth it.

There was a time when I would have gotten drunk anyway, to hell with the hangover…

He was getting old. He'd turned sixty-three last birthday. Sixty-three. That meant he'd been in love with Elizabeth Craigdon for close to forty years…

And what do I have to show for it? We aren't together. She's not my wife. She bore me a daughter and didn't even tell me. Ditto with not telling me about her son, her firstborn. Who keeps secrets like that from someone they love? Had I known I would have celebrated Ashton's arrival—for her. The woman I love. No wonder we aren't even talking…

Not only did he miss her company in his bed, he missed her companionship in his life. Her gentle humor, the way she understood him better than anyone else. The fun times they had together, dining out, dancing, going to live theater, the opera, concerts…

It had been more than six months since he'd been to any kind of show. He and Elizabeth had gone to see *Carmen*. It was one of their favorite operas. He was filled with a sudden yearning to do something special, to go out, to socialize. To remind himself he was still alive.

Switching on the television, he picked up the remote and connected to the Internet. He pulled up the Opera Australia website and checked out their current list of performances. His gaze snagged on the word *Carmen*. His heart skipped a beat. It was playing in Sydney at the Opera House that Friday night! It was a sign!

He wanted to go. But who would he go with? There was no way he'd go alone. Maybe he could ask his daughter? Sophia loved live shows. Yes. He'd call Sophia.

Mind made up, he pulled out his phone and dialed her number before he had any second thoughts. It was late enough in the afternoon that she should have finished school. He hoped she wasn't in a staff meeting or something like that. Now that he'd made the decision to get himself off his couch and go out, he wanted to lock it in and he needed Sophia's acquiescence to do that.

Her phone rang out and he'd braced himself for it to go through to voicemail when she answered.

"Hi, Uncle… Dad. What are you up to?"

"How are things?"

"Fine." She sounded bemused.

He understood her reaction. He rarely phoned her. "Good."

"Is something the matter?" she asked, her tone filling with concern.

He hurried to reassure her. "No, of course not."

"Okay."

"Listen," he said in a rush. "I just wondered if you would come to the opera with me this Friday night?"

"The opera?"

"Yes. They're performing *Carmen.* I love that opera."

"Don't you normally go to those things with Mom?"

He bit his lip. He and Elizabeth had done their best to keep their estrangement away from the notice of their kids.

"Yes. Of course. But… I just thought it would be nice if I went there with you. For a change. If you want."

Embarrassment flamed across his cheeks. He'd made a real mess of that. He was on the verge of telling Sophia not to worry about it when she spoke again.

"I've never been to the opera, but I love live shows. I guess it might be fun."

Archie's heart leaped with excitement.

"The only thing is, I can't do this Friday. Jarrod and I have made plans."

Archie's excitement immediately fizzled. He compressed his lips, filled with disappointment.

"That's okay," he managed. "Perhaps another time."

"You bet."

"Have a good weekend, honey."

"You too. Dad."

Archie ended the call and then stared at his phone, feeling depressed. He'd really been looking forward to going to *Carmen.* Maybe there was someone else he could ask?

Maybe Isabella would like to come with me…

Brightening, he scrolled once again through his contacts and dialed his niece's number.

Chapter Fifteen

eeling heartened, Archie once again listened as the call dialed out.

"Uncle Archie! What's going on?"

He grinned at Isabella's enthusiastic greeting. "Not much, but it's nice of you to ask. What's going on with you?"

"I'm back in Brisbane and busy hitting the shops. I'm trying to find pieces to decorate our new townhouse."

"You and Raine finally found somewhere to live?"

"Yes. It's gorgeous. A little two-bedder with awesome views of the river and not far from Raine's work. It's perfect."

"I'm so happy for you," Archie said, meaning it.

"Thank you, Uncle."

There was a pause and then she asked, "Um, is everything all right? You're not calling with bad news, are you?" She laughed a little, but he heard her sudden tension.

"No, of course not. As far as I know, everyone's fine. I just…"

"What is it?"

"I was calling to ask you if you wanted to accompany me to the opera this Friday night, that's all. But you're in Brisbane, so of course you can't. Don't worry. It's all good."

His words came out in a jumbled rush. He was surprised she'd made head or tail of it. But she simply laughed, this time with relief, and replied.

"Oh, too bad. I would have loved to have gone with you. Maybe next time."

"Really?"

"Yes."

"Well, great. I love the opera. Your mother and I used to go all the time."

"Yes, I remember. Daddy couldn't stand it. Mom was so pleased you didn't feel the same. Why can't she go with you now?"

Archie thought about giving her a glib response or putting her off with a lie, but he was tired of all the subterfuge. He went with the truth.

"Your mother and I aren't talking at the moment."

"Oh, no! That's awful! You two get on so well and with all that's been going on, now more than ever you need each other."

Her words warmed him. "Thank you, Isabella. I appreciate that."

"Do you mind me asking what you're arguing about?"

He sighed. "It's kind of complicated. It's been going on for a while."

"Well, I hope you work it out."

"Thank you. So do I. Unfortunately, I don't think it's going to be in time to make the opera this Friday night."

"Listen, why don't you call an escort service? I'm sure they'll have a lovely lady who'll be willing to accompany you to the show."

He gasped in shock. "An escort service! Isabella! I'm not looking for…that kind of thing. I just want to go to the opera."

Her laughter rang in his ear. "Oh, Uncle! You're so quaint! Escorts will be whatever you want them to be. If all you're looking for is a woman to take to the opera, then that's what you request. Yes, some of them offer more…intimate services, but it doesn't have to be like that. If all you want is companionship for the evening, then you let them know up front and that's fine."

He frowned as the idea slowly sank in. "Really? She wouldn't expect me to… You know."

Once again, Isabella laughed. "No, not at all. There are many escorts who don't offer sex as part of their service. It's up to the individual girl."

Archie felt a modicum of relief. "Well, that's interesting to know."

"So, what about it? Are you going to give someone a call?"

"I wouldn't even know how to go about looking for someone like that."

He could almost see Isabella roll her eyes. "Uncle! For goodness sake! What century are you living in? All you have to do is call one of the escort agencies and tell them what you're looking for. You can call or book online. It's all very discreet and professional. In fact, I can even recommend an agency to you, if you like."

Archie didn't want to contemplate how Isabella would have the name of a reputable escort agency at her fingertips, but the idea of using an escort service to attend the opera was growing on him. It would mean he could leave the house with a purpose and hopefully shake off his doldrums. It would also prove he didn't need Elizabeth in order to go out and have a good time. That last thought cinched it.

"Okay. Give it to me."

"Bravo!"

He smiled at the approval he heard in Isabella's tone. She gave him the name and phone number of an agency. He took down the details and thanked her.

"No worries. Happy to help out," she replied.

"Thank you again. And take care."

"You, too."

Archie brought the call to an end and then sat there staring at the phone.

I can't believe it. I'm actually thinking about arranging to take an escort to the opera! How delightfully...naughty.

All of a sudden, he felt young again and he laughed out loud at the sheer thrill of it. Reaching for his highball, he downed the contents for Dutch courage and once again reached for his phone. He put in the number Isabella gave him and waited for someone to pick up.

It was far easier than he'd anticipated. In short order, he arranged for a mature woman to meet him in the city for a night at the opera. He was assured of the utmost discretion and was advised that for an additional sum, the woman was his for the night.

Archie blushed.

She's talking about sex... If I want, I can pay to sleep with the woman...

No. This wasn't about sex and he couldn't imagine wanting to cheat on Elizabeth. There had been way too much of that already. This was only about him feeling lonely and wanting to do something fun. A night out at the opera with a beautiful woman ought to do it. Even if that woman wasn't the love of his life.

⌒

To Elizabeth's relief, Ashton was excited about the thought of accompanying her to the opera. He seemed to have thrown off his bad mood and was now in high spirits.

"I've never been to an opera before," he confided. "In fact, I've never been inside the Opera House. Is it as cool on the inside as it looks on the outside?"

She smiled. "Yes. It's beautiful. An architectural masterpiece and an amazing and vibrant performance space. Well worth experiencing." She guessed that growing up in the country meant that he'd missed a lot of what Sydney had to offer. She vowed to make that up to him.

He looked handsome in the designer tux, pristine white dinner shirt and black bow tie she'd bought for him to wear. His thick black hair was shiny clean and he'd even shaved for the occasion. As she climbed out of the taxi that had dropped them at the bottom of the Opera House stairs he held out his arm toward her in a gallant fashion.

"Mother."

"Thank you, Ash," she murmured and slipped her arm inside his.

She'd taken particular care with her wardrobe, spending a ridiculous amount of time pulling dresses off their hangers, sizing them up and then discarding them. In the end, she'd settled on something new, bought while she waited for the tailor to make alterations to Ashton's suit.

The black velvet sheath fit her like a glove. Sleeveless, it kissed the floor even with the aid of her four-inch heels. It clung to her curves and smoothed out her bumps and did everything a five thousand dollar dress ought to. She couldn't have been happier with her selection and it seemed Ashton approved too.

"You look sensational, Mom. I'm going to be the envy of every man in the room." He smiled widely and she was filled with pride.

This man is my son.

All those years ago she never imagined she'd ever see him again, let alone get to spend time with him, get to know him. It was a blessed gift she had no intention of squandering. She'd steal whatever moments she could with him. At some point he'd return to his life in Tamworth. After all that's where he lived. Until then, she'd make the most of it. Including tonight.

She pulled her phone out of her evening bag and opened

it to the camera. Tugging on Ashton's arm, she brought him to a halt.

"Let's take a moment to get a photo to commemorate the occasion."

He immediately shook his head and held up his hands. "Sorry, Mom. I don't do photos."

She frowned. "What do you mean, you don't do photos?"

He shrugged. "Just that. I don't like having my photo taken."

She stared at him, thinking he must be joking, but his expression remained serious. She frowned again. "You mean it? You really don't want me to take a photo?"

"Yes. I really mean it. If you don't mind, I'd like you to put that phone away."

"But I don't have any photos of you! Not a single one! I know that was my fault, but still… I'd like to make up for lost time."

"No." His tone remained firm, his expression unmoving.

Elizabeth was filled with bewilderment. She'd never met anyone who was so averse to having their photo taken. It was strange. But now wasn't the time to contemplate that. She was at the opera. With her *son*. The son she never thought she'd see again. She'd missed forty years of his life. She was determined to enjoy every moment she spent with him.

They walked up the steps together and were the recipients of more than a few stares. She could tell some people thought they were a couple. She smiled at the thought.

Just inside the Opera House, she ran into a friend. Well, not really a friend. An acquaintance, more like it. She and Julia weren't close. The few times they'd shared conversation while chairing several charities together, Elizabeth had been taken aback at the woman's ability to whine almost constantly about everything. Beside Julia stood her long-suffering husband, Eric.

Julia's eyes widened with surprise and her gaze immediately went to Ashton. She opened her mouth and Elizabeth could almost see the battle going on behind her eyes. She wanted to ply Elizabeth with questions about the handsome stranger on her arm, but courtesy dictated otherwise.

"Elizabeth! How lovely to see you! That dress is just divine!"

The woman leaned in to peck Elizabeth's cheek and then stood back again. The avid curiosity in her gaze continued, unabated. Knowing the woman was just dying to ask who her date was, Elizabeth made the introductions.

"Thank you, Julia. I'd like you to meet my son, Ashton."

The woman's mouth formed a perfect "O." Her eyes flared wide with surprise. Elizabeth could almost see the woman doing the math, trying to figure out their age difference, but of course, she was much too well bred to ask the questions that were no doubt clamoring to get out.

Elizabeth merely smiled calmly and turned to Eric. She made a comment about the weather. Eric answered, agreeing it had been a very mild summer. With a not-so-subtle nudge, Eric dragged his wife away. She left, staring over her shoulder toward them, the questions still burning behind her eyes.

"One of your friends?" Ash asked, a wry smile turning up his lips.

"Don't worry about her. We barely know each other." Elizabeth dismissed his comment.

They moved over to the bar and Elizabeth asked Ashton what he wanted to drink.

"I'll have a rum and Coke, thanks."

Elizabeth put in his order and asked for a glass of champagne. The drinks arrived a few minutes later and she paid the barman and then offered the rum to her son.

"Thanks," he said again and then looked around him.

"Geez. Talk about a fancy affair. I've never seen so many rich people."

Elizabeth glanced surreptitiously around them and hoped no one had overheard. It wasn't Ashton's fault he'd been raised without the social niceties, but still… She hoped he wouldn't embarrass her.

"Hey, isn't that one of the Craigdon's over there? That old guy? Yeah. What's his name again? Archie?"

Elizabeth froze. There was no way Ashton could be right. Archie would never have come to something like this on his own.

"Who's that woman with him?" Ashton whistled low in his throat. "She's a stunner."

Elizabeth's heart took off at a gallop as she looked in the direction Ashton indicated. Her chest tightened on a stutter of disbelief. Sure enough, Archie stood on the other side of the room with a beautiful young woman beside him. As if sensing her interest, the pair of them turned and looked right at her. Elizabeth immediately dropped her gaze, flustered and confused.

Okay, so the woman probably wasn't that young. But even from a distance Elizabeth could tell the age gap was close to thirty years. Blinding hot jealousy surged through her. She gasped and had to turn away.

What is he doing here and who is that woman? Don't tell me he's moved on… After everything we've been through, everything we've meant to each other… We love each other, darn it. At least, I thought we did…

With her heart breaking, Elizabeth pasted a smile on her face and nodded to friends and acquaintances as they made their way to their bar. There was a murmur of voices in the crowd and she was sure they were all talking about her and Archie. While no one knew they were romantically linked, it was still a surprise to see them with other partners. That had never happened before. It was no surprise that they caused a fuss now.

Gripping Ashton's arm like her life depended on it, Elizabeth prayed for the courage to see this through with her head held high and her pride intact. In the same breath, she prayed for the night to be over.

Archie returned from the bar carrying two glasses of champagne and had just offered one to his date when he sensed someone looking at him. He turned slightly and caught Elizabeth's shocked gaze. She immediately looked away, but not before he saw the flush of embarrassment color her cheeks. He was just as surprised as she was.

Though they both adored the opera, it hadn't occurred to him she'd attend on her own.

But she isn't on her own...

His gaze slid to the handsome man who stood beside her. It was Ashton. Her son. The son Archie hadn't known she'd had. The son she'd kept a secret from everyone, even Henry. Archie risked another glance in their direction. They'd moved away, toward the stalls. Ashton's arm was draped protectively around her shoulders.

Jealousy surged through him. Archie had heard through the servants' gossip mill that Elizabeth was spending all her time with her long-lost son. Lavishing him with expensive gifts, fawning over him. Now she was here with him at the opera. It was an insult.

This was *their* thing. It didn't matter that Archie was also there with a date. That was different. He'd paid Alexandra to be there. It wasn't like he preferred her company over Elizabeth's and yet, that's the way it was for her and her son. Or so it seemed.

She still hadn't made up with him. He'd bared his heart to her, told her what he wanted, what he needed and she'd turned her back on him. They hadn't spoken since the confrontation outside his house. Maybe that's the way she wanted it? Maybe now that she had Ashton in her life she had no intention of making up with Archie? Maybe her son was enough… Was the important one.

The sudden thought filled him with a rush of pain. He'd spent years loving Elizabeth from a distance, never being able to openly declare his love. Now he faced the very real possibility he never would. The pain of it made him groan aloud.

Alexandra touched him on the arm, her eyes filled with concern. "Archie, are you all right?"

He managed a smile that was closer to a grimace. "Yes. I'm fine. A bit of indigestion. Nothing to worry about."

He'd been both relieved and surprised when he'd met Alexandra in the street not far from the Opera House. She was everything he'd requested. Tall, beautiful, mature. He hadn't asked her age, but she looked about thirty-five. She wore a sparkling silver-sequined dress that clung to her curves and emphasized her tiny waist. Her cleavage was enticingly on display, but not in a trashy way. In fact, no one there would guess she was an escort. Isabella had been right.

Now Alexandrea accepted his explanation without question and sipped her champagne. "What show are we watching?" she asked with only mild curiosity.

"*Carmen*. And we call it a performance, not a show. Do you know it?"

"No. What's it about?"

Archie opened his mouth to explain, but then decided against it. *What does it matter if she enjoys the performance or not? It's not like I'm going to see her again.*

"Just watch it. I'm sure you'll catch on before too long," he said instead.

She shrugged in an offhand way and took another sip from her glass. Archie did the same. His gaze strayed around the crowd of opera goers, unconsciously searching for Elizabeth again. He thought he caught a glimpse of her up near the front, but he might have been mistaken. No doubt she was too caught up in Ashton to give Archie another thought.

Archie's shoulders slumped in defeat. *Maybe I shouldn't have given her that ultimatum? Maybe I should have accepted whatever scraps she was prepared to offer?*

No! The thought was forceful and immediate. He wanted more than a clandestine affair. He'd lived like that for too many years already. He loved Elizabeth with everything that he was. He wanted to call her his own. If he gave in now, he'd forever blame himself for not sticking to his guns, or trying harder to win her over to his side.

But perhaps he could make the first move, extend the olive branch? After all, she'd come to him and he'd chased her away. No wonder she hadn't been back. Yes, that's what he'd do. First thing in the morning. He'd go and see her, take a picnic basket… Invite her on a date. Even if it was only in her backyard. She'd always loved spending time in her garden, reading a book beneath one of the shady oak trees, her head resting close to his…

Decision made, he felt immediately better and gave his date a wide smile. "Are you ready to head inside?" he asked and offered Alexandra his arm.

"Are you all right?" Ashton asked.

The concern in her son's eyes filled her with warmth. It was nice to have someone worried for her.

"Of course."

"I'm guessing you weren't expecting to see Archie with another woman. Am I right?"

She bit her lip and nodded, surprised at his perceptiveness.

"How long have you been lovers?"

Her gaze flew up to his. "What are you talking about?"

"Come on, Mom. I'm not blind," he chided.

"I don't know what you're talking about," she said coolly. After all, what else could she say? No one knew about her long-term romantic entanglement with Archie. Not even their children.

Ashton merely shrugged as if it were of no consequence. "I don't care one way or the other, but it's obvious there's something going on between the two of you. That night after the engagement party when you introduced me, he looked like he wanted to kill me. There's only one reason a man gets that look in his eyes. Jealousy."

He gave her a meaningful look. She lowered her gaze and played with the straps on her evening bag.

How could Ashton have worked it out? He barely knows us! And yet he's been able to see what no one else does… Not even our families…

And then he was smiling, that boyish smile that showed off his white teeth and the dimple in his cheek. The smile she found hard to resist…

"Come on, Mom. Time to 'fess up. I promise I won't tell anyone."

There was something about him that made her want to take him into her confidence. Maybe it was because he was her son, her flesh and blood and they had so much time to make up. Maybe sharing something so personal, something she hadn't told anyone else, would bring them closer, like people who'd shared a traumatic experience. Whatever it was, she suddenly found herself wanting to talk to him about it. Taking his arm, she led him away from the crowd until they were partly concealed behind a huge ceramic urn that housed an even larger potted plant.

"Okay. Yes, you're right. Archie and I are…lovers. But you mustn't breathe a word. No one else knows."

"How long has it been going on?"

"Years."

"As in, five, six? Ten?"

"Twenty-three."

Ashton blinked in surprise. "You've been having an affair for twenty-three years and no one knows? What the hell's wrong with these people?"

Elizabeth looked away. "What I meant to say is, no one knows it's still going on. Our families are aware we had an affair many years ago. They know that Sophia is Archie's daughter."

Ashton grinned. "Whoa! This keeps getting better! You and Archie did the deed and produced a baby?"

Elizabeth gritted her teeth. The re-telling of this part of their history wasn't something she was proud of. After all, they'd both been married to other people.

"It happened a long time ago and there were…extenuating circumstances. It wasn't a simple matter of getting a divorce and running away together. There were other people involved. Children. Spouses."

Ashton nodded knowingly. "Oh yes. I can see how that might have complicated matters."

The sarcasm that lined his words irritated her. She suddenly regretted taking him into her confidence. He was acting like an immature twit. She didn't know what she'd expected, but she'd been hoping for something closer to understanding. Instead she felt like he was judging her.

She looked at her son. Amusement at her expense still glittered in his eyes. "You know what, forget about it," she said.

Ashton grabbed her around the arm. "Oh, no! Please, Mom. Tell me more! I want to hear all the juicy details. I want to know *everything*."

She shook her head. "I don't think so. I've said enough."

He gave her his puppy-dog eyes. "Please, Mom. I've

already missed out on so much of your life. I want to know about you. What makes you sad? What makes you happy? What's shaped you? You've spent a lifetime without me. Sharing even the tiniest tidbits with me helps me feel closer to you. Like I matter."

Elizabeth stared at him and felt a twinge of remorse. It wasn't his fault he knew nothing about her; had missed forty years of her life. She sighed quietly.

"I've been in love with Archie for a long time, but like I said, it was complicated. We were both married to someone else. Now we're finally on our own, free to choose each other, to tell the world of our love."

"I don't understand. Why are you still hiding your feelings? Why aren't the two of you together?"

Elizabeth's shoulders slumped. "Good question. I want to… Believe me, I want to."

"Then why can I hear a 'but'?"

"You're right. There is a 'but.' The problem is, I can't even articulate the reasons to myself. I love Archie so completely. There's never been anyone else. At least, not since I realized how I felt about him. But now that it's possible for us to be together in every sense, I'm scared."

"Of what? Are you scared of what people might think? What your children might think?"

"A little," she admitted. "But mostly I'm scared that our relationship might not work."

"But you've been in love for twenty-three years. Maybe even longer."

"Yes. But haven't you heard about people who were together for years and years—not married, but together and in love? It's working for them, but then when they finally make it official and get married, they break up. It happens often enough to be a thing. Do you know what I'm talking about?"

"Yes, of course. I have friends who were in a de facto

relationship for ten years. They decided to get married when the first child arrived. Within a year they were divorced."

"See!" Elizabeth cried, feeling justified. "That's exactly what I mean! What if that happens to me and Archie?"

Ash stared at Elizabeth and hardly dared to believe his luck. He'd been wracking his brain for a way to get closer to her, prove he was indispensable and now she'd handed him the very opportunity he'd been searching for. She was in turmoil about her relationship with Archie. They'd been lovers for decades and now they weren't even talking. Lucky for him he could give her some advice… And hopefully keep her the hell away from Archie.

"You're right to be concerned," he said grimly, compressing his lips. "That happens to a lot of people. Not only to my friends, but to plenty of others, too. It's weird and no one can explain how it happens, or why… But there's no denying it. As you said, it's a thing."

Elizabeth looked as overwrought as he hoped she would. "You see? Now you understand my reluctance to make things public! What if it all falls apart?"

Ashton shrugged. "Only you can decide if Archie's worth taking that chance. If you want my advice, I'd leave things the way they are. You've made it work for the two of you for more than twenty years. Why change a good thing? Why take the risk you might mess everything up and lose what you have forever?"

In a deliberate effort to show disinterest, he looked around at the crowd that was beginning to move into the theater. "That's only something you can answer, Mom. But know this: No matter how things turn out for you and Archie, you'll always have me. I've spent my whole life waiting for you, wondering, loving you from afar. I'm not going anywhere."

The smile she gave him was filled with love. She reached out and cupped his smooth cheek in her palm.

"Thank you, Ash. You're so sweet. I don't know how I survived without you."

This is going so much better than I hoped… And now she's trusted me with her secret about her and Archie… No doubt I'll find some way to use that to my advantage… Watch out, Archie! I'm coming for you!

Pasting a smile on his face, he winked. "The good news is, now you don't have to. I'm here to stay."

"So you're not returning to Tamworth?"

"No. There's nothing to keep me in Tamworth anymore. You're stuck with me whether you like it or not."

She smiled. "Oh, I like it. I like it a lot. I missed out on your first forty years. I'm not going to miss out on another minute more."

"That's my mom!" he cheered.

She flushed, but he could tell from the way her smile widened that she felt good. She linked her arm with his and together they headed for the stalls.

Chapter Sixteen

rchie pulled his car to a halt outside Elizabeth's house. He'd thought about parking around the back and coming in through the servant's entrance like he'd done so many times before, but too much time had passed since they'd been on an even footing and he no longer felt certain of his welcome. Instead, he collected the overflowing picnic basket off the back seat and then climbed the wide stone steps to the front door. He looked around for Elizabeth's Audi, but couldn't see it. That didn't mean she wasn't home. She sometimes parked it in the garage. He hoped that was the case right now.

He'd spent most of the night after attending the opera thinking about what to say. Their relationship was so tenuous at the moment, he didn't want to upset her by saying the wrong thing. He wanted her to know he loved her and he'd take whatever she was willing to give. Pride be damned, he was done with holding out for a public declaration. He hoped that might come in time but it wasn't the most important thing.

In the meantime, he wanted her back in his life—on any terms. He needed her by his side. His one true love, his soul mate. He only hoped she felt the same way.

After seeing her with Ashton the night before, he was no

longer certain how she felt. She sure seemed taken with the man. Archie felt bad about feeling jealous of her son, but he couldn't help it. *He* wanted to be the one escorting her to the opera, dammit! After all these years, he'd earned the right!

He set the basket down near his feet and lifted his hand to turn the doorknob and then decided to knock. A short time later he heard footsteps, but they didn't sound like Elizabeth's. The wooden panel opened, revealing Ashton on the other side. Dressed in a navy-blue polo shirt and crisp white shorts, he looked as smart as he had the night before. His face registered his surprise.

"Archie! What are you doing here?"

"Hello, Ashton. Is Elizabeth in?"

"I'm afraid not," the man said, pulling the door closed behind him. He crowded Archie on the top step, dwarfing him by at least fifty pounds and five or six inches.

Refusing to be intimidated, Archie held his ground. "When will she be back?"

Ashton glanced at the picnic basket and then shrugged. "I don't know. She might be gone all day. She went into the city. She said something about wanting to buy me a surprise. Something that would make me smile. I can't imagine what it could be. She's already been so generous." His eyes widened with false sincerity. "Did you know she bought me a violin worth more than three hundred thousand dollars? Of course, she didn't tell me that. I did some research on the Internet. On top of that, she bought me a Porsche!" He threw up his hands and grinned. "I mean, who does that? I can't believe how much she loves me."

Archie's temper ignited. He wished he could wipe the smug look off the man's face.

How dare he act like he owns this place! Like he's the center of Elizabeth's world! He's known her for five minutes! Who the hell does he think he is?

"You… You imposter!" Archie sputtered. "You might have convinced Elizabeth you're her long lost son, but I'm not quite as gullible. I want proof that you are who you say you are. I demand a DNA test!"

Ashton merely rolled his eyes. "Oh, not you too! Join the queue, old man. And while you're at it, be sure to tell your lover about your demand for my DNA. She got quite upset when I told her two of her beloved children were pressuring me to hand over a sample."

Archie tensed in surprise. *How does he know Elizabeth and I are lovers? Surely she didn't tell him? A stranger. Someone she doesn't even know… Especially when she continues to resist my pleas to tell her children… How could she tell this jerk?*

As if privy to his increasingly distressed thoughts, Ashton smirked. "Oh, yes, I know all about your secret affair. And even about your love child. Sophia, right?" Ashton grinned and waggled a finger in front of Archie's face. "Naughty boy."

Archie looked at him, aghast. He couldn't believe Elizabeth had told this…this *stranger* things she'd kept secret for so many years. She refused to tell their children, and yet someone she'd barely known for five minutes had her full confidence! It was outrageous!

As Archie struggled to come to grips with the onslaught of emotions that poured through him, Ashton sneered.

"That's right, old man. I'm in. You're out. It's time you realized that. How about you do us both a favor and drop dead? It would save Elizabeth the trouble of telling you she no longer wants you in her life."

Archie gasped in pain. "You're wrong! I don't believe you! Elizabeth and I love each other. We've been in love for years. There's no way she told you that!"

Ashton merely shrugged. "Believe what you want, but don't blame me when she finds the courage to tell you how she really feels. Why do you think she's kept your little affair a secret all this time? The reason she doesn't want anyone to know is because she knows it's coming to an end. She has me now. I'm all she needs."

The noise in Archie's head made it impossible to hear the rest of what Ashton said. Archie saw the man's lips moving, but he couldn't make out the words. Holding his hands over his ears in an effort to block out the noise, he abandoned the picnic basket and turned and stumbled down the stairs. Ashton's cruel laughter rang out behind him.

Joel's fingers were tense with anticipation as he tore open the envelope containing Ashton's DNA results. Isabella had told him Christopher had offered to call in a favor and expedite the results, but in the end there was no need. Instead of months, it had taken a couple of weeks and now he held them in his hand. He'd been fielding calls from Isabella almost on a daily basis as she called for an update. In the end, he'd told her to stop.

"I'll call you as soon as I know anything," he'd promised.

Grudgingly, she'd agreed. In fact, she'd done them both a favor and returned to Brisbane. Joel was relived. There, she was Raine's problem.

Joel tugged the single sheet of paper out of the yellow envelope and scanned the contents. His gaze was drawn to the paragraph that set out the likelihood of the donors being a match.

He read: *The two samples were scientifically compared. It was proven they were a three percent match. It is highly improbable that the two samples are related.*

Joel's heart skipped a beat. Adrenaline rushed through him. He punched the air in triumph.

"Yes!"

His partner shot him a sideways glance. "Someone's had good news."

Joel grinned. "You bet." He immediately reached for his phone and called Isabella. He tapped his fingers impatiently on the desk as he waited for her to pick up. To his disappointment, the call went through to voicemail.

"Issy. It's Joel. I've got news. Call me."

He pushed away from his desk and headed for the tea room. He'd barely filled his coffee cup before Isabella phoned him back.

"Sorry. I had an armful of boxes. What have you got?" she said when he answered.

"Are you sitting down?"

"Shit. You mean that jerk's Mom's son?"

"Just kidding. No. He's not."

"Joel!" she shrieked in protest! You nearly gave me a heart attack. Are you sure?"

"Yep. According to the results, he had a three percent probability of being related. That's nothing. Whoever he is, he sure as hell isn't Mom's long lost baby."

"We need to tell her."

Joel grimaced. "Yeah."

"Who's going to do it?"

"Not me."

"Joel!" Isabella protested. "We're in this together! I'm not doing it on my own!"

"Issy, I'm just not good at that kind of stuff."

"That's nonsense and you know it, Joel Craigdon! For heaven's sake, you're a cop! You give people bad news all the time."

"Yes, but they're not my mother. She's going to be devastated."

"Yeah. She is." Issy sighed on the other end of the phone. "But we still need to tell her. She's turning her life inside out for him. Did you know she got him a puppy?"

Joel frowned. "What?"

Issy sighed again. "Oh, don't worry about it. The puppy's the least of our problems. How are we going to get him out of Mom's house?"

"I'm sure that won't be a problem. Once he knows the gig's up, he'll be only too willing to leave. Especially if I threaten him with criminal charges."

"Yeah! Let's do that. It's no more than he deserves. What an asshole. Preying on an unsuspecting elderly woman like that. It makes my blood boil." She paused and then added, "Do you think he's done it before?"

"Maybe. He's very smooth. Not at all nervous. That makes me think this isn't the first time. Leave it with me. I'll do some digging. See if anyone else's reported a similar crime."

"Are you going to report what he did to Mom?"

Joel bit his lip. "Let's talk to her first. She deserves to know before we do anything else."

"Agreed." Isabella sighed. "I guess I'd better book a ticket to Sydney."

"Let me know what flight you're on. I'll meet you at the airport."

"Gee, thanks. What a good big brother you are."

"You got that right."

By the time Joel collected Isabella from Mascot Airport a couple of days later, he had more to report.

"I did some digging on Ashton, or whatever his name is. Seems like there's been a string of similar offenses around Sydney over the past ten years. Might be even more victims out there than what's been reported. A lot of the people I contacted were too embarrassed to speak with me. They felt stupid for being so gullible. From their physical description, I'd guess we're talking about the same perp. I tell you, this guy's smart. He has his *modus operandi* down pat."

"How does he even know about these people?" Isabella asked. "That kind of information isn't on a public database."

"You're right. Which means he has access somehow. Maybe he works in a government department, or is close to someone who does."

"Whose jurisdiction does this kind of thing come under?"

"The department of Family and Community Services."

"They have some explaining to do."

"They might not even know their systems have been breached. Or this guy could be legitimately authorized to access those databases. The fact he's chosen to use that information as a way to defraud people is hardly their fault."

Isabella sighed and stared out at the passing traffic. It was mid-afternoon, though it felt a lot later. The sky was heavy with dark clouds. Any moment it looked like the heavens would open up and drench them. She turned back to Joel. "So, what's the plan? How are we going to tell Mom?"

"I've called Callum and brought him up to speed. He's agreed to meet us at Craigdon Manor."

"Good. It's always good to have Callum around in a crisis."

"Yep. Sure is. I've also told the others. Jett's at work until six and then he has to get home to look after the kids. Danielle's started taking night classes. Something to do with pottery. Or maybe it's ceramics. Hell, I wasn't really listening. Nicholas is at home with a migraine. Harper wouldn't even let me speak with him. Sophia wanted to be there when we told Mom, but she's at school until after three and then she has a staff meeting she can't get out of. I told her to call by later. Once Mom hears what we have to say, she'll need all the support we can give her."

Isabella compressed her lips into a thin line. She was dreading the upcoming confrontation, but it had to be done.

"What about Ashton?" she asked. "Do we know where he is?"

"As far as I know, he's still there. When I called Mom earlier to check if she'd be home, she told me he was outside by the pool."

Isabella grimaced. "I'll just bet he was."

Joel shot her a glance. "Don't worry, Issy. His days of sponging off the Craigdons are about to come to an abrupt halt. I've arranged for an arrest team to be waiting right down the road from home. They wanted to come with me now, but I didn't want to alarm Mom unnecessarily. She's not exactly young. We don't want to give her another heart attack."

Isabella looked at him. "You're right. After losing Dad that way, and that scare with Mom, we can do without more of the same."

"The boys will wait for my call. As soon as I give them the all clear, they'll descend upon Craigdon Manor and arrest the son of a bitch."

"Good riddance," Isabella said.

Elizabeth heard the crunch of tires on the driveway outside and looked up from the rose bush she'd been pruning. Callum's car came to a halt at the bottom of the wide stone steps that led up to the front door. Elizabeth smiled at the unexpected surprise. Earlier, Joel had called her and asked if she'd be home. She didn't realize Callum was also stopping by.

Setting aside her secateurs, she tugged off her gardening gloves and then wiped her hands on her pants. Before she had a chance to greet Callum, another car pulled up. Joel and Isabella climbed out. They murmured greetings to Callum and then the three of them turned to face the front steps. They wore equal expressions of dread.

A frisson of alarm snaked through Elizabeth's belly. She frowned.

"Don't be silly. I'm sure it's nothing," she mumbled under her breath. Still, it was unusual for three of her children to be in attendance at Craigdon Manor this time of day during the week without a specified reason. When Joel had asked her if she'd be home, she didn't think to ask him why and he hadn't offered an explanation. Now they were here. All three of them. What was even more alarming was that Issy had come from Brisbane.

Elizabeth hurried into the house. She washed her hands at the sink in the downstairs bathroom and then hurried toward the entryway. She opened the front door just as her children reached the top step. She gazed at them closely, trying to read their expressions, searching for a clue. But there was nothing.

She pasted a smile on her face and did her best to remain calm. "Joel! Callum! Issy, what are you doing here? I thought you were in Brisbane?"

Isabella kissed her on the cheek. "Hi, Mom. I was. I flew in about an hour ago."

"An hour ago? You came straight here?"

"Yes."

Elizabeth peered behind her. "Where are your bags?"

She lifted an oversized leather handbag that hung off her shoulder. "I have everything I need in here. I'm not staying long. Just tonight. I have to be back in Brisbane tomorrow."

Elizabeth's anxiety ratcheted up another notch. This was getting stranger and stranger. "Oh. Okay."

"Hi, Mom." Callum leaned in and kissed her on the cheek. "How are you doing?"

"I'm fine, Callum. How are you?"

"Fine."

He moved past her and she found herself enveloped in Joel's arms as he gave her a brief hug.

"Hi, Mom. It's good to see you."

"You too, Joel." She gave him a pointed look. "What's going on? What's this all about?"

Joel sidestepped her questions. "Can we come inside?"

Nerves swirled in Elizabeth's stomach.

Something's wrong… Oh, God. Please don't let it be one of my children… I couldn't bear it if anything happened to one of them…

Isabella saw the look of panic cross her mother's face and knew they were going to have to get this over with before her mother dropped dead of fright. She could tell Elizabeth knew something was up. After all, it wasn't everyday she had three of her children turn up unannounced on her doorstep. Isabella glanced at Joel who gave her an imperceptible nod. She swallowed a sigh of relief. Good. Joel had also noticed their mother's growing distress.

Let's get this over with…

Isabella forced a smile. "Where's Ashton?"

"I don't know," Elizabeth replied in a distracted voice. "I think he might be upstairs."

"Let's go into the music room," Joel suggested.

The three of them followed their mother into the room she'd made her own. For as long as they could remember, this was the place where she liked to spend her time. Playing music, doing needlework or just reading a book—the room had always been her sanctuary. Now they were about to destroy her peace, maybe for a long, long time.

Isabella shot Joel a glance. He looked grim. She caught his eye and as if aware of her thoughts, he frowned and then offered her a half-shrug. It was too late to suggest they meet somewhere else now.

"Would anyone like tea?"

They answered "no" in chorus.

"What about coffee? Or maybe a cold drink? I could have Amy make us some lemonade?"

Callum touched her gently on the arm. "No thanks, Mom. We're fine."

Elizabeth twisted her hands together as if she wasn't quite sure what to do with them and then promptly seated herself on the couch. Isabella sat beside her. Callum took the armchair opposite. Joel remained on his feet.

Their mother's gaze moved over the three of them. She gave them a tremulous smile. "Okay, so now you have me worried," she said. "What's going on?"

Issy looked at Joel. They'd decided on the way over that he'd do the talking. Not only did he have experience with these situations, he also knew more of the facts. As he cleared his throat, their mother straightened her spine and stared him in the face, a mixture of fear and anticipation warring in her gaze.

c⁓

Elizabeth clasped her hands tightly together to hide their trembling. She stared at Joel and willed him to speak.

"I'm sorry to have to tell you this Mom," he began in a somber tone.

Straight away her thoughts went to the children who were absent. Her hand went to her throat. "What happened? Who's hurt? Please don't tell me it's one of your brothers or your sister. *Or is it Archie?*"

"No, Mom. It's nothing like that," he hurried to reassure her.

She leaned back against the couch and breathed a sigh of relief. "Oh, thank God. You had me so worried."

"It's Ashton."

Elizabeth frowned. "Ashton? But he's upstairs."

Joel nodded. "Yes. He's not injured. In fact, no one's

injured. The thing is, Ashton's not who he says he is. He's not your son."

Elizabeth's mouth gaped. She felt lightheaded. Thank God she was sitting down or she might have just fallen over.

"What… What are you talking about?"

Isabella squeezed her hand. "Mom. I took some hair samples. Joel sent them to the lab. Ashton isn't related to you by blood. He can't be your son."

Elizabeth stared at her daughter and tried to make sense of what she'd said. "You took some hair? Whose hair?"

"Yours and Ashton's."

"H-how? When?"

Isabella drew in a deep breath and let it out on a sigh. "A couple of weeks ago. I went into your bathroom and pulled some hair out of your brush. I did the same thing with Ashton's. Then Joel sent them off to the lab to compare the DNA. They didn't match."

Elizabeth sat frozen to the spot. Isabella's expression filled with remorse.

"I'm sorry, Mom."

"For what?" Elizabeth rasped. "For going against my wishes and stealing something you had no right to, or sorry that the man I believed with all my heart was my son turns out to be nothing more than a con artist." She blinked and sat up straighter, glaring at her children.

"That's what you're all saying, isn't it? That he's conned me into believing he's my son?"

Joel nodded, his expression somber. "Yes, Mom. And you don't have to take our word. The lab test proved it beyond doubt. Worse still, this doesn't seem to be his first time."

Callum put his arm around her shoulders. Elizabeth was grateful for his support.

"Though we were suspicious, this has come as a huge shock to all of us Mom," Callum said in a low voice. "And if results had confirmed he *was* your son, we would have celebrated that. None of us wanted this to happen."

"Then why did Isabella and Joel go out of their way to run the test?" she asked.

Isabella's gaze remained focused on the carpet. "I don't know what you want me to say, Mom. I'm sorry, but I had to know. We knew nothing about this man. If he'd turned out to be my half-brother, I would have accepted him as such. But I had to know for sure. We all did."

Elizabeth started in surprise. "So you were all in on this? All six of you?"

Joel cleared his throat. "In fairness to Callum, he didn't express an opinion either way. As for the rest of us, yes. We all wanted to know."

Elizabeth's chest was tight with anxiety and unshed tears. She felt like her heart had been ripped out and trampled.

For nearly a month, she'd reveled under the knowledge she'd been given her precious son back—but that had all been a lie. Instead, she was the brunt of a big fat joke. How Ashton must have laughed at her. Must still be laughing at her.

Oh, God…

She bent her head forward in defeat.

Chapter Seventeen

atching from an upstairs window, Ashton had been filled with curiosity as three of the Craigdon siblings climbed out of cars and headed inside. The last time he'd seen so many of them in one place had been at the engagement party. He wondered about the occasion that had brought them there.

The sight of Joel and Isabella together filled him with unease. He hadn't forgotten the conversation he'd had with them when they'd asked him to submit to a DNA test. Callum had been friendlier toward him at the engagement party, but that didn't mean he wasn't also harboring suspicions. It was important for Ashton to stay on top of any developments, particularly if it necessitated a quick getaway. He'd hoped this might turn into something more permanent, but it looked like that wasn't to be the case. With that thought in mind, he left his room and headed for the stairs.

Taking care to muffle his footsteps as he crossed the travertine tiles, Ash heard the murmur of voices coming from the direction of the music room. He slowed his steps and moved closer. The door was half-open, making it easier for him to hear. Isabella was talking. Then it was Joel. Ash caught the words "hair samples," "lab" and "DNA."

His heart started pounding so loudly it was difficult to hear what they said. He made an effort to draw in some deep breaths, but the blood rushed through his ears.

The gig's up…

He was flooded with disappointment. He'd been enjoying his time at the Craigdon mansion. Had started to think of it as home. Now it had come to an end.

Oh, well. I guess I should have known it was bound to happen sooner or later… Too bad it was sooner rather than later…

But there was no point thinking like that. Now that everyone was aware of the truth, it was time to go upstairs and pack. Decision made, he turned on his heel and hurried back the way he'd come. He had no way of knowing how much time he had before they came gunning for him, but it was best not to waste time.

Pulling his Louis Vuitton suitcases—courtesy of Elizabeth—down from the top shelf of the walk-in wardrobe, he tossed in his designer clothes, shoes, and cologne. The Rolex, the solid gold cuff links, the custom-made tux, his new phone. Finally, he grabbed the violin. Thank God he'd parked the Porsche around the back, along with Rusty. If he went down the servant's stairs he could leave without anyone seeing him.

With one last look around the room to ascertain that he'd left nothing behind, he set the violin case on top of one of his suitcases and then rolled them in front of him, pulling the door closed behind him.

Time to find a new sucker to take advantage of…

Joel looked at his mother and frowned with concern. She was so pale and still. He understood she'd just suffered an awful shock, but they'd had no choice but to tell her. It was unthinkable that they let her continue to think that interloper was her son. That didn't mean Joel wasn't filled with guilt knowing he was responsible for the devastation on his mother's face.

"What happens now?" Elizabeth asked. Her tone was low and dull, almost as lifeless as her eyes.

Joel cleared his throat. "I'll go and talk to Ashton, tell him the game's up. And then I'm going to arrest him for fraud."

Elizabeth's head snapped up. "Arrest him? Surely you don't have to do that."

Joel held onto his patience. "Mom, we have no choice. This isn't the first time he's conned a vulnerable woman. He needs to be stopped. What he did was a crime. He needs to pay for that and I'm going to do all I can to see he does."

She opened her mouth as if to protest further, but then closed it again. Joel moved toward the door.

"You said he was upstairs. In the east wing?"

"Yes," Elizabeth responded quietly and with sad resignation.

Joel gave a brief nod of acknowledgement and left.

Isabella moved closer to her mother and reached out for her hand. "This has all come as a terrible shock, Mom. How are you holding up?"

With an effort, Elizabeth held back the sob that made it difficult to breathe and managed to nod. "I'm fine."

Isabella gave her a wry smile. "You're not fine, Mom. But I give you points for courage."

Elizabeth's lips twitched reluctantly. Now that the initial shock was over, other emotions had begun to drift in. The overriding one was embarrassment. She considered herself to be an intelligent, switched-on woman. And yet she'd been taken in by a conman.

"I've been such a fool," she admitted quietly.

"No, Mom. Never. Don't ever say that again. Ashton's

slick and charming and knows what he's doing. He's done it many times before. How were you to know he was lying?"

"But you were suspicious of him from the start!"

"Yes, but it was different for me. I had no emotional connection to him. You *wanted* him to be your son. Perhaps that clouded your judgment. But don't be too hard on yourself. Your reaction was totally understandable. And though it's probably cold comfort, like I said, you weren't the only one to be taken in by him."

Elizabeth managed a small smile. "Thank you, Isabella. I appreciate your effort to make me feel better about this."

"Issy's right," Callum added. "You had extra incentive to believe what Ashton said. Giving up your baby was a traumatic experience. No doubt Ashton's arrival, claiming to be your son, brought all of those sad memories and emotions back. You were overwhelmed at the thought of having him back in your life. I'm betting most mothers who gave up a baby for adoption would feel like that. There's nothing to be embarrassed about having those emotions. They come from the heart."

Elizabeth felt a fresh wave of tears behind her eyes. She blinked to hold them back. "Come here," she choked.

She held out her arms and Isabella and Callum moved into her embrace. They hugged each other for a long moment.

"He's gone."

Joel's somber announcement caused them all to pull away. Elizabeth looked at her son in consternation.

"You mean, Ashton?" she asked.

"Yes. He's nowhere to be found. I checked his room. It's been cleaned out. There's nothing there but the bed linen. He must have overheard us. Whatever the reason, he's gone."

"What about the officers you said were planted down the road?" Isabella asked.

"Yeah. I spoke to them. They were waiting for me to give

them the go ahead to move in. They saw a red Porsche tear out of here about ten minutes ago. They weren't sure whether to pursue it. They decided to wait for my call, which is exactly what they were told to do."

His shoulders slumped on a sigh. "It's my fault. I was the one who set up the rules of engagement." He glanced at his mother. "I wanted the chance to tell you what we'd discovered before the police came charging in."

"Thank you, Joel. I appreciate your thoughtfulness," Elizabeth replied.

"Yeah, too bad it's meant our perp's got a head start on us. Anyway, he won't get far in a car like that. It will stick out like dog's balls."

"Joel!" Elizabeth admonished.

"Sorry, Mom. What I meant to say is, we'll find him. He won't get away with doing this ever again."

"I'm glad," Elizabeth murmured. And she was. She didn't want another mother to have to feel the way she did right now—like her heart had been broken...and right now she wasn't sure if it would ever heal.

The most devastating realization was that she'd held on so hard to the belief Ashton was her son because she wanted it to be true. It was just like Issy had said. Elizabeth had been desperate to cling to the hope this man was her son, the child she'd abandoned within an hour of his birth so many years ago.

She felt so stupid. She should have listened to Joel and Isabella. They knew right from the outset something wasn't right. If it weren't for their persistence, they would never have discovered the truth. She owed them an apology.

"Joel. Issy. I'm sorry. I should never have doubted you. I also shouldn't have forbid you for wanting to know the truth. I should have wanted that confirmation, too."

Isabella leaned over and gave her another hug. "There's no need to apologize."

"Issy's right," Joel added. "Don't feel bad. You were duped by a professional. That's not your fault."

Elizabeth grimaced. While she appreciated their response, that didn't make her feel any better. What it did do was fill her with a sudden determination and an almost-physical yearning to track down her real son. He was out there somewhere. She was sure of it and she was going to do all she could to find him.

The first place she'd start was the department of Family and Community Services. She recalled Ashton telling her that's how he'd started his search for her. There was every chance he'd been lying, but it had enough of a ring of truth to it, that it might just be correct. Either way, it was a starting point.

Ignoring the murmur of conversation between her children, she pulled her iPad toward her. She opened up a search engine and with her heart in her throat, typed in the following phrase: *How can I find my adopted child?*

Joel stared at the computer screen in front of him and silently cursed. It had been a week since Ashton had disappeared. Joel blamed himself for letting the asshole get away. He should have gone in hard at the outset and soothed his mother's frayed nerves after the disclosure of what they'd learned. Instead the prick had overheard enough to hightail it out of there and though his phone had initially pinged off several phone towers around Sydney, for the past three days, the trail had gone cold. Either the asshole's battery was flat, he'd switched his phone off, or more likely, he'd left the city.

Joel had been in contact with the local police in Tamworth and had brought them up to speed. He made it clear Ashton Walker was a person of interest in a string of frauds and was wanted by the police.

"Does he have any priors?" the detective who'd introduced himself as Malcolm Bennett asked.

"I don't think there've been any convictions though we believe he's done this before. I've put his name through our database. I came up with nothing. It's possible he's using an alias, though I tracked him back to Tamworth with information he volunteered."

"So he's a local, is he?"

"Apparently. He claims his parents were Todd and Jennifer Walker. Dad was a local farmer. Mom was a music teacher. According to newspaper articles I found, they were well-known in your local area. Have you heard of them?"

"Yes. As a matter of fact, one of my kids took piano lessons from Jennifer. She was an excellent teacher. We were all very sad when she died."

"Yes. At least she didn't live long enough to see how her son turned out."

"It's strange," Detective Bennett mused. "I remember meeting Ashton Walker a few times when I dropped off my daughter to her lesson. He loved to work in his mother's garden. He had a bit of a reputation for growing prize-winning roses. No one else's came close. It must have had something to do with the love and attention he gave them. He was always doing something with them. He was so mild-mannered and softly spoken. It's hard to believe we're talking about the same bloke."

Joel frowned. The detective's description of Ashton didn't gel with his. "What did this Ashton look like?" he asked on a sudden whim.

"I don't know. Average height, average build. Sandy-brown hair. Freckles. Nothing that would make you look at him twice. He kind of blended in, you know."

Joel's frown deepened. The Ashton described by Bennett didn't sound at all the same as the man who'd moved in with Joel's mother and pretended to be her son.

"If I find a photo of this bloke, can I send it through to

you?" Joel asked. "I just want to be certain we're talking about the same man."

"Sure. No problem."

Joel ended the call and immediately dialed Isabella. "Do you have any photos of Ashton?" he asked as soon as she answered.

"Hello to you too, brother." Her tone was dry.

He flushed but wouldn't be deterred. "I need a picture of Ashton."

"Am I allowed to know why?"

Quickly, he filled her in on his conversation with the Tamworth detective.

"Sounds a bit strange," she replied when he'd finished. "They sound like completely different men. I can't imagine Ashton spending so much time with roses. He didn't seem the least bit interested in Mom's garden."

"Yes. And then there's the physical description. The Ashton we met was impressive. Tall and well built. He also had dark hair. Something's not adding up."

"Well, you said he's done this kind of thing before under several aliases. What's the bet 'Ashton Walker' is just another one?"

"You're right. There's every possibility of that. It's just that, he knew so much about Walker's past, his family. Why would he go to that bother, researching it in so much depth? It was just a name. Mom would not have been expected to recognize it. She hadn't seen him since he was born. He could have given her any name—his real name—and she'd be none the wiser. It doesn't make sense."

"Perhaps he's smarter than he looks?" Isabella mused. "Perhaps that was part of the game. Making up a whole persona, a whole life. Remember he goaded you into looking into this background. He even volunteered the information."

"You're right. I used the information to do some Internet research. It was a simple matter to track him down from there and verify his information. It checked out. That's why I wasn't suspicious right away."

"See! That's what I mean! He's smart. He covered his bases, just in case someone bothered to check his story. Someone like *you*."

"Yeah, I guess. You could be right. Anyway, I need a photo. Do you have one?"

"No, but I'm sure Mom does. She spent nearly every waking moment with him while he was there. I can't imagine she didn't take some photos."

"I'll call her now," Joel said.

"No worries," Isabella murmured in a dry tone.

Joel blushed and then added, "Thank you, Issy. I appreciate your help."

"Like I said, no worries."

As soon as he ended the call with Isabella, Joel dialed his mother. He tapped his fingers impatiently on his desk while he waited for her to answer. Finally she did.

"Mom. It's Joel."

"I know that, dear. Your name came up on my screen."

"Good. Look, I need you to do me a favor. Can you send me a picture of Ashton?"

"He wouldn't let me take any," she responded in a quiet voice. "Now I know why."

Joel cursed under his breath. "Dammit. You don't have a single photo?"

"As a matter of fact, I do. I took one when he wasn't looking. He was sunning himself by the pool. He's wearing sunglasses, but I think anyone who knows him would recognize him. Why do you need it?"

"I'm chasing up a few leads," he answered vaguely.

"Are you any closer to catching him?"

Once again, Joel kept his answer deliberately vague. "Maybe. I've been talking to a detective in Tamworth. He might be able to help me narrow down the search."

"I guess that's good you're making progress," she said in a dull voice.

Joel squeezed his eyes shut. He hated that she sounded so despondent. He hated even more the reason for it. His anger at the man who'd caused it burned brighter.

I'm coming for you, you prick. You don't get to treat my mother like that. You've broken her heart all over again. I'm not going to let you get away with that…

"If you can send me that photo, Mom, I'd really appreciate it. The sooner the better."

"Yes, Joel. No problem. I'll send it to you right away."

"Thank you. Oh, and Mom?"

"Yes?"

"Call Archie." With that, he hung up.

Chapter Eighteen

*E*lizabeth stared down at the phone in her hand, completely taken aback. Joel's final words still rang in her ears. Why would he say something like that? *Call Archie.* It was strange. Had he guessed they were still together? That they were still in love? That the affair she'd owned up to hadn't come to an end? Had never ended? That their recent estrangement was tearing her apart?

But if so, how would he know they were still a couple? And why now? What had happened that he suddenly thought the need to tell her that? *Call Archie.* Had Archie said something to him?

Her phone beeped and she jumped. She looked at the screen. It was a message from Joel.

Mom. The photo?

"Oh, damn. I forgot."

She scrolled through her photos and found the one she'd taken of Ashton by the pool. She'd taken it back when she'd absolutely believed he was her long-lost son. Given his phobia about having his picture taken, she'd had to take the photo from afar. His black hair was slick and wet, glinting in the light. His broad chest was tanned and muscular. She could remember thinking at the time that he must work out, even though she hadn't seen any evidence of that. In fact, he didn't do much of anything other than the occasional hit of golf and sunning himself by the pool. She'd supposed he must have a job. After all, how else had he taken care of himself before he'd arrived there? But he'd never spoken of his life in Tamworth or what he did there and she hadn't felt she could ask.

Now of course she knew exactly why he'd been reluctant to share anything personal. Or play the piano, or the violin. He probably couldn't play any instrument. He was a fraud, a pretender, a con artist of the worst kind. He preyed on women who were still riddled with guilt over a decision they'd made forty years ago. Women who'd give anything for their son or daughter to forgive them.

She'd been no different. She'd spent hundreds of thousands of dollars on a car, clothes, a violin. She would have gladly spent millions to have her son love her.

But the dream had come crashing down around her the day Joel told her it wasn't real. *He* wasn't real. She was still trying to get over her devastation. Putting her energies into finding her real son was the only thing keeping her sane. Two days ago she'd received an envelope from the department of Family and Community Services. It had taken her by surprise. Ashton had told her he'd been searching for her for more than a year. Just something else he'd lied about.

She still hadn't found the courage to open it, but now was probably the right time. Her anger at being duped by a conman made her all the more determined to get to the truth. If she knew who her real son was she wouldn't be taken in again by a scheming liar, out to get whatever he could. Never again would she be made a fool of.

Decision made, she stood and walked over to her piano. She'd left the envelope on top. It sat there, a benevolent reminder that inside lay the information she'd dreamed about for so long. A name, an address. Maybe even a phone number. The woman from Family and Community Services had urged her to speak to a counselor.

"You think you're prepared for this, but experience shows that's not always the case. Finding out the details of the child you put up for adoption can be a massive shock. All of a sudden, they're real. They exist. They have a life. All the things you've wondered about. You're about to find out the truth about all that. But most of all, you're going to find out how they feel."

"What do you mean?" she'd asked.

"I mean, you might get into contact with them and they don't want to meet. They might not even want to talk with you on the phone."

"But there was no veto on his file. You said so," Elizabeth reminded her.

"Yes, and that's something positive, but sometimes people change their minds. And that's their right. We all process things in different ways. Some people are happy to be reunited with their birth mother, others not so much."

Elizabeth had been taken aback. In all her imaginings of a reunion with her son, none of them had included him not wanting to meet her. Now it was all she could think about. It was what had held her back from tearing open the envelope and making contact right away.

She hated feeling so cowardly. It reminded her that she still hadn't made up with Archie, done what he'd asked of her. But the desire to know the name of her son was overwhelming.

With a deep breath, she reached for the envelope and tore it open. There was a single sheaf of paper inside. With shaking hands, she pulled it out and then reached for her glasses. With her heart in her throat, she focused on the black type, blinking several times to stop it from blurring.

She had to read it three times through before the words sank in.

Vaughan Barrington.

Her son.

Such a strong name. And one she was strangely familiar with. Her step-son Christopher was also a Barrington. *What a coincidence.* 'Barrington' wasn't an unusual name by any stretch, but it wasn't garden-variety common either. She couldn't help wondering what Vaughan looked like. Did he take after her, or David? Was he married? Did he have children? Had he tried to find her, or David? Did he even know he was adopted? Perhaps that was the reason he hadn't placed a veto on his file…

Fear clawed at her insides. She couldn't bear the thought of coming this far and being turned away. The woman at the department had cautioned her against getting her hopes up in case her son didn't want to see her, or failed to meet her expectations. *What expectations?* She didn't care who he was or what he did, whether he was married, gay, straight. He was her son. Her *son.* She'd love him unconditionally, no matter what.

As the initial shock from the contents of the envelope wore off, she read again the lines she thought she'd never get to read. She had the name and address of her son. There was no telephone number, but that was all right. She could write to him. And maybe, just maybe, he'd write back.

Ash Walker was pissed. As he sped through the streets in the middle of the night, he thumped his fist against the steering wheel in frustration. He'd returned to his dead end job at the department of Family and Community Services and his dump of an apartment. It felt cramped and squalid since his time living in the luxurious surroundings of Craigdon Manor. Even poor Rusty appeared bewildered at his sudden change of circumstances. If only those busybodies—Joel and Isabella Craigdon—hadn't poked their noses in where it wasn't wanted…

Just the thought of the two conniving individuals made his blood boil. He'd had it all planned out. He'd convinced Elizabeth he was her son. She'd called off the blood hounds. He'd tossed a few lies in Archie's direction in the hope the old man would scamper away and hide. Elizabeth might wonder what had happened, but Ash would be there to comfort her and assure her she was better off without a man who pressured her with ultimatums… No matter how long he'd been in her life.

But now his deception had been uncovered and he'd been forced to steal away like a thief in the night, taking with him a decent amount of collateral, but even that didn't measure up to the lifestyle he'd left behind. Anger boiled inside him. Someone had to pay.

He floored the accelerator. The Porsche leaped forward. No doubt the police had been alerted by Joel to what had happened and probably were on the lookout for Ashton's car. It was the reason he'd switched off his phone. He'd seen enough cop shows to know they could track him that way.

There was always the chance Elizabeth had been too embarrassed to make a formal complaint. After all, he'd gotten lucky that way before. That's why he hadn't yet parted with his car. There was no way he'd ever afford another one. He wasn't keen to get rid of this one unless he absolutely had to.

Taking a corner way too fast, he depressed the accelerator further and enjoyed the surge forward as the powerful engine took hold. The road ahead straightened out and he took full advantage. This time of night there was very little traffic and he let the car have its head. As trees whizzed past in the darkness, he began to laugh.

His time at Craigdon Manor might have only lasted a few weeks, but he couldn't regret his decision to deceive Elizabeth. This had been the best time of his life. Of course, he'd go on and find another sucker to take advantage of, but he couldn't imagine any of them coming close to what he'd had with the Craigdons. It was too bad it had all come to an end.

He took a sharp bend in the road and then surged forward again. In the distance, he saw the outline of Archie's mansion peeking out from behind the trees. Though it wasn't nearly as impressive as Elizabeth's home, it was far from shabby.

Archie…

It had been laughable how that stupid old coot had tried to stand up to him. As if the poor bastard stood a chance. Ha! What a joke. It would serve him right if Ashton turned the tables on him; did something to show him exactly who was boss.

As he drew closer to Archie's house, an idea began to form. Slowly, a smile tugged at his lips until he laughed out loud.

Yes! It's perfect! It will serve the old man right!

Flicking on his indicator, Ashton turned into Archie's drive. He dimmed his lights and used the moonlight to guide him up to the front door. As his plan took hold, he detoured toward the garage, hoping to find what he needed inside.

He tested the door and found it open. Yes! Luck was with him! Feeling his way forward in the dark, he felt around for a light switch and found one right inside the door. He flicked it on, taking the chance that Archie would be tucked up in bed this time of night and wouldn't notice anything untoward. There were two cars in the garage—a sedan and a four-wheel drive. The walls were lined with shelves. Moving closer, Ashton spied tools, boxes, oil drums and…*voila!*

Jerry cans stood in a neat row on the concrete floor beneath one of the shelves. Ashton picked one up. It was full. Loosening the lid, he bent low and took a sniff.

Petrol. Just what I need…

He hunted around a bit longer and found a box of matches along with a few other odds and ends.

Yes!

Adrenaline surged through him. Anticipation flooded his

veins. He pocketed the matches, collected a Jerry can and after killing the light, crept back out of the garage.

He looked around him. The night was quiet and still. One good thing about living on a few acres was that there were no close neighbors looking in. He could get in and do what he wanted to and nobody would know. The thought made him chuckle with delight.

Working quickly and guided now only by moonlight, he tried doors around the perimeter of the house until he found one that was unlocked. Easing open the door, he made his way inside. He'd never been in Archie's house before, so he followed the lights. Most of the downstairs was in darkness. He looked into the only room where there was a light on and found it empty.

This time of night it made sense that Archie would be upstairs in bed. Asleep, no doubt.

Good. That will make this even easier…

It didn't take him long to find Archie's bedroom. The door was open and he heard gentle snoring from within. He walked far enough into the room to ascertain it was in fact Archie asleep in the bed and then moved slowly away. At the same time, he loosened the lid on the Jerry can and started pouring fuel all over the floor.

Closing the door behind him, he poured a trail of fuel down the stairs until the Jerry can was empty. Then he lit a match. Staring at the tiny flame, a smile came to his lips. He tossed the match on the floor. Within seconds, it ignited. Flames started licking at the floor.

As he watched the fire begin to take hold, his quiet laughter rang out in the darkness.

Take that, Archie Craigdon! Not so brave now, are you?

It had been a long time since Christopher Barrington had been to a Barrington family function. Oh, an invitation was always extended by his mother to the latest celebration, but he usually politely declined. Though he'd been adopted by Frank Barrington when he was twelve and was the oldest of the Barrington children that didn't mean he always felt like he belonged.

He'd spent his life trying to get his biological father to recognize him and that had come to naught. Henry Craigdon had gone to his death still thumbing his nose at his firstborn, refusing to acknowledge their relationship.

That still had the power to hurt, but they were now more than a year past Henry's death. As time went on, the wound of rejection was slowly healing. Christopher had Elizabeth to thank for that, along with some of her family. Noah, in particular, seemed willing to extend the olive branch.

Christopher was tired of the anger and angst that for so long had churned him up inside. During his latest discussion with Elizabeth, he'd almost convinced himself to give it up. To withdraw the suit against Henry's estate and to walk away and get on with his life—what was left of it.

He'd turned forty-one a week ago. His mother had insisted they celebrate together as a family. They'd all shown up—his half-brothers and half-sisters. His Barrington siblings. They'd patted him on the back, shared some drinks, wished him well. They were their usual effervescent, boisterous, genuine selves. Every one of them had grown up knowing he was adopted, but that hadn't mattered to them.

Of course, he wasn't the only kid Evelyn and Frank had adopted. That's just the kind of people they were. In the early days of their marriage, when they thought they couldn't have children, they'd adopted another boy. Vaughan was only a year younger than Christopher. He'd spent the first eleven years of his life in foster homes. His foster parents hadn't always been kind to him. Even now, all these years later, it angered Christopher to know how some people thought it was okay to abuse children.

He and Vaughan had gotten lucky with Frank, and Christopher's mother had been only too happy to expand her family. When they were blessed with several biological children a couple of years after Vaughan's adoption had been finalized, they'd impressed upon each child that they were all equal in their eyes. No one treated anyone differently. They were all Barringtons. That was a testament to the way his mother and adoptive father had raised them.

No, not adoptive father. Frank Barrington had been more of a father to him than Henry ever was. Frank had taken him in, accepted him unconditionally, had even given him his name. As far as good and decent went, Frank was streaks ahead of Henry Craigdon. Frank deserved to be called "Dad."

Christopher had wasted so much time—years—wishing things were different—hoping that something would change Henry's mind; that one day he'd come to his senses and welcome Christopher with open arms, even beg his forgiveness. But those things hadn't happened and now they never would. It had taken a long time—more than a year, in fact—but Christopher had finally gotten there. He'd also come to value his Barrington family.

Despite the attitude from Frank and his mother, Christopher had resisted their gentle encouragement for him to accept he was as much a Barrington as any of them. He'd been so caught up in his resentment and anger toward Henry, he'd closed himself off from his real family—the family who'd always loved him unconditionally. He could remember a time not that long ago when he didn't feel he belonged anywhere. Now he knew that was more the bitterness talking.

Now that the lawsuit had been settled in his mind during the chat with Elizabeth, he could close the door on that part of his life and concentrate on the blessings he'd been given in the form of the Barrington family. Henry Craigdon was an asshole, then and now. He didn't deserve a son like Christopher. And that was that. His mother would be both relieved and pleased to know Christopher had reached this understanding. She and Frank had long counseled him about accepting Henry for what he was and letting go of whatever Christopher couldn't change.

He passed through the small town of Broken and anticipation flooded his veins. The streets were mostly empty, with only the occasional car passing him by. It wasn't that late, but Broken was like that most of the time. A sleepy rural town nestled in the lush southern highlands where people knew each other and called each other by name.

Over the years, it had grown in popularity with people from the city who favored the area to set up their country homes. No doubt some visitors thought the Barringtons were one of them. After all, they lived in a house every bit as grand as their neighbors. But the locals knew Frank and Evelyn had set up home decades earlier and had raised their family there. They were as much a local family as any of them and people from the area regarded them as such.

A few more miles just south of the town and he arrived. He flicked on his indicator and turned into the long paved driveway that led to the Barrington house. An impressive five-foot-high sandstone wall spanned either side of the entryway. A large and shiny engraved metallic sign announced the property as "Barrington Estate."

That might seem a bit ostentatious, but in this part of the world, an easy ninety minutes' drive south of Sydney, appearances mattered. Barrington Estate wasn't the only multimillion dollar property in the Broken neighborhood.

Not that Frank and Evelyn were pretentious. In fact, despite the incredible wealth Frank had acquired over his many years in mining, they remained humble and modest in their private life. Except for the grand house and the nice cars, they lived quite simple lives and often invited the less fortunate into their home. It wasn't unusual for them to throw a barbecue on the lawns of the estate and invite all of Barrington Mining employees and their children for a fun-filled day.

As Christopher's headlights swept up the driveway, they bounced off the white rendered walls of the mansion. It was every bit as grand as Craigdon Manor—probably even grander. The Hamptons-inspired home stood on thirty acres of lush, southern highlands land. Tall stately poplars lined either side of the road, all the way up to the wide circular driveway that widened right in front of the house.

With nine bedrooms and ten bathrooms, there was plenty of room for everyone. Coupled with an indoor heated swimming pool, a games room, home theater, eleven-foot cathedral ceilings and plenty of natural light it was a home to be envied. Christopher could recall several visits over the years from journalists employed by various home magazines wanting to do a story on the Barrington house.

His mother took pride in the haven she and Frank had created for their family, but she didn't purposefully seek out the attention owning such a prestigious residence often invoked. To them, it was just their home.

Most of his brothers and sisters had moved out. There were only the younger ones still at home. Recently, he overheard his parents discussing the possibility of turning the place into a respite center for troubled kids. God knows, they had the room and there were plenty of needy kids.

Christopher pulled alongside the curb of the curved driveway and switched off the ignition. Though he preferred to stay away from family celebrations, he'd made a special effort this time round to attend his brother's fortieth birthday. Vaughan's birthday had fallen a few weeks earlier, but the family had left it until now to celebrate the occasion.

Christopher had chosen to see in his fourth decade, perched on a barstool at his favorite seedy hangout, with nothing but a bottle of scotch for company. But Vaughan had always looked at life differently. He was a glass half-full kind of guy. He had an irrepressible optimism that was even more remarkable given what he'd endured during the first eleven years of his life.

With a sigh, Christopher opened the door and climbed out of the car. Bracing himself for the onslaught of family who'd soon be upon him, he headed for the front door. The first person he ran into was his mother.

"Christopher. Honey, it's so nice to see you." Evelyn hugged him and then pecked him on the cheek. "Thank you for making the effort. Your brother will be so pleased."

Christopher twisted his lips into an imitation of a smile. "Yeah, well Vaughan's the only reason I'm here."

His mother pouted. "Surely not the only reason?"

He opened his mouth to answer, but she pressed a finger to his lips. "Uh uh. Don't say it." She smiled and linked her arm with his. "So, how was your drive down?"

Christopher shrugged. "It was okay. The worst of the traffic had already gone by the time I left. That's what's so good about leaving Sydney an hour or so after everyone else."

"Well, I'm glad you're here. Now all of my children will be together under the same roof for once. That hasn't happened since last Christmas."

He rolled his eyes and she poked out her tongue. At sixty, his mother was still playful enough that he couldn't help but smile.

"Come," she said. "Let's go and find your father. Then you can wish Vaughan a happy birthday. That is, if you can get anywhere near him. He invited more than a hundred friends and at least half of them seem to be women."

Christopher chuckled. "Good old Vaughan. He's always been a ladies' man."

"You're right," his mother agreed easily. "It's just too bad he won't choose one. I'm going to be the oldest grandmother in the world by the time you two get around to it."

Several hours later, Christopher found himself heading back to Sydney. Despite his misgivings, he'd managed to enjoy himself. It had been nice to catch up with his siblings, and Vaughan seemed to have had a great time. He'd even managed to give Christopher some advice about letting go of the grudge he'd held so long against Henry Craigdon.

For once Christopher had been able to discuss the whole sorry saga without combusting with anger. In fact, if he took the time to really examine what he felt, he'd probably identify it as resignation. Anyway, it was progress, whatever it was.

Christopher's mother had pleaded with him to stay the night, but he'd politely declined. Though he loved his family, a few hours spent with them all in one place was enough. At some point, one of them would be sure to ask him about his single status. Then the discussion would turn to the fact he drank too much and was often abrupt to the point of rudeness. His younger sisters took great delight in telling him he'd never catch a woman if he continued to go round with a perpetual frown on his face.

Christopher supposed it was his own fault that he'd earned the unofficial title of the Grouch among his younger siblings. He couldn't remember a time in his life when he'd felt particularly jovial. In fact, until recently, the happiest he'd felt was when he was making others miserable.

What does that say about me? I ought to be ashamed. Mom and Frank would be horrified if they knew some of the things I've been up to…the trouble I've caused…

A hot wave of shame washed over him. The only thing he had to console himself with was the fact his Craigdon siblings had weathered his dirty tricks and come out the other side. Driving back to Sydney along the quiet freeway, he was filled with a determination to turn his life around. He'd spent the first forty-odd years feeling angry and bitter at the hand he'd been dealt. That was all about to end. It was time to change his attitude and make up for lost time.

With that thought in mind, he turned off the freeway and headed in the direction of Richmond. It was late, but Elizabeth had impressed on him more than once that he was welcome at her home any time, day or night. She kept a spare key under the mat beside the back door. It had been there for years. No doubt his half-brothers and sisters had made good use of it from time to time when they were younger.

He rubbed his eyes with his knuckles and yawned widely. He was tired. It had been a long night. Hell, it had been a long year. He was more than an hour away from his apartment on the other side of the city. The thought of spending the night at Craigdon Manor held an appeal he couldn't deny. Not only was it a lot closer, it would give him a chance to tell Elizabeth in person that he'd come to a decision. He couldn't wait to talk with her over breakfast.

As he drove the streets, quiet and still, he felt cocooned from the rest of the world. Classical music played through his stereo, lulling him, soothing him, calming his troubled soul. It was like everything around him was conspiring to support him in his decision to turn his life around.

Archie's mansion loomed up in the distance, less than a mile from Elizabeth's house. As Christopher approached, a faint orange glow filled the sky. Slowing, he stared out the window, trying to get a better look. The light was all wrong. Strange, eerie. Totally out of place.

"Fuck!"

All at once, his brain registered what he was seeing. Archie's house was on fire!

Chapter Nineteen

With his heart thumping double time and adrenaline rushing through his veins, Christopher sped up Archie's driveway. At the same time, he fumbled for his phone and dialed 000.

"This is Edith. What is your emergency?"

The woman's voice sounded so calm and collected in his ear, totally at odds with the panic that held him tense.

"Fire! My uncle's house is on fire! Hurry! Send the fire brigade!"

"No problem, they're on their way. What's your address?"

For a moment, Christopher went blank. He had no idea about the house number. All he could remember was the road.

"It's on Windsor Road, in Richmond. I don't know the number. But hurry! Please!"

"Is there anyone inside?"

"Yes! At least, I think so. My elderly uncle. He might be stuck inside. Please! You need to send someone fast!"

"They're already on their way," the calm voice soothed. "Are you there now?"

"Yes! I just arrived! I'm going to see if anyone's inside."

"Sir! Stay where you are! It might be unsafe. Wait for the fire brigade to arrive. They're trained for this kind of thing. They'll be there in a few minutes."

Christopher brought his car to a stop right outside Archie's front steps. By now the flames had grown higher and were eating into part of the roof. Thrusting his phone into his pocket, he jumped out of his car and ran toward the house, shielding his face from the heat.

"Help! Someone! Help me!"

Christopher froze. His gaze moved upward to the second story. He saw the shape of a man—*Archie?* The smoke and haze made it impossible to know for sure, but there was no doubt someone was up there. Someone who was about to burn to death if he didn't do something.

Mind made up, Christopher pulled off his dinner jacket and wrapped it around his head. Leaving a gap for his eyes, he took care to cover his mouth and nose. It would do neither of them any good if he succumbed to smoke inhalation before he managed to pull off the rescue.

"Help! Please, someone! Help!"

The voice had grown weaker and urgency ripped through Christopher's gut. The faint sound of sirens could be heard in the distance, but there was no time to wait. The fire had taken hold and was roaring across the roof. Christopher had no way of knowing how far it had entered the house, but he had no choice but to breach the perimeter and do what he could to make it to where the man was trapped.

With quick panting breaths, Christopher went in low, doing his best to avoid the smoke. Guided only by memory and the faintest orange-glow light from the fire, he crossed the entryway and headed for the stairs. Almost immediately he was engulfed in thick smoke as it billowed up the stairwell. Already, flames had made their way to this part of the house. Time was running out.

He calculated Archie was in the third room along the second-floor hallway that faced out into the driveway. As he ran past one closed door after another, he yelled out.

"Archie! Where are you? Archie!"

"In here," came the faint reply a little further ahead.

Christopher's eyes stung. His lungs burned. He sucked in what little oxygen was still available in the smoky air and pressed forward. He came to the room where he'd guessed Archie was inside and put his shoulder to the door. It was hot.

"Fuck."

The fire must have already made it inside…

There was nothing else for it. He had to get through. Archie was behind that door, fighting for his life. With no further thought for his safety, Christopher wrapped his jacket over the doorknob and turned. The door came open just as a large piece of burning timber fell from the ceiling. The flames quickly spread across the hardwood floors and began licking at a rug.

The fire had already taken hold and the room was well alight. Through the thick smoke, Christopher saw Archie cowering by the window, almost as if he'd been weighing up his chances of surviving the jump.

"Archie!" Christopher shouted above the roar.

The old man turned his head in Christopher's direction. Relief flooded his face. That quickly changed to terror when another piece of the ceiling hit the floor.

"We have to get out of here!" Christopher yelled.

Archie nodded. He looked around him, seeking a way through. The flames were consuming everything in sight.

If we don't get out of here soon, we're both going to die…

The thought was enough to give Christopher the impetus to move forward. With his jacket still covering his mouth and nose, he got down low and crawled across the floor. On the way, he snatched the bedspread that had somehow been spared the flames. He threw it around Archie and then dragged him back the way Christopher had come.

Another beam fell out of the ceiling and landed not three feet away. With adrenaline pouring through him, Christopher increased his efforts to get both of them out of the room. The door was only yards away… Four… Three… A rumble and creak of timbers above them and *crash*… Two… One…

They were there, fighting through heat and the smoke, batting away the embers that were lodging themselves in the bedspread.

Out in the hallway, choking for breath, Christopher looked around him. The stairwell was now fully engulfed in flames.

"Oh, fuck."

There was no way down.

Still, he refused to give up. He dragged Archie a little further away and then bent low to his ear.

"Is there another way out of here?"

"The back stairs," Archie wheezed.

His eyes were bloodshot and his skin was as pale as ash, but at least he was still alive. With renewed determination, Christopher shouted, "Which way?"

"That way," Archie pointed.

Christopher peered through the smoke. Though visibility was almost non-existent, it appeared the fire hadn't made it down that far yet. A surge of relief went through him.

We can do this… We're going to get out of here… It's going to be all right…

No sooner had he finished the thought than a loud crash almost deafened him. His gaze flew to Archie. "What the hell was that?"

"I'm not sure, but I think it's the roof. It's falling in on us!"

On another burst of adrenaline, laced liberally with fear, Christopher grabbed Archie by the arm and began hauling him along beside him.

"Come on! Move it! We need to get the hell out of here!" Christopher shouted.

Archie did the best he could but there was no way he could keep up with Christopher.

If we don't move faster, we're going to be trapped…

And then Archie cried out in pain and fell hard. He writhed on the floor, grabbing at his leg.

"What it is?" Christopher asked, his pulse rate frantic.

"My knee. I've hurt it. It's bad. I can't move."

"*No, no, no!* Archie, you can't do this to me! We have to get out of here!"

"I'm sorry. I can't move. The pain's too bad. You go. Leave me."

Fuck.

Christopher might have done some low acts in his time, but this wasn't going to be one of them. Here was a chance to redeem himself, to apologize for all the wrongs he'd done. Besides that, there was no way he was leaving the old man to die, no matter what Archie said.

With a muffled curse, Christopher bent and picked Archie up in his arms. Still crouched low, he stumbled forward toward the backstairs. With his eyes stinging and his lungs burning, he focused on putting one foot in front of the other until they finally made it to the end of the hallway. A closed door was at the very end of it.

Christopher tested the handle. It was warm, but not hot. Slowly, he opened the door and peered through the crack.

It's clear!

Relief poured through him. The fire hadn't made it this far back. But they weren't out of danger yet and it wasn't going to be easy getting an injured Archie down the stairs. There was nothing for it but to carry him. Any other option would slow them down.

Hoisting the old man across his shoulders, Christopher made his way down the stairs. The pitch blackness made it even more difficult. He closed his eyes and tried to imagine one stair following another. Finally they reached the bottom. Another door blocked their exit.

Setting Archie down, Christopher once again tested the doorknob and found it cool. With his heart surging with anticipation, he turned it.

It was locked.

"Oh, fuck. Archie! The door's locked."

"Yes," Archie wheezed. "Locked up before I went to bed."

Refusing to be defeated, Christopher moved Archie further back. Taking a few seconds to gather his focus, he charged toward the door and put his shoulder to the wood.

"Fuuuck!"

It felt like all of his muscles had been torn from the bone. Fire raged through his shoulder. But he refused to die like this, caught in a stairwell, when they were so close, so close…

Gritting his teeth, he tried again, screaming out in pain each time his injured shoulder connected with the unforgiving surface. It took three attempts, but finally the wood splintered.

"Yes! Oh, fuck yes! We're almost there, Archie. We're going to get out of here!"

Ignoring the pain, Christopher charged at the door again. This time, the lock broke free. Gasping for breath and with tears pouring out of his eyes, Christopher pushed the door open and was hit with a blast of cool night air.

He immediately turned and collected Archie in his arms and carried him out of the house. Christopher managed to stumble ten or twelve yards before his legs gave out. They collapsed on the manicured lawn, heaving and gasping for breath. Christopher heard a shout. With the last of his strength, he waved his hand in the air to get attention.

"Help! We're over here! We need help!"

The last thing he remembered was catching a glimpse of a paramedic as she made her way toward them. Before she'd even reached them, he blacked out.

The sound of Elizabeth's phone ringing tore her from a deep sleep. For weeks she'd struggled each night to relax and clear her mind enough to allow herself to drift off. Finally she'd succumbed to the urgings of her doctor and had taken a couple of sleeping pills. As she sat up in bed and fumbled for her phone, her head felt like it was stuffed with cotton wool.

This is why I've never been a fan of sleeping tablets…

The thought struggled to make it through the fog clouding her brain. The phone kept ringing. She glanced at the clock on her bedside table.

Two-forty-eight…

"For heaven's sake!" she muttered. With a sigh, she answered the call.

"Hello?"

"Mom! Mom! Where are you?"

At the sound of Joel's frantic voice, Elizabeth came wide awake. "I'm at home. Where else would I be?"

"Oh, thank God!"

The relief in his voice was palpable. A frisson of apprehension sparked through her veins. "What is it, Joel? What's happened?"

She heard her son sigh heavily on the other end of the phone. "It's Archie. There's been a fire. At his house. I wasn't sure… That is, I thought there might be the possibility you were there…"

A buzzing sounded in her ears. She had no time to think about what Joel said. All she heard were the words "Archie" and "fire." Her heart thumped with alarm.

She gripped the phone harder as panic ratcheted through her veins. "Is he all right? Please, Joel. Please tell me he's all right!"

"I'm not sure, Mom. He's been taken to the hospital, along with Christopher. That's all I know."

With a cry of alarm, Elizabeth collapsed against the bedhead. "Oh, God! Oh, no! Not Archie! Please, God! Let him be all right!"

"I'm on my way over, Mom. I'll take you to the hospital."

She was filled with relief. Her state of mind was dire, and coupled with the sleeping pills, she wasn't at all sure she could drive herself.

"Thank you Joel," she said, then took a deep breath to gather her wits.

"I'm only a few minutes away. Hurry up and get dressed."

With that, Elizabeth ended the call and threw herself out of bed. As fast as she could, she stumbled to her walk-in wardrobe and started pulling on clothes. She couldn't have said what she'd chosen. All she knew was by the time Joel's car swept into the driveway and pulled up at the house, she was waiting for him on the top step. She hurried down to meet him.

The air smelled strongly of smoke. Though she couldn't see Archie's house through the thick stand of trees that separated them, she imagined the worst. It took her two tries to open the door. She plopped down inelegantly on the seat and sighed.

Joel looked at her with concern. "Are you all right, Mom?"

She focused on not slurring her words. "Of course I'm all right. Just get moving. We need to get to Archie."

Joel continued to look worried. "It's just that you seem a little…out of it."

Elizabeth blew out her breath on a groan of impatience. "Oh, for heaven's sake, Joel! I took a couple of sleeping pills before I went to bed. I wasn't expecting to be woken in the middle of the night. I'm still a bit groggy, okay?"

He nodded slowly with comprehension. "Okay."

"Now, can we get moving? Please?"

To her relief, Joel put the car in gear and spun the tires on the pavement. The car shot forward down the driveway and out into the street. The roads were three-in-the-morning quiet. They passed only the occasional car. The whole way, Elizabeth stared unseeingly out the window to the darkness and prayed Archie would be all right.

Please, God. Don't let him die. Not now. Not like this. We've waited all our lives to be together. Now we finally can be. I'm nothing but a poor sinner, but I beg you to show some kindness. I need the chance to say I'm sorry. Poor Archie! We've barely spoken all these weeks… My fault, not his. My stupid pride. I was upset he hadn't told me about Logan. As if I had the high moral ground on secrets. Ha! Poor Archie! A fire! Please, God. Please keep him alive…

The desperate thoughts went round and round inside her head until she thought she might scream from frustration. No matter how hard she prayed, Archie's life was in the hands of a higher power. She was reminded of the night Callum had been born and the promise Henry had made to God.

Spare my son and I'll give him back to you. I'll make sure he devotes his life to God…

It was a promise Henry should never have made. It wasn't his life to bind. Fortunately, Callum had found the strength and courage to make up his own mind and was now living the life he'd chosen. Elizabeth needed to do the same. It wasn't for her to beg and plead and make bargains with God. How totally arrogant! How presumptuous! Considering all the things she'd accused Henry of.

We're kidding ourselves if we think we have any say in it… That we should *have any say in it… Thy will be done… Right?*

Archie's life was in God's hands and that's the way it had to be. It was up to Him to decide. All Elizabeth could do was hope and pray God chose to spare the man she loved with all her heart.

Chapter Twenty

The trip to the hospital was the longest of Elizabeth's life. The last time she'd felt like this, she was rushing to the emergency department to see Sophia, desperately hoping her youngest child was still alive after being attacked by a madman in her home. Thankfully, Sophia had pulled through and Elizabeth could only hope and pray Archie would too. Joel didn't have any information on his injuries, just that he'd been pulled from the house alive.

"I still can't believe it was Christopher who saved him," she mused, staring out at the night as Joel negotiated the road. "I hope Christopher isn't badly hurt."

"Whatever his injuries, they aren't life threatening. It was Christopher who called me."

"How did he happen to be there at that time of night? He doesn't live anywhere near either of us."

"Apparently he'd been to Broken earlier that night. He was visiting his parents. They were celebrating a fortieth birthday at the family home. One of their kids. I don't know which one. Christopher was asked to spend the night, but decided to drive home. Got tired so decided to stay at your place. Lucky for us, he did."

Elizabeth shook her head slowly from side to side and breathed out her disbelief. "I don't know what brought him past Archie's house at that moment, but I'm so glad he was there and noticed." She paused and then added, "Have you called Archie's sons?"

"Yes. Well, I called Noah. He was going to call his brothers. They're going to meet us at the hospital."

"Do the police know what caused it?"

"No, not yet. The place has been pretty much destroyed. It will take the investigators hours to pick through the debris to formulate a theory." Joel shot her a grim look. "Let's hope it wasn't arson."

Elizabeth started in surprise. Her heart skipped a beat. "You think it could be?"

"It's always a possibility."

Elizabeth stared at him in confusion. "But who would do such a thing?"

Joel looked at her. He quirked an eyebrow. "You really can't think of anyone?"

"No, of course not! Who do you mean?"

"Didn't we just reveal Ashton to all and sundry as a criminal?"

"But he had no gripe against Archie! Besides, he was pretending to be my son. I can't believe he'd go from that to a full-on criminal."

Joel shot her a wry smile. "A full-on criminal? What's that, Mom? You mean fraud isn't criminal enough?"

She blushed. "You know what I mean, Joel. It's one thing to try and dupe an old lady out of some money, but arson… To set someone's house on fire knowing they might be inside…" She shuddered. "Surely Ashton wouldn't do something like that."

"Well, I for one, wouldn't put it past him," Joel muttered.

"I take it the police haven't found him?"

Joel's expression turned grim. "No, but we will. I'm not giving up until this asshole's behind bars. And if he's responsible for the fire, that's even more reason to lock him up."

"You don't know he was involved yet, Joel."

"That's right. But if he is…"

"I'm still so upset at myself for falling for his lies," Elizabeth murmured.

Joel glanced at her. "Mom, we've been over this. It wasn't your fault. He was a professional con artist. You weren't his first victim."

She sighed. "You keep saying that. It doesn't make me feel any better."

"Well it should. It's meant to. It means other people have been just as gullible as you."

She gave him a dry look. "Are you sure that's meant to make me feel better?"

Joel flushed. "Okay, so I'm not good with words. I'm a cop. What do you expect?"

She reached over and patted his hand. "It's all right, Joel. I understand. And thank you."

"For what?"

"For trying to take my mind off Archie."

"Did it work?"

"No, but it's better than being locked away in silence with my thoughts."

"He's going to be okay, Mom."

She shook her head. "You don't know that, Joel."

Joel turned the car into the hospital parking lot. That time of the morning, they had the place almost to themselves. The drive over had helped to clear Elizabeth's head. The fogginess had gone, but the hard ball of dread in her stomach and the fear and uncertainty that filled her veins remained.

She climbed out of the car on feet that felt like they were filled with lead. Joel came around her side and took her arm. She leaned against him, grateful for the support. They entered through the public entrance of the emergency department. Unlike the parking lot, the ED was teeming with life.

A crying baby, red in the face, screaming like its lungs were on fire. Its mother doing her best to calm the child, but looking tense with fear. A man with blood pouring from a wide gash on his forehead. He held a dirty handkerchief to the wound, moaning loudly. A middle-aged woman with her ankle stuck out at an odd angle sat quietly in a wheelchair, her foot elevated. There were many others in various states of ill health. Elizabeth was grateful when Joel led them straight up to the triage nurse.

"We're here to see Archie Craigdon. He was brought in by ambulance about an hour ago. Do you know where he is?"

"Are you his son?" the nurse behind the counter asked.

"No. His nephew. We're still waiting for his sons to arrive."

She tapped on the keyboard in front of her and looked at the computer screen. "Did you say Archie Craigdon?"

"Yes."

"I can't find anyone under that name. Are you sure he was brought here?"

"Yes," Joel said.

"Try Archibald," Elizabeth suggested.

The nurse tapped the keys again. This time they were successful.

"Okay. Yes, we have an Archibald Craigdon." She read the notes on the screen. "He's currently in surgery. I'll have someone come and collect you and take you to another waiting room. As soon as he can, the surgeon will find you there and let you know what's going on."

At the nurse's words, Elizabeth's knees buckled. She would have fallen if it weren't for Joel's supportive arm around her.

"Oh dear God! Surgery?"

"I wish I could tell you more," the nurse said kindly. "Take a seat. I'll call someone."

"What about Christopher Barrington?" Joel asked. "Was he brought here?"

"Is he a relative of yours?" the nurse asked.

"Yes. My half-brother."

Once again, the nurse tapped on her keyboard. "Yes. He was brought in by ambulance shortly after your uncle. He's also in surgery."

Joel looked at Elizabeth. Her heart sank at the nurse's words. *Archie and Christopher. Both of them hurt. Both of them fighting for their lives...*

She clung to Joel's arm. They'd barely made it across the ED waiting room before Flynn, Noah and Logan burst through the automatic doors. As one, they scanned the waiting room. The minute their gazes landed on Elizabeth and Joel they rushed over.

"How is he?"

"What happened?"

"Can we see him?"

Elizabeth was relieved Joel was there to fend off their worried questions.

"He's in surgery. That's all we know. Same with Christopher."

"Shit."

"What was Christopher doing there?"

"Surgery? That doesn't sound good."

"How long have they been in there?"

Joel held up his hand. "Fellas, please. One at a time."

"What happened?" Flynn asked in a more controlled tone.

"We don't really know. There was a fire. Christopher happened to be driving past and saw it. He called 000 and then fought his way inside the house and dragged Uncle Archie out. From what I can tell, he saved your father's life."

"Shit," Logan said and then shot a glance in Elizabeth's direction. "Sorry," he mumbled.

She waved his apology away. A little cursing was the least of her worries at the moment.

"Thank God for Christopher. What was he doing there?" Noah asked.

"Apparently he was traveling back from Broken. He'd been to a family celebration. One of his brothers turned forty," Joel supplied.

"Talk about lucky," Flynn said. "What do we know about Dad's injuries?"

"Nothing. Only that he's in surgery. The nurse couldn't tell us anything more."

"What about Christopher?" Noah asked.

"I'm not sure the extent of his injuries," Joel answered. "The nurse said he was in surgery too, but I think he's going to pull through. He's the one who called me to let me know what had happened."

"Thank God for Christopher. Let's hope he's okay," Noah said.

"How soon will they give us an update on Dad?" Logan asked.

Joel shrugged. "The nurse said someone will come and get us and take us to another waiting room. One closer to the theater, no doubt."

Joel had barely finished speaking when a young woman dressed in surgical scrubs and with a stethoscope around her neck came up to them.

"Are you the relatives of Archibald Craigdon?"

"Yes," they all said simultaneously.

"I'm Doctor Potter. I've just come from the operating theater."

Elizabeth jumped to her feet. "How is he?"

"Are you his wife?"

"No, I—"

"I'm one of his sons," Flynn interrupted. "Whatever you have to say can be said in front of all of us."

"Very well. He suffered extensive smoke inhalation. His lungs were in pretty bad shape. He also has a bruised medial ligament in his knee which will repair itself over time. On top of that, he suffered a minor heart attack on his way here in the ambulance. We've replaced one of his valves and added a stent. He's going to be sore for a few days while his lungs heal, but otherwise, it appears he'll be fine."

Elizabeth pressed a hand against her chest, almost fainting with relief.

"Oh, thank God! Thank you God!"

Joel put his arm around her and squeezed her shoulder. She drew in a deep breath and eased it out through dry lips. Slowly, the adrenaline that had poured through her system began to recede.

"He's going to be okay Mom," Joel murmured. "He's going to be okay."

"What about Christopher Barrington?" Noah asked.

"He's doing well. Minor smoke inhalation. A broken collarbone and some torn ligaments in his shoulder. Painful, but not life threatening. We've repaired the ligaments. The collarbone will heal by itself. He's going to be sore for a while, but he'll be fine."

It felt like hours before Elizabeth was allowed to see Archie. She'd waited with barely restrained patience for his sons to have their time with him. At Joel's urging, they eventually left to find coffee. She entered the room filled with fear of what she might find. The moment she caught sight of his pale form covered almost to his chin with a hospital sheet, her legs nearly gave out again.

"Archie! Oh, my goodness!" she gasped, bringing her hand up to her mouth in an effort to hold back a sob. Tears came to her eyes.

He looked so frail and old. He was only three years older than her, but right now he looked about a hundred. The trauma of being caught in the fire had taken a lot out of him. On top of that, he'd had a heart attack. An oxygen mask covered his nose and mouth. An IV bag ran fluid into his vein. And then his eyes fluttered open and he saw her. He gave her a weak smile.

She was beside him in an instant, taking his hand in hers. She brought it up to her lips and kissed his fingers.

"Oh, my darling! You gave me such a fright! I can't believe how close I came to losing you!"

"Still here," Archie rasped. "Tougher than that!"

"Of course you are!" Elizabeth agreed. "It's going to take more than a bit of smoke and a little heart attack to keep you down."

Archie closed his eyes and then got caught up in a coughing fit. It sounded like he was dragging up a lung. Elizabeth cast around for something to help him. She spied a water jug and cup and half-filled it with water. Carefully pulling the oxygen mask to one side, she held his head in one hand and the cup in the other and helped him take a few sips.

"Enough?" she asked.

He nodded. "Thanks."

She set the cup down on the table that stood beside his bed and set the mask back in place. Feeling suddenly out of her depth, she moved away and then picked up the chair by the window and brought it back to the bed. She perched on the edge of it and tried to get a hold of her nerves. There was so much she wanted to say to him, but where did she start?

"Don't get yourself worked up, Lizzie. It's going to be all right."

His gentle words were her undoing. Tears rushed to her eyes and spilled over, warm and salty on her cheeks. She jumped back up and held him carefully, resting her head lightly on his chest.

"Oh, my darling! I'm so sorry! I've been such a stubborn fool! I don't know what I was thinking! Why did I make this so difficult for us! I love you with all my heart! I always have! I should never have kept our love a secret. I should have found a way. From now on, we're going to live our love out in the open. You have my word."

Archie offered her a shaky smile. His eyes glinted with tears. "You don't know how long I've waited to hear you say that," he rasped. "I love you, too."

Openly sobbing, she kissed whatever skin she could access: his eyes, his cheeks, his forehead. Every single part of him was loved by her. She couldn't believe it had taken his near-death for her to realize how much she wanted to declare their love to the world as well as to him. Archie started coughing again and once again she helped him sip from the cup. When he was finished, she lowered his head gently back down to the pillow.

He closed his eyes on a sigh, obviously exhausted.

"You've been through so much. You need to rest," she murmured. "Are you in pain?"

"No. I'm fine," he rasped. "Just tired."

"I should go."

His eyes flew open. "No! Please! Stay."

Nodding, she drew the chair up closer to the bed and sat down. Once again, she reached for his hand and held it tightly. After coming so close to losing him, she didn't want to let him go.

"What happened with Ashton? Flynn told me he'd left."

Elizabeth flushed with embarrassment. "He didn't leave. He's on the run. Turns out he was an imposter. Joel ran a DNA test. Ashton—if that's his real name—isn't my son."

"Oh, Lizzie. I'm sorry."

She squeezed his hand. "No, Archie. I'm sorry. I should have listened to you. To all of you. I was too caught up in my desire for him to be my son. I shut everyone out. It was wrong."

"He told me you'd tossed me over. That you didn't want to be with me. That's why you kept refusing to make our love public. At least, that's what he said."

Elizabeth stared at Archie in shock. "Ashton told you that?"

"Yes."

"When?"

"Does it matter?"

"It does to me."

Archie took another shuddering breath. "I came over to see you the morning after the opera. You weren't home. Ashton met me at the door."

"Oh, Archie!"

He gave a sad smile. "I came over to tell you I didn't care anymore about a public declaration. All that was important was that I had you by my side."

Tears burned in her eyes. She lifted his hand up to her lips and kissed it. The tears spilled over, dampening her cheeks.

"Oh, Archie! I don't deserve you! I love you so very much."

Silence fell between them. She listened to his raspy breaths. Long moments passed. She thought he'd fallen asleep. A few moments later, he startled her when he spoke in a low, conversational tone. His eyes remained closed.

"My brother always stole my girlfriends. Even when we were teenagers. He'd come home and badger me until I told him about my latest crush and then he'd go out of his way to charm them and claim them for his own. As we got older, he'd go so far as to sleep with them and then he'd brag to me about it."

She gasped, taken aback by these fresh revelations. Of course, she'd known for a long time how malicious her husband could be, but to do that to his brother! It was unspeakably cruel.

"Of course, it was the same with you," Archie added quietly. "He knew right from the beginning that I was in love with you. It was only a matter of time before he came to me and told me what it was like to fuck you."

Elizabeth gasped, both from the surprising vulgarity and the words. "I never slept with Henry before we married!" she protested.

Archie opened his eyes and regarded her somberly. "I guess that's why he married you."

Elizabeth shook her head, lost for words. She recalled how happy she'd been during the first few months of her marriage. Okay, so it hadn't taken her long to realize Henry didn't love her like she loved him, but she'd always thought he had genuine affection for her. Now it was clear she'd been nothing but a prize, a trophy wife. A one-up against his brother. That realization made her sick.

As if sensing her distress, Archie opened his eyes. He reached out and cupped her cheek. "Don't go getting upset over what's incredibly ancient news. Focus on the here and now. You and I are together still and blissfully in love. We'll be together, loving each other, for the rest of our lives. So take that Henry! Look who's had the last laugh."

Chapter Twenty One

The afternoon light was fading and evening was close on its tail. Elizabeth left Archie sleeping and made her way down the corridor to the nurses' station. A young Asian nurse dressed in smart navy-blue scrubs sat behind the desk. She looked up as Elizabeth approached and gave her a friendly smile.

"May I help you?"

"Yes. Um, I was wondering if you could tell me where I can find Christopher Barrington. Is he on this ward?"

The nurse nodded and turned around to consult a whiteboard behind her. "Yes. He's in bed fifteen. Head past the water cooler. It's the second door on the right."

"Thank you."

Elizabeth followed the directions and found Christopher propped up in the bed beside the window. His right arm was supported by a sling. There were three other patients in the room. Two of them had visitors. The third one was snoring.

Christopher smiled wryly as she approached. "Fancy seeing you here."

She smiled back. "I was thinking the same thing." She moved up beside him and pecked him on the cheek. "How are you?"

Christopher moved as if to shrug and then stopped himself with a grimace. "I'm fine. The shoulder's a bit sore, but I'll live."

She drew up a chair beside the bed. "I'm so glad."

"How's Archie?"

"He's going to be okay." A rush of emotion overwhelmed her. "I don't know how to thank you, Christopher. You saved his life."

"I did what anyone would do. It was nothing."

She touched him on the arm, her gaze steady on his. "No, Christopher. It wasn't nothing. It was heroic. You risked your life. There are plenty of people who wouldn't have had the courage to do what you did."

Christopher compressed his lips. "I'm just glad he's going to be all right."

Three people wearing equally worried expressions filled the doorway. The woman and one of the men looked around her age. A younger man stood behind them. Elizabeth frowned. Christopher looked across at them and smiled.

"Hey! What are you guys doing here?"

"Christopher! Are you okay? We got here as quickly as we could. Thank God you're all right!"

The older woman who'd spoken rushed over to Christopher's side and gave him an awkward hug.

"I'm fine, Mom. But thanks for asking. It's good to see you."

The older man stepped forward and squeezed Christopher's arm. "How are you holding up, son? You gave us all a fright."

"Sorry, Dad. I didn't mean to."

The younger man moved to the end of the bed. He grinned at Christopher. "Haven't you heard? You're all over the news! You're a hero, bro!"

Elizabeth stared at the man. There was something about him that appeared familiar. The shape of his face, the chiseled jaw, the brilliant green of his eyes…

Christopher touched her hand to get her attention. "Elizabeth, I'd like you to meet my parents—Frank and Evelyn Barrington. The other idiot is my brother, Vaughan. He turned forty a few weeks ago and now he thinks…"

A rush of noise filled her ears, blocking out the rest of Christopher's words. She stared at the man at the foot of the bed.

Vaughan… Vaughan Barrington… My son….

She could see the resemblance so clearly now. While David's hair had been much lighter, the caramel-gold shade of Vaughan's was striking. Her gaze roved over him, cataloguing the rest of his features. The generous mouth, the strong nose, the sound of his voice… It was all David. She'd found him, her son. He stood only a few feet away from her, totally oblivious.

Her heart beat so hard she thought she might be having a heart attack. This wasn't the time or the place. The letter she'd penned to him still sat on her desk, waiting for her to find the courage to post it. Now she knew who he was, had seen him with her own eyes, but that didn't make things any easier…

Stumbling to her feet, she pushed away from the chair and muttered some excuse about leaving them to their visit. She blindly left the room and found herself out in the corridor. She wanted to go back to Archic, but her head was in such a turmoil. She needed to get away, somewhere she could think.

The shock of coming face to face with her son had blindsided her. She couldn't even think straight. The walls felt like they were closing in on her. Her chest was tight.

I need to get out of here… I can't breathe…

As she stumbled toward the lifts, there was one thought that crystallized in her mind.

I can't tell anyone about this. At least, not yet. Not until I've had time to process it, to decide what to do…

She hated the thought of another secret between her and Archie and she swore she wouldn't keep it from him for long, but right now the thought of sharing her discovery with anyone was overwhelming. She needed time to think.

At last she made it out into the cool evening and dragged in great gulps of air. She leaned against a light pole. The tightness in her chest slowly eased. When she felt able to walk again, she made her way across to a bench off to one side of the emergency department. She'd come there with Joel. She'd have to call one of her children to come and collect her.

No, she'd call a cab. She couldn't bear to face anyone at the moment. Not until she'd had a chance to come to terms with the knowledge her son was Christopher's half-brother. She might have been fooled by Ashton, but this time there was no doubt in her mind. Vaughan Barrington was her beloved son.

Elizabeth waited until the last Craigdon family member was seated around the large dining room table before calling them all to order. The only ones missing were Isabella and Raine, who were both in Brisbane and of course, Archie. Climbing to her feet, she tapped her wine glass with a spoon. The murmur of conversation immediately ceased. The rest of them were there: Jett and Danielle, Callum and Grace. Joel and Sheridan, Nicholas and Harper, who now had a pronounced baby bump. Their wedding would take place the following Saturday. Sophia and Jarrod sat side by side, holding hands.

Christopher sat next to Joel. He'd been discharged the day before. The white sling across his chest and around his shoulder stood in stark contrast to his black-collared shirt. Elizabeth had called him and asked him to come, and though he'd initially declined her invitation, she'd insisted, telling him it would please her very much if he were there. Despite his presence reminding her all too sharply of Vaughan, she wanted Christopher to hear what she had to say. As far as she was concerned he was part of their family and after saving Archie's life, they'd be forever in his debt.

Archie's sons and their respective partners were also seated around the table. Flynn and Jayde, Noah and Ayla, Logan and his girlfriend, Mia. Elizabeth's heart filled to overflowing at the knowledge they were all so lucky in love. She'd seen them all at various times at the hospital as they'd taken turns to visit their father. They were as grateful to Christopher as she was for what he'd done.

She cleared her throat, suddenly beset with nerves at the thought of what she was about to reveal. After long hours looking at things from many angles, she'd decided to keep the discovery of her son a secret a little while longer—at least until Archie was discharged from hospital and was well on the road to recovery.

In the meantime, she'd called them all together to finally make a public declaration of love. A part of her wished Archie was there to see it, but she didn't want to wait any longer. This day had been long enough in coming as it was. She was filled with another rush of nerves.

Don't be silly! This is my family! They're not going to disown me, stop loving me, whatever.

In fact, she secretly hoped they'd be happy for her and Archie. They all now had firsthand experience about what it was like to fall in love. They also knew that no one got to choose who they fell in love with. She hoped that knowledge would help ease their shock over what she was about to tell them.

Several pairs of eyes looked at her expectantly. She cleared her throat again. "Thank you all for coming. I appreciate the effort you've made."

"How's Archie?" Callum asked.

"He's doing well," she replied. "I saw him earlier today. He's started to complain about the food, so it's my guess he's feeling much better."

The muted laughter helped ease her nerves. It had been three days since Archie's admission to hospital. While the doctors were happy with his progress, they wanted him to spend another few days there to ensure his damaged lungs and the wounds from his recent heart surgery had healed.

Elizabeth had spent the past three days fielding questions about Archie's health status and trying to avoid the unspoken questions in the eyes of their children. It seemed they all sensed there was something more between her and Archie, but no one knew quite what it was, or had the courage to raise the issue.

It was time to come clean. To tell them how she felt. How Archie felt. Their love had been more than twenty-five years in the making. For Archie, he'd loved her for even longer than that. She still felt guilty that she'd refused to acknowledge his importance in her life…until now.

Her stomach clenched on a fresh wave of nerves. Delaying the moment a little longer, she directed her gaze to Christopher. "On behalf of all of us here, and Archie, I want to thank you from the bottom of my heart. If you hadn't been there, hadn't risked your life to drag Archie out of that fire, he surely would have died. We owe you a debt of gratitude, Christopher. You've had my love since I met you as a young boy, and you'll have my love and support for the rest of your life."

There was a murmur of agreement from around the table. Christopher merely inclined his head to acknowledge the comments. Elizabeth drew in a deep breath and spoke again.

"There's something else. You're all aware of the affair I had with Archie that produced your sister, Sophia. What you don't know is that our love for each other didn't end with Sophia's birth."

"What are you trying to say Mom?" Sophia asked.

Elizabeth drew in another breath and then blurted it out. "Archie and I are still in love. We've loved each other all this time. Before Sophia was born and afterwards. Even now."

For a moment the shocked silence was so complete there wasn't a sound in the room. Elizabeth gave them all a few moments to absorb her announcement. She regained her seat and calmly folded her hands in front of her. Now that the truth was out there, she felt nothing but relief.

"Did Dad know it was still going on?" Nicholas asked.

Elizabeth nodded. "Yes."

Though he'd accused me of being unfaithful some years before I actually broke my wedding vows, but I'm done with all of that. Henry's dead. I'm not going to drag up ancient history. One of us has to be the bigger person. It sure as hell was never Henry…

"No one's going to judge you Mom," Callum said quietly. "We all know Dad had numerous affairs. I'm not condoning your actions, but Dad was far from a saint."

There was a general murmur of agreement from her children. Then Flynn spoke up.

"There was cheating from both of our parents, too. Neither of them could claim the high moral ground. It's sad and messy and I wish to God everyone had honored their wedding vows, but that's the way it is."

Flynn looked at Elizabeth. "I'm glad you and Dad have found each other and that your love has been sustained over all these years. It can't have been easy and yet, here you are, all these years later, still in love." He looked at Jayde and then reached for her hand. He kissed the back of her knuckles. "I hope and pray I feel the same way about my wife twenty-five years down the track and that she feels the same way about me."

Jayde framed Flynn's face with her hands and kissed him

full on the lips. "'Til death do us part, buddy. You're stuck with me forever."

Everyone laughed and the tension eased. Conversations resumed. Wine glasses were filled. The meal was served and people busied themselves with enjoying the rare steak, mushroom sauce, baby potatoes, buttery corn, and green beans that had been provided by Amy. And though several of them protested that they couldn't possibly fit in dessert, the white chocolate mousse with fresh cream and strawberries served in individual parfait glasses soon disappeared.

After the plates had been cleared away, Elizabeth suggested they retire to the music room for coffee and liqueurs. When they were all seated, she stood and moved to the middle of the room.

"I appreciate your support for me and Archie. It means a lot to me. I wish I'd trusted you with our secret a long time ago. Archie urged me to tell you all many times over the past twelve months. I resisted. I was scared," she admitted. "Scared how you'd react. That you'd be upset, disappointed. I should have given you the benefit of the doubt. You're all fine people, kind and generous and loving and…" She paused, feeling choked up. Drawing in a breath, she finished. "And I'm so grateful for that."

"You're welcome Mom."

"We love you, Mom."

The chorus of support was heartfelt and she swelled with love and pride. And then she looked at Christopher and remembered there was something else that needed to be finalized.

"I want to talk to you all about Christopher's lawsuit."

There was a general grumbling among the crowd. Elizabeth held up her hand. "Please, hear me out. We all accept Christopher is part of this family. As such, he's entitled to a piece of your father's estate."

"He wants eighty-five million dollars. I'm all for settling the lawsuit, but I think he's over-reaching just a little bit," Jett said dryly.

Elizabeth glanced toward Christopher. He gave her an imperceptible nod. She looked back at her children. "You're right. Christopher and I have been talking. I propose a settlement of ten million dollars—the same amount Jett, Joel and Callum received. How do you all feel about that?"

She moved her gaze from child to child. They all offered a nod. When she got to Christopher, she paused. "Christopher? What do you think?"

Christopher sighed. "As you know, it was never about the money. Ten million is more than generous. Thank you. I accept."

Elizabeth sighed softly with relief. "Good. Now, there's something else."

Jett groaned. "I'm not sure I can handle any more of this."

"Jett, be quiet," Elizabeth gently admonished. "Now, where was I?"

"You were about to hit us with something else," Sophia said, rolling her eyes.

Elizabeth clucked her tongue. "Enough of that attitude from you, Sophia Craigdon. You were raised better than that."

"Mom! Just get on with it!" Callum laughed.

"Right. Yes." She turned to face Logan. "This next part has to do with you."

Logan offered a nervous smile. "Oh, hell. What have I done?"

"You're going to sign Craigdon Enterprises over to Nick."

"What?" Nick gasped. "Mom, that's not fair! Dad left the company to Logan!" Nick's gaze flew to Logan's. "I didn't put her up to this! I knew nothing about it, I swear!"

"It's all right, Nick. I believe you," Logan soothed. He

looked at Elizabeth. "Thank you for raising the issue of Craigdon Enterprises, Aunt Elizabeth. It's something I've wanted to talk about with everyone for some time."

He stood and faced them. "As you know, I've never had any interest in Craigdon Enterprises. Not then; not now. I now understand why Uncle—Dad left it to me, but that doesn't change the way I feel."

He turned to Nick. "Craigdon Enterprises was your passion. You worked there for years before you'd even left school. It should have been yours. And it will be. I agree with Aunt Elizabeth. It belongs to you."

Nicholas looked like he'd been hit between the eyes with a sledgehammer. "Really? Are you sure? I mean... It's part of your inheritance. You don't have to give it to me. I... I could buy you out...maybe. I don't know where I'd get the money, but I could figure something out."

Logan held up his hand. "Nick, stop. Please. Keep your money. I don't want it. And I don't want the company, either. It's yours. Lock, stock and barrel. Now quit going on about it and just say thank you."

Nicholas continued to look stunned, but a smile slowly crept across his face. "Thank you," he breathed. "I don't believe it... I... I just don't believe it. *Whoopee!*"

He punched the air in triumph. Everyone laughed. Elizabeth eased out a breath and felt herself relax. Everything was going to be all right.

Jett and Danielle and Callum and Grace had already left when Elizabeth found Joel in the kitchen. She'd noticed when she'd revealed her ongoing affair with Archie that Joel didn't appear to be shocked. She had a sneaking suspicion he'd guessed the truth long before she'd come clean. He turned as she entered, his coffee cup in hand.

"I needed a refill," he said. "Do you want one?"

"No, thank you. If I have any more caffeine, I'll be up all night."

Joel grinned and sipped from his cup. "Lucky for me, it doesn't affect me like that. I can drink black coffee and go straight to bed and sleep the whole night through."

Elizabeth chuckled. "Lucky you." And then she sobered and looked him straight in the eye. "You knew, didn't you?"

"Yes."

She was relieved he didn't bother to pretend confusion over her question, or to deny it. Even so, she was curious.

"What gave us away?"

He looked at her as if he didn't quite believe she'd asked that. "Really, Mom? I'm a cop. Trained in the art of observation. Ever since you told us about Archie being Sophia's father, it became obvious. The way you were together—so comfortable and familiar. The way Uncle Archie was always here. And when he wasn't here, you were at his place. That's why I was so frightened the night of the fire. Christopher had told me how he'd rescued Archie, but I had no idea if you were still inside. The possibility terrified me."

"What about Jett? He's a cop, too."

Joel gave her a droll look. "I'm sure you won't be surprised to hear he knew all about it, too."

Elizabeth shook her head in disbelief. "Why didn't either of you say anything?"

Joel shrugged. "It wasn't our place. For some reason you wanted to keep it a secret. That was fine with me. It was none of my business how you lived your life. After the heartache you put up with from Dad, I didn't begrudge you your happiness."

Elizabeth smiled tremulously, overwhelmed with emotion. "Thank you, Joel. You're a good son. I love you so much."

"I love you too, Mom. You take care of yourself. And Uncle Archie."

"You bet."

"By the way, I've received a call from someone in the arson squad. An accelerant was used to start the fire at Archie's home."

Elizabeth gasped. "So it was arson?"

"Yes."

"Do the police have any suspects?"

"Yes."

She hardly dared to ask. "Ashton?"

"I'm sorry, Mom. Someone saw a red Porsche speeding away from the property around the time of the fire. That's not inconclusive proof, of course, but it's not looking good for him. They've located him and are bringing him in for questioning about the fire and…the other stuff."

Elizabeth nodded with resignation. "I feel stupid for being taken in by him, but I'm pleased he won't be able to deceive anyone else. What he did wasn't right. He needs to take responsibility for what he did."

"Don't worry, Mom. He'll be taking responsibility, all right. By the time we finish with him, he'll be lucky to be out of jail in time to celebrate his fiftieth birthday. And if he's responsible for starting the fire… Let's just say he'll be in jail for a lot longer than that."

Elizabeth's smile was tinged with sadness. "Hopefully by then he'll have learned his lesson."

Joel pecked her on the cheek and drifted away. Elizabeth returned to the music room that was now empty of occupants. She moved over to the piano and ran her fingers randomly over the keys.

"I used to love to listen to you play. It always had a way of calming me down."

Elizabeth turned at the sound of Isabella's voice. "Issy! Oh, honey! It's so wonderful to see you! When did you get in?"

"My flight landed an hour ago. I caught an Uber and came straight here."

"You should have called someone! One of us would have been happy to meet your flight."

Isabella shrugged. "It was no bother, Mom. I wanted to come here and see how you were. And Uncle Archie and Christopher. How's everyone holding up?"

"We're getting there slowly. Christopher's here. He was discharged yesterday. And Archie's going to be all right, thank goodness. If anything had happened to him…"

She shuddered. Isabella regarded her with a quizzical expression. Elizabeth blushed. "Do you know about me and Archie?"

Issy nodded. "Yes, Mom. I know. Joel told me everything. He called me while I was on my way here."

"Ah. Well, that's good."

"What I don't understand is why you kept it a secret all this time? Especially since Daddy died. You and Uncle Archie have loved each other for a long time. I thought you'd be glad you could finally bring it out in the open."

Elizabeth sighed. Slowly, she sat down on the piano stool. "I was. I am. I don't know why I kept it from you all for so long. I guess, when your father died, we were all thrown into chaos. Life was turned upside down. So many shocks and surprises… There just didn't seem to be a good time.

"Archie wanted to, of course. He'd been pressuring me to go public almost from the night we buried your father. But I resisted… To tell you the truth, I wasn't sure how you'd all react. Whether you'd be mad. I'd spent so long wanting to be with Archie, I couldn't bear the thought my children didn't approve. Then there was my fear that if we finally made it official it would somehow jinx us. There are plenty of people who've been together for years and the moment they make it official, something changes. They split up. I didn't want that to happen to us. So I kept putting it off."

"Is that why you and Uncle Archie have been at odds with each other this past month?"

She gave Isabella a wry look. "You noticed that, huh?"

Isabella grimaced. "Archie mentioned something about it. He even invited me to the opera with him…"

Elizabeth sighed wearily. "We'd recently argued again about coming clean to you all. Archie gave me an ultimatum: Either I tell you all about us—my children and his—or we were through."

"Oh, Mom! That must have been tough."

"It was. But when I found out Archie was hurt—maybe even fighting for his life—the first thought I had after praying he'd be all right was regret that I hadn't done as he'd asked. He wanted me to show him how much I loved him by making our relationship public and until then I'd resisted. I was so filled with regret at the thought that I might never be given the chance to make it up to him. It nearly killed me."

Isabella stepped forward and patted her hand. "Thankfully that didn't happen. Uncle Archie's going to be fine and the two of you are going to live a long and happy life together. I'm sure of it."

Elizabeth gave her daughter a grateful smile. She couldn't believe how close they'd grown since Henry had died. Her relationship with Isabella had been strained for so many years. Elizabeth had only discovered the reason why, after Henry's death. He had a lot to answer for. She hoped he regretted the evil he'd done while he was still alive.

"You know, there's one thing I've always wondered about," Isabella mused.

"What is it?"

"Why was Daddy so convinced Nicholas wasn't his? You once told me it took you two years to act on the declaration of love from Sophia's father. Now I know that was Uncle Archie.

But Nick was born way before that. Why didn't Daddy believe you?"

Elizabeth's shoulders slumped on another sigh. "I never really knew the answer to that. All I can think of is that he saw something he thought was more than it was."

"What do you mean?"

"About four years before Sophia was born, Archie came to me and bared his heart. He told me how he'd loved me from the moment he'd seen me and he couldn't live without me in his life. He… He kissed me then. A kiss filled with pent-up passion and love. I was so surprised, for a few moments, I kissed him back. Then I realized what I was doing. I pulled away and told him it was wrong. We were both married. There couldn't be anything between us, no matter how we felt."

Elizabeth sighed softly. "We were out in the rose garden. I can still smell their perfume, sweet and heavy on the summer breeze. I think Henry saw us. That's why he thought there was something going on. I was already six weeks pregnant with Nicholas, although I didn't know it at the time. When he was born later that year, Henry obviously thought he belonged to Archie. Nothing I said would change his mind. In the end, I gave up trying. I knew the truth. That's all that mattered."

Chapter Twenty Two

*E*lizabeth ran a brush through her hair and tried to quell her nerves. She felt jittery, uncertain, even shy.

This is ridiculous! I'm sixty years old! Archie and I have been lovers for decades. So, why do I feel like a bride on her wedding night?

It was Archie's first night home from hospital. Flynn had offered to collect him. There was no question he'd be staying at Craigdon Manor. Apart from the fact his home had been destroyed in the fire, now that their love was out in the open, there was no need for him to be anywhere else.

Flynn's offer meant Elizabeth had time to drive into the city and search for a new nightgown. Something light and floaty, that was both flattering and sexy. Though the doctor had urged Archie to take things slowly—and she'd vowed to go easy on him—she also wanted to blow his mind.

It had been so long since they'd been together. Weeks that felt like years. She'd missed his companionship, his quick wit, his warm presence in the bed beside her… His love. But now he was home and she was determined to make this night special.

It had taken her a few hours, browsing the inventory, moving from one store to the next, but finally she'd found what she was looking for. A gorgeous off-white silk and chiffon peignoir with matching nightgown. She smoothed her hand over the fabric. It looked just as good on her as it had in the shop. She was pleased with her purchase and hoped it would have the desired effect.

A sound in the bedroom behind her reminded her that Archie was waiting for her. With a quick spray of her favorite perfume and a final primp of her hair, she switched off the light in the bathroom and left. The lamps on the bedside tables gave off a soft yellow glow. The room, though generously proportioned, now felt cozy and warm. It was like they were cocooned away from the rest of the world with no one in it but them. She smiled at the image.

"What are you smiling about?" Archie asked in a tender tone.

"I'm just so happy we're together again." She came toward him. Her peignoir billowed out behind her. Archie's gaze scanned her from head to toe. His eyes flared wide with appreciation.

"Wow. No wonder you took so long in there. You look amazing."

His voice was already husky with desire. She smiled again, this time with satisfaction. Shimmying out of the peignoir, she let it drop to the floor and then climbed on the bed. The spaghetti straps of her low-cut nightgown helped support her generous breasts. The form-fitting bodice, embroidered with antique lace, cupped and lifted her cleavage, leaving a fair amount of pale skin on display.

Archie reached out and stroked one finger across her chest and then moved his hand further over to cup and caress her breast.

"You're so beautiful," he rasped, still a little hoarse. "I can't believe you're mine."

"Yours, now and forever and always," she whispered.

Framing his beloved face with her hands, she kissed him, softly, tenderly with all the love she felt inside. She'd come so close to losing him. The nightmare of what might have happened still weighed heavily on her mind. It was only through a sheer act of will that she forced the dreaded images from her head.

He stared at her with eyes that were already shadowed with desire. The familiar spark surged through her. Her nipples tightened. After all these years, she wanted him so much.

"It's not too soon, is it?" she asked.

"No, the doctor cleared me for gentle exercise. He said I could pretty much do whatever I was doing before, so long as I don't overdo it."

She gave him a teasing smile. "I guess I can be gentle. And I promise I won't tire you out."

With that, she started on the buttons of his nightshirt. When they were all undone, she spread the cotton fabric wide and stared down at the three small wounds on his chest. Tenderly, she touched them. The bandages had been removed before he'd been discharged, but the incisions had been covered with small white dressings. Flynn had passed on the doctor's instructions to keep the wounds clean and dry for a few more days. Next week the stitches would be removed.

"We should be thankful for that fire," Archie murmured.

Elizabeth frowned. "Why on earth would we be thankful for a fire that destroyed your house and almost everything in it?"

"The doctor told me I was a heart attack waiting to happen. Hardened arteries that were bound to cause a blockage. Without the fire, I would never have ended up in hospital. I could have suffered a major heart attack at any time."

Elizabeth shook her head. "Thank God you didn't. I don't know what I would have done if you'd died. We were still estranged. There was so much I hadn't said. I would have lived with the guilt of that all my life."

He lifted his hand and gently stroked the hair away from her face. "Don't upset yourself, Lizzie. It didn't happen. I'm here, alive and well. We've said all that needs to be said. Tonight's about new beginnings. Tonight's the first day of the rest of our lives."

"Amen," she whispered.

With that, she lay down beside him and he gathered her into his arms. Their lips met and melded. In short order, Archie pulled off her nightgown and flung it away. She helped him undress. Their movements were frantic, like they were teenagers. And then they were skin to skin.

Elizabeth sighed. *Archie.* Her safety and security. The love of her life. Her rock. There was nowhere else she'd rather be.

They kissed again with warmth and increasing passion. Heat centered in her core. She moved restlessly against him. His erection pressed against her belly, reassuringly thick and hard.

"Make love to me, Archie."

Rising above her, he kissed his way across her breasts. He paid particular attention to her nipples, loving them with his tongue. He knew every part of her body so intimately and yet, on some level it felt like their first time. She guessed it had something to do with the fact that for the first time they could love each other, knowing there was nothing between them— not spouses, not children, not secrets… Just the two of them, together for all time.

When Archie entered her, she reveled in the feeling of having him deep inside her, stroking her innermost walls. It had been so long since they'd loved each other this way. Silently, she vowed never to let anything come between them again. Life was too short. She wanted to spend every minute of it loving the man who was her life.

Afterwards, when they were both fully sated and trying to catch their breath, Archie drew her in close against his side.

"Flynn told me about the family meeting. That you told all of them about us."

"Yes. They took it better than I expected. I should have trusted them enough to tell them a long time ago."

"You were scared. I understand that. I'm just glad it's done now. We can love each other as we please with no more secrets and subterfuge. I've had enough of that to last a lifetime."

Her heart clenched. She thought about Vaughan.

It's time… I have to tell him…

Coming up on her elbow, she looked at him. Something in the seriousness of her expression must have registered. He frowned.

"Lizzie? What is it?"

"There's something I have to tell you. It's about my son."

"The baby you had when you were young?"

"Yes. The thing is… I've truly found him."

Archie's eyes widened with surprise. "Wow."

She gave him a tiny smile. "Yes. Wow."

"So who is he? Where does he live? Does he know about you?"

"I don't have all the answers yet. For now, it's enough that I know who he is."

"Am I allowed to know his name?"

Elizabeth drew in a deep breath. "It's Vaughan. Vaughan Barrington."

Archie's expression didn't change. It was obvious the name meant nothing to him. Elizabeth told him the connection.

Archie gasped. "He's Christopher's half-brother? Are you kidding?"

Elizabeth shook her head. "No. It came as a shock to me, too."

"Wow. I mean… Wow."

"Yes."

"Who else knows?"

"No one."

"What are you going to do?"

"I don't know. I'm going to sit on the information for a bit until I know what I want to do with it. I'm in no rush. Now that I know who he is, I can take my time deciding on my next step. Right now, I want to concentrate on us. We have a lot of time to make up."

The shock slowly disappeared from Archie's face, followed by an expression filled with such tenderness, it snatched away her breath.

"Thank you for telling me," he said.

She smiled and reached for his hand. "No more secrets, right?"

"Right."

Pulling slightly away from her, he moved across the bed and opened the top drawer of his bedside table. Reaching inside, he pulled out a black velvet jeweler's ring box.

Elizabeth's eyes went wide with surprise. "Archie! My goodness! When did you have time to buy this?"

"I've had it stored on a shelf in my wardrobe for almost a year. Fortunately I'd taken to keeping it in the glove box of my car which I'd left parked outside in my driveway the night of the fire. I was at your place as often as I was at mine. With Henry and Janelle gone, I wanted to be ready. Finally we could be together, as husband and wife." He gave her a rueful smile. "It's taken a little longer than I anticipated, but now the time has come."

He stared at her, his eyes intense, filled with longing and love. "Elizabeth Craigdon, will you marry me?"

"Yes! Oh, Yes!" she cried and threw her arms around him.

Their lips met in a soulful kiss, filled with the passion and tenderness that had been a hallmark of their relationship for more than two decades. All these years later, the deep and abiding love was still there.

Slowly, reluctantly, Elizabeth ended the kiss and drew away. She looked down at the ring that was still in Archie's hand.

"It's beautiful," she whispered.

Archie pulled the ring out of the box and then lifted her left hand. The ring slid onto her finger with a minimum of effort.

"A perfect fit," she breathed.

"I had it specially made by a jeweler in the city. I designed it myself."

"Oh, Archie!"

"The diamonds remind me of your sparkle and light. The rubies remind me of your lips. The two sapphires represent your beautiful eyes and the heavy gold band is strong and durable—just like our love, it will withstand life's challenges for all eternity."

By the end of his little speech, she had her hands up to her mouth and tears filled her eyes.

"Hey," he protested gently, "I didn't mean to make you cry."

"They're tears of joy," she whispered and kissed him softly again on the lips.

The kiss turned heated and his lips moved over hers. He slanted his mouth against hers and deepened the kiss. Slowly, he pulled away.

"You're so beautiful," he whispered.

She blushed. "I'm sixty years old."

"What, you think I don't know that? Age is just a number. It's what's in here that counts." He pressed a hand to his heart. "You'll always be the girl that I fell in love with and I'll love you until I die."

She put her arms around him and her eyes filled with love. "You're my one and only, Archie. My one true love. You're my life."

He pulled her closer and rested his cheek on the top of her head. She buried her face against the warmth of his neck. Like two pieces of a puzzle, she fit neatly into the crook of his arm. It had always been that way. They were the perfect match. She thanked God they'd reconciled before it was too late. After all the heartache of the past year, she looked forward to the future, living each day with the man she loved beside her.

Note to Readers

I do hope you have enjoyed reading Elizabeth and Archie's story. If you've enjoyed this book, I would really appreciate it if you could leave a review at Goodreads and your favorite digital retailer. Every review increases visibility and helps other readers to find books they enjoy.

Receive a free book when you sign up for my newsletter if you like to receive news on upcoming stories, release dates, book launches and other snippets. I love to receive feedback from my readers. Please feel free to contact me at chris@christaylorauthor.com.au.

Want more Craigdons? The Barrington Series is a spin-off series of the Craigdon Family Series. The first book in this series, *Broken Lives*, is Christopher Barrington's story. It is due for release late 2021. Please join my newsletter if you would like to receive updates on my latest book releases and other news.

http://www.christaylorauthor.com.au/

About the Author

Chris Taylor grew up on a farm in north-west New South Wales, Australia. She always had a thirst for stories and recalls writing her first book at the ripe old age of eight. Always a lover of romance and happily-ever-afters, a career in criminal law sparked her interest in intrigue and suspense. For Chris to be able to combine romance with suspense in her books is a dream come true.

Chris is married to Linden and is the mother of five children. If not behind her computer, you can find her doing the school run, taxiing children to swimming lessons, football, ballet and cricket. In her spare time, Chris loves to read her favorite authors who include Richard North Patterson, Sandra Brown, Kathleen E Woodiwiss and Jude Devereaux.

You can find out more about Chris and sign up for her newsletter at her website:

http://www.christaylorauthor.com.au